THE GROVES OF ACADEME

Books by Mary McCarthy

Mary McCarthy

THE GROVES
OF ACADEME

New York

HARCOURT, BRACE & WORLD, INC.

PRINTED IN THE UNITED STATES OF AMERICA

TO

Jess   *Kevin*

Augusta   *Jay*

ACKNOWLEDGMENTS

The author wishes to thank *The New Yorker* for permission to reprint Chapter One, and the Guggenheim Foundation for the fellowship that made some of this work possible.

Atque inter silvas academi quaerere verum

Horace, Ep. II, ii, 45

THE GROVES OF ACADEME

An Unexpected Letter

WHEN HENRY MULCAHY, a middle-aged instructor of literature at Jocelyn College, Jocelyn, Pennsylvania, unfolded the President's letter and became aware of its contents, he gave a sudden sharp cry of impatience and irritation, as if such interruptions could positively be brooked no longer. This was the last straw. How was he expected to take care of forty students if other demands on his attention were continually being put in the way? On the surface of his mind, this vagrant grievance kept playing. Meanwhile, he had grown pale and his hands were trembling with anger and a strange sort of exultation. "Your appointment will not be continued beyond the current academic year. . . ." He sprang to his feet and mimed the sentence aloud, triumphantly, in inverted commas, bringing the whole force of his personality to bear on this specimen or exhibit of the incredible.

He had guessed long ago that Hoar meant to dismiss him, but he was amazed, really amazed (he repeated the word to himself) that the man should have given himself away by an action as overt as this one. As an intellectual, he felt stunned not so much by the moral insensitiveness of

the President's move as by the transparency of it. You do
not fire a man who has challenged you openly at faculty
meetings, who has fought, despite you and your cabal, for
a program of salary increases and a lightening of the
teaching load, who has not feared to point to waste and
mismanagement concealed by those in high places, who
dared to call only last week (yes, fantastic as it seemed,
this was the background of the case) for an investigation
of the Buildings and Grounds Department and begged the
dietitian to *unscramble*, if she would be so good, for her
colleagues, the history of the twenty thousand eggs. . . .
A condolatory smile, capping this enumeration, material-
ized on his lips; the letter was so inconsonant with the
simplest precepts of strategy that it elicited a kind of pity,
mingled with contempt and dry amusement.

Still, the triteness of the attempt, the jejuneness and
tedium of it, tried forbearance to the limit; at a progressive college, surely, one had the right to expect something
better than what one was used to at Drake or Montana, and
the very element of repetition gave the whole affair an
unwarranted and unreal character, as of some tawdry farce
seriously re-enacted. He had been in the academic harness
long enough, he should have thought (and the files in the
college office could testify) to anticipate anything, yet
some unseen tendril of trust, he now remarked with a
short harsh laugh, must have spiraled out from his heart
and clung to the President's person, or simply to the idea
of decency, for him now to feel this new betrayal so keenly.

For the truth was, as Mulcahy had to acknowledge,
pacing up and down his small office, that in spite of all
the evidence he had been given of the President's unremit-

ting hatred, he found himself hurt by the letter—wounded, to be honest, not only in his *amour propre* but in some tenderer place, in that sense of contract between men that transcends personal animosities and factional differences, that holds the man distinct from the deed and maintains even in the fieriest opposition the dream of final agreement and concord. He had not known, in short, that the President disliked him so flatly. It was the usual mistake of a complex intelligence in assessing a simple intelligence, of an imagination that is capable of seeing and feeling on many levels at once, as opposed to an administrative mentality that feels operationally, through acts. Like most people of literary sensibility, he had been unprepared, when it came down to it, for the obvious: a blunt, naked wielding of power. And the fact that he had *thought* himself prepared, he bitterly reflected, was precisely a measure of the abyss between the Maynard Hoars of this world and the Mulcahys.

The anomalies of the situation afforded him a gleam of pleasure—to a man of superior intellect, the idea that he has been weak or a fool in comparison with an inferior adversary is fraught with moral comedy and sardonic philosophic applications. He sat down at his desk, popped a peppermint into his mouth, and began to laugh softly at the ironies of his biography: Henry Mulcahy, called Hen by his friends, forty-one years old, the only Ph.D. in the Literature department, contributor to the *Nation* and the *Kenyon Review*, Rhodes scholar, Guggenheim Fellow, father of four, fifteen years' teaching experience, salary and rank of instructor—an "unfortunate" personality in the lexicon of department heads, but in the opinion of a number of his colleagues the cleverest man at Jocelyn and the victim, here as elsewhere, of that ferocious envy of mediocrity for excellence that is the ruling passion of all systems of jobholders.

Mulcahy's freckled fist came down on the desk. A tall, soft-bellied, lisping man with a tense, mushroom-white face, rimless bifocals, and graying thin red hair, he was intermittently aware of a quality of personal unattractiveness that emanated from him like a miasma; this made him self-pitying, uxorious, and addicted also to self-love, for he associated it with his destiny as a portent of some personal epiphany. As a prophet of modern literature in a series of halfway-good colleges, he had gladly accepted an identification with the sacred untouchables of the modern martyrology—with Joyce, the obscure language teacher in Trieste; with tubercular Kafka in Prague, browbeaten by an authoritarian father; with the sickly, *tisane*-drenched Proust; with Marx, even, and his carbuncles; with Socrates and the hemlock. He carried an ash-plant stick in imitation of Joyce's Stephen Dedalus; subscribed to *Science and Society*, the Communist scholarly publication; and proclaimed the Irish, his ancestors, to be the ten lost tribes of Israel. The unwholesome whiteness of his long, pear-shaped body, the droop of his trousers, his children's runny noses and damp bottoms, his wife's woman's complaint, the sand sprinkling the lashes of his nearsighted, glaucous eyes, which had made him the butt of students, were not antipathetic to him but on the contrary lovable, as a manifesto of ethical difference, like the bleeding holy pictures of his childhood, the yellowed palms from Palm Sunday, the vessel of holy water blessed by the Pope. A symbolist,

he was purposefully saturated in a sort of folkish traditional poverty of the lower middle class, in the Freudian
family romance—the steam of the tea-kettle and the laundry tub; diapers drying on the radiators and on the
rusty shower rod of the bathroom; nightgowns, kimonos,
medicine cabinets; the smell of unaired closets; nose rags,
cleaning rags, lint, broken toys, potties. He and his wife
together dearly loved a midnight "spread," candy bars,
frosted cupcakes, nuts and pickles, second helpings of
mashed potatoes; he was defiantly conscious of a porous
complexion, bad teeth, and occasional morning halitosis.

All this, in a progressive community where the casserole
and the cocktail and the disposable diaper reigned, where
the handsome President and his wife entertained with
sherry or sat, Bennington-style, on the floor, listening to
Bach and boogie-woogie, had, as he was perfectly aware,
a heretical flavor, a pungent breath of class hatred and
contempt. He knew, without being told, that he and his
wife were criticized for the condition of the children's
clothes, little Mary Margaret, as every wife on Faculty
Hill could say positively, having been sent home *twice*
by her first-grade teacher with a note calling attention to
the absence of buttons from her dress. But except, he supposed, for the courage of the outstanding boy in his Proust-
Joyce-Mann course, he might have remained ignorant of
the sobriquet, Dr. Stuck-Up, pinned on him by the campus
rowdies, in reference to the bits of toilet paper (the result
of cuts when shaving) that sometimes stuck to his chin
during the eight-o'clock tutorials, and of the newest slander, spread only ten days ago, that the Student Self-Help

Bureau made excuses not to send him sitters, because the girls complained of the smell of urine in the house.

"Bravo!" he impulsively murmured, blowing a saturnine kiss from his fingertips. *"Bis, bis!"* The critic in him, he thought, could not help applauding the *consonantia* of the President's action; any other dénouement to the saga of his stay at Jocelyn would have been lacking in inevitability. Moving to the casement window, he stared out across the snowy amphitheatre of the campus, down the long line of hemlocks, to the arch of the Administration Building, where the President had his paneled offices. "I congratulate you, Maynard Hoar," he softly apostrophized, "Carleton College, B.A., Wisconsin, Ph.D., disciple of Alexander Meiklejohn, lover of the humanities, guitar-player, gadfly of the philosophical journals, defender of academic freedom! Accept my felicitations on the clean-cut way you have handled this disagreeable task!" Pondering, he drew out his watch, inherited from an uncle in Tammany, glanced vaguely at it, hearing the Phi Beta Kappa key jingle; he was feeling more than half tempted to take the letter over to the main hall and post it on the faculty bulletin board, before the arrival of his eleven-o'clock tutee could force him to maturer reflection.

The conviction that it would embarrass Hoar to have the letter made public had come to him just now in a flash, as though by divination. *Hoar was counting on his silence.* He knew this to be true by a sixth political sense, by a depth-sounding of the bureaucratic character, without yet knowing why, or what use to make of the discovery. A man in Mulcahy's *position* (he mimicked the President's reasoning), a man with Mulcahy's *unfortunate* record, could not *afford* to proclaim this *new* dismissal from the housetops; he could be reckoned on, in fact, to go quietly, with a letter of recommendation as his price. Mulcahy smiled. What the President apparently did not know, he thought with satisfaction, was the finality of his instructor's predicament—the literally scores of fruitless letters Mulcahy had written and had had written for him during the year and a half between jobs, when he had lived with his mother-in-law in Louisville while his wife clerked in a department store and he stayed home and wiped the snot from the children's noses and worked on the Joyce concordance that no commercial publisher believed in. During that year and a half, he reflected, he had had a salutary foretaste of what he could expect in the future from the old friends and teachers who had stood by him thus far, but with what pipe-pulling, pursing of the lips, frowning airs, and due consideration! Jocelyn, their letters now apprised him, was his last chance, though they did not put the *caveat* in so many words but inquired deftly after Catherine and the children; praised Maynard Hoar, "a humanist and a gentleman," who was having a hard time, so they heard, between an unruly student-body and an unsympathetic board of trustees; and finished by chiding their friend Hen, half playfully, for "an engaging tendency, apparent already in your undergraduate years, to go off half cocked."

Mulcahy's jaw tightened. He felt a sudden stiffening of the will. What these well-wishers augured for him, what he could augur for himself, he very simply and calmly declined, with thanks. To be fired at this juncture, when he was halfway to tenure, was unthinkable. Consequently, he refused to be fired. The moment he had enunciated this principle, in a cool and dispassionate inner voice, he recognized that from the very beginning he had never taken the President's letter seriously, never intended to be fired, and had been inwardly self-possessed and resolute while outwardly excited and incoherent.

Yet it was just this incoherence and illogic, he perceived, beginning to pace the floor again, that constituted the strength of his position. That clear sense of blame and wrong, of the unjustified and the unwarranted, that at the beginning of any dispute dominates the imagination and orders the facts of the case into an appearance of sequence became, as he knew, gradually blurred and was finally lost irrecapturably as the quarrel unfolded in all its organic complexity; he feared this development in the present case, this attrition of the issues, and saw that, in order to win, it would be necessary to shut his mind even to its own settled purpose, to be furious, voluble, contradictory, incapable of "listening to reason." What was required, in a word, was just that obstinate feigned *madness* of Hamlet's, the rejection of all outcomes and explanations, the determination to make trouble, to be inconvenient, obstructive to the general weal, like a sidewalk demonstrator who declines to "move on" when the word from above is given.

And for that matter, Mulcahy said to himself, dropping into his swivel chair and commencing to polish his glasses, who had the more to lose by publicity, he himself or the college? Was it not Maynard Hoar, precisely, who could not "afford" to have it known that he had got rid of an inconvenient critic—Maynard Hoar, author of a pamphlet,

"The Witch Hunt in Our Universities" (off-printed from the *American Scholar* and mailed out gratis by the bushel to a legion of "prominent educators"); Maynard Hoar, the photogenic, curly-haired evangelist of the right to teach, leader of torch parades against the loyalty oath, vigorous foe of "thought control" on the Town Meeting of the Air? Especially when it so happened that the inconvenient critic had been under fire, not so long ago, by a state legislature for "Communistic, atheistic tendencies," as evidenced by a few book reviews in the *Nation,* of all places, a single article in the old *Marxist Quarterly* ("James Joyce, Dialectical Materialist"), and a two-dollar contribution to the Wallace campaign. A faint speculative gleam appeared in Mulcahy's eyes; he lodged a third peppermint in his cheek and tapped musingly with a pencil on his teeth, a quick rat-a-tat-tat of estimate and conjecture.

Confronted with a charge of bias, Hoar, of course, would forensically repudiate any political motive in the termination of the contract, but rumor, working in secret, might tell a different story. . . . Mulcahy's pale eyebrows wryly lifted; he shrugged off a twinge of conscience: in the split modern world, he lightly posited, we are too often the dupes of appearance; let us look at the underlying reality. A year and a half ago (cf. the Convocation Address), Jocelyn had been officially enraptured to welcome Dr. Mulcahy to its staff, as an exemplar, a modern witness to the ordeal by slander, etc., etc., *passim* (see also the New York *Times* magazine for the fearless administrator's account of the factors that influenced his decision), but since then Dr. Fuchs had confessed; Mr. Hiss had been convicted; Mr. Greenglass and others (including a former Jocelyn physics student) had been tried for atomic spying; Senator McCarthy had appeared; at Jocelyn there had been a suicide among the former Students for Wallace, an attack from a Catholic pulpit, the withdrawal of a promised gift, a deepening of the budgetary crisis. And though the college still officially counted on "a swing of the pendulum back to the old native freedoms," Hoar, only this winter—under pressure, it was said, from the Alumni Fund Chairman—had reluctantly removed his name from the Stockholm Peace Petition. Mulcahy laughed comfortably. To those familiar with Maynard Hoar's history, he ventured to predict, the dismissal of an outspoken teacher, at this turning point in the college's affairs, might seem a *leetle* too opportune, especially if it could be shown that the teacher in question had engaged in political activities of the type now considered suspect.

Mulcahy sprang blazing to his feet. Surely (he saw it all now) he had been observed at the meeting of the Partisans for Peace, which, it so happened, he had gone to, with no special enthusiasm, at the invitation of a former colleague and fellow-Joycean who was scheduled to speak on the program. He looked in now and then on such affairs out of contempt for mob opinion, as a sheer exercise of his individual liberties, but would Hoar dare deny that his instructor of literature's presence there had been duly noted and reported on the campus by some vigilant F.B.I. agent?

He clapped his hand to his head. "*Dummkopf!*" he cried. "*Dummkopf!*"—awestruck at his own blindness. The clue had been in his hands as long ago as the Christmas reception. Hoar had tipped him off, but he, of course, had been too witless to heed it. He began to laugh intemperately, till the tears dampened his eyes, recalling the holiday scene in the President's living room, the damnable Swedish *glögg* and *pfeffernuesse,* candles, yule log, holly, students dressed as waits singing outside the window, and within, on an oak bench, Maynard Hoar, in heavy ribbed sweater, genially asserting that he could as soon, *in these times,* as president of a small, struggling college, appear at a "peace" rally as be found playing strip poker on Sunday in a whorehouse (laughter). How he, Henry Mulcahy, could have heard these words and failed to apply them to himself passed human understanding; disgust, he supposed, with the falsity of the tone, with the specious air of rueful openness, must have palsied his own powers of inference. Or possibly, he appended, his inner censor had simply declined to pass such rubbish as affecting himself in any fashion. What retort had Hoar expected from him anyway—explanations, promises of amendment, apologies?

Yet the joke was on Mulcahy this time, he had to admit, chuckling. Here he had been scrupling about ascribing bias to the President when the President had not scrupled to put that bias on record. There could be no doubt, certainly, he interjected, sobering, that he had been warned by Hoar, in public, before witnesses, and that he had seemed deliberately to ignore that warning; worse still, to repulse it. For some flippant demon had led him, of all people present, to frame an answer to Hoar. He had wondered aloud idly: Was Christianity compromised by the Magdalen? To which Hoar had replied, in a voice of cogent rebuke, "I'm unable, Hen, to identify myself with Jesus. *I don't know about you.*"

Nor, prompted memory, a precisian, was that all. Had not Hoar—yes, on that identical occasion—gone on to lay down the principle that the president of a college dedicated to free teaching methods had a duty, in times such as these, not to engage irresponsibly in political activities that could imperil the whole academic structure and in which (school principal's keen, probing gaze; measured pause for emphasis) he had *no deep belief.* Seeing how everything fitted together (whom else could this homily have been meant for?), Mulcahy fetched a sigh. The picture of the liberal educator in action was more damning than even he had supposed. It was a case, plainly, for the A.A.U.P. Grievance Committee, a clear instance of political pressure, complete with dates and witnesses. The evidence had been there all along, but he himself, in some recalcitrant part of his moral fiber, had been unwilling to see it. Preferable for humanity's sake, he thought, frowning, to believe that a teacher was being fired because of a personal vendetta than to know that a public man like Hoar was a lie, from springing curly hair to the soles of his moccasin shoes!

Mulcahy made a grimace of disgust, conscious suddenly of a moral distaste not only for this nasty specimen of the genus careerist impaled on the pin of discovery but for the task of exposing it to the public eye. And also, for the first time, strangely enough, he felt a certain chill objective sympathy or commiseration for a man who could sink so low, as for an inching worm on which the heel is descending. The certainty that Hoar was delib-

erately using him as a scapegoat to satisfy the reactionary trustees and fund-raisers afforded him no joy, but,
rather, sorrow for the race of men in general and for
this particular example of the human kind. And the fact
that he, Henry Mulcahy, had it within his power to ruin
the man forever, at least in liberal circles (*make no
mistake*, he said to himself bitterly, factual proof is unnecessary; the charge, the mere charge, will be sufficient), inclined him to fellow-feeling. He had seen, he thought,
too much of venality in the course of his academic experience to regard Jocelyn's president as exceptional or
exceptionally deserving of punishment. Not being an ideal-
ist, he was indifferent to the law of the talion; regrettably,
perhaps, but indubitably, he lacked the taste for blood.

And the *threat* of exposure in such cases, as one scarcely
needed to remind oneself—a pinched, wintry smile sharpened his diffuse features—was generally more effective
than the act. Seated at his desk, he tilted his fingertips
together in a contemplative triangle, and leisurely allowed his passion to cool—a favorite amusement of his
spare moments and an intellectual tonic. *Live and let live*,
he finally opined, was the most politic motto for the occasion. Maynard Hoar confronted with charges in a faculty
meeting or before the A.A.U.P. would have no recourse
but to fight, but Maynard Hoar in his office, respectfully
urged to "reconsider" by a little ad-hoc committee
("Think, President Hoar, is this the best moment, in the
very thick of the battle for academic liberties, to let out
a dissident teacher, the father of four children? Is there
not, in these times, an obligation to avoid even the appearance of yielding to popular pressures?") was still, one

would guess, open to persuasion. . . . Mulcahy sighed, forgoing the satisfaction of a joined battle; he was conscious of submitting to practicality as to an austere virtue.

The President (it was always well to remember) had the legal power not to reappoint anyone short of the professorial rank, and though a legal power was scarcely a moral imperative, how many ardent defenders (were the case to be argued in public) of the President's inalienable right to fire whom he pleased—for the color of his hair or his hatband—would not throng eagerly forward to speak against Mulcahy in the name of lily-white principle, and in the front ranks of the defenders of principle would he not find friends, who had dined with him, who had played with the children, who would be delighted now to lend him money, to write to a friend, the head of an adult-education project and fix him up with a splendid job, teaching nights to illiterates?

A terse laugh broke from him, and at almost the same moment, the two timid knocks he had been expecting sounded on the door. A young girl's face appeared, looking frightened. "Dr. Mulcahy?" "Come in, Sheila," he instructed kindly, taking pains as usual to speak in a soft, solicitous voice. Folding her heavy coat over the back of the side chair, the girl sat down, put her books on the arm, and crossed her thin hands tensely in her lap. She was pale, round-shouldered, reticent, a freshman, the daughter of a commercial artist, whom she reverently invoked as "Daddy." Her trial-project was American naturalism. Mulcahy's spectacled eyes assessed her, half pitying: a typical Jocelyn student of the paying sort that had been admitted in the fall by an over-lenient registrar.

The thin, blond hair, he observed with interest, was done in a new fashion, braided around her head in two petering-out pigtails—the style of the President's wife.

He raised his eyebrows a trifle. This visible sign of the Presidential influence affected him very unpleasantly; he took it as a bad omen for himself and his cause. At the same time, he felt quite detached and made note of it merely as a symptom, a corroboratory straw in the wind. "So that is how the land lies," he thought, giving an inward whistle. He felt decision form in him, like a clot. While the girl watched him, rabbit-scared, he refolded the President's letter, creased it incisively with his thumbnail, and dropped it into his file. He performed this action very slowly and deliberately, conscious that the girl would be thinking that the document he was suppressing must have something to do with her grades. "Now Sheila," he said to her, smiling, idly prolonging her mystification, "I see you are fixing your hair differently."

The girl's face brightened with a start; she glanced at the file somewhat doubtfully, as if seeking a connection. Then she looked up at him and blushed. "Do you like it?" she shyly asked. "Very much, Sheila," he replied in a grave tone. "It reminds me of my three little girls, with their pigtails. Do you know them, Sheila?" The girl nodded several times and spoke breathlessly. "I've seen them with you in the Co-op, Dr. Mulcahy. They're *darling*."

Mulcahy leaned forward, spontaneously moved. "You must come some time and see the baby boy, Sheila. You'll like him." "I'd love to," breathed the girl. "I love babies." "He's sick this morning, though, Sheila," he confided. "His mother is sick too." Impulse had been propelling him,

almost against his will. He felt himself gliding, by rhythmic
easy stages, into the girl's confidence; the knowledge that
there, in the file, lay that which would disrupt her faith
in officialdom gave him a sense of power over her and
all her virgin classmates, and the fact that he had no
intention of letting her in on that knowledge allowed him,
he calculated, to carry her to the very verge of discovery
with perfect safety to himself. Yet now a slight shifting
of the girl's weight in her chair made him imagine that
he had lost his hold on her. Conscious that his delivery
had become somewhat false and saccharine, he darted a
mistrustful glance into her eyes; what, he thought angrily,
did the young care for sickness and sorrow? Very likely,
thanks to the Sitters' Bureau, she had already had an
earful of his domestic cares. Her eyes, however, were
starry with sympathy and a sort of joyous gratitude; two
anxious furrows had appeared between her fuzzy brows.

"How awful, Dr. Mulcahy," she whispered. "I know
just how you must feel."

A smile touched his lips, a trifle coldly. "I doubt
whether you do, my dear," he retorted, stung to shortness
by her innocence, her protected life, her "Daddy." He
regarded her, narrowing his eyes, feeling pity for her
inexperience, her weak, soft, waxy soul, plastic to all im-
pressions, to himself, to the Hoars. "I doubt whether you
do," he lightly repeated.

The girl looked at him curiously, waiting for him to
go on. He felt a harsh desire to initiate that innocence,
to ply it with brute facts, like drink. At the same time, he
was aware that he ought to titillate her no longer. Her
aroused curiosity was a temptation, which, having sa-

vored it, he must now in wisdom put aside. According to
academic usage, the man must disappear into the pedagogue. He chose a book from her chair-arm.

"Sherwood Anderson," he announced, reading from the
spine. "And how did you like Windy MacPherson?" Yet
even as he was speaking, he felt another, irresistible force
take hold of him, not rudely but almost playfully, like a
spring breeze. "Look, Sheila," he murmured quickly, as
if fearful of being overheard or interrupted. "Would you
like me to tell you a secret?" The girl nodded, straining
forward. He had consolatory visions of student petitions,
torchlight parades, sit-down strikes in the classroom. He
held her in suspense for a moment—like a conductor, he
thought, with raised baton over the woodwinds of her feelings. "This morning, I was fired from Jocelyn."

CHAPTER II

Mulcahy Has an Idea

WHAT THE student, Sheila McKay, replied to his confidence was: how terrible, Dr. Mulcahy; how awful to have to break such a piece of news to your wife. Among the still-filial section of the student-body, the Mulcahys were acclaimed as a very devoted couple, an ideal couple, the girls said; so wrapped up in each other. They were popular, especially, as chaperons at the regular Saturday night dances, with the fat girls, pale girls, pimpled boys, chinless boys who stiffly paired off in the drafty gymnasium decorated with bows of crepe paper, while the rougher element, scornful of the old self-play phonograph or cheap three-piece band, of the basketball nets and the Indian clubs, drove off in its convertible to Gus's roadhouse or put on its pork-pie hat and buttoned its windbreaker and hitchhiked down the state highway to York or Lancaster or up to Harrisburg or chipped in on a gallon of red wine and made love on the couches of the darkened social rooms. In the brightly lit gymnasium, however, Catherine Mulcahy, née Riordan, led off with a boy-student, her pale-rimmed spectacles folded in their case for the night, her long heavy straight brown hair wound up high with a

Spanish comb from which a white-lace mantilla descended.
She wore her wedding-dress, a white satin and net con-
coction with a short train; crystal drops sparkled at her
ears; lipstick outlined her thin lips; and the pale, somewhat watery blue of her eyes, the sharp cut of her nose,
which ordinarily had a secretarial quiver, were lustered
and softened with excitement and a heightened sexual
aplomb. "Doesn't Mrs. Mulcahy look *beautiful?*" the girls
cried to their escorts, identifying Catherine's triumph over
four children, housekeeping, and poverty with their own
trepidant emergence from the chrysalis of slacks and blue
jeans, with the innocent magic of parties, rouge, low
dresses, music, with everything silky, shining, glossy, trans-
figured, and yet everyday and serviceable, like a spool of
mercerized cotton or a pair of transparent nylons reinforced at heel and toe.

And Dr. Mulcahy, by the serving-table, quaffing fruit-
juice punch and crunching cookies, waving jubilantly to
his wife, arguing the quantum theory with a physics or a
pre-med student, impressed for the boys and girls the die
of authority on the gala, as a more personable teacher
could not have done. This ugly, a-social man, at home and
suddenly garrulous in their midst, shedding his terrors
for them as his wife shed her spectacles, imparted to each
and every dancer a sense of privileged participation, of
having been chosen and honored, as though their act of
choice in inviting him set them under a new dispensation,
eventfully apart from the rest. These were not the remarkable students but the diffident, unoffending minority
who, anywhere else but Jocelyn, would have been on top
of the heap; and the knowledge that here the prerogative

of extending the invitation weekly, of securing a sitter for
the children, fell to them, of all people, rather than to their
elders and betters, made them feel almost apologetic; their
undeserved good fortune, surely, was a reflection on the
Jocelyn system of values.

In the eyes of such mild maiden freshmen as Sheila
McKay and her two roommates, the dances came slowly
to be conceived as an object-lesson to the college; this,
declared the minority, timidly presenting its bill of par-
ticulars, is what we would like Jocelyn to be. To have a
good attendance became urgent and exemplary, as winter
closed in and beer-cans piled up in the leaf-choked rain-
pipes of the boys' dormitories and the poker-playing
crowd kept the girls in the neighboring building awake all
night Saturdays and swaggered in, unshaven, to Sunday
breakfast in commons, boasting of no-hours sleep. Prose-
lytization for the dances went on, concomitantly, at an intensified pace in the girls' rooms—*"Don't* go to Phila-
delphia *this* weekend; stay and go to the dance!" Having
been taught by their mothers that the girl was always at
fault if the boy drank or took liberties, the missioners
applied this principle to the social situation at Jocelyn,
and, perched on the foots of beds, in pajamas, with cold
cream on their faces, in the bathroom with soap-dish and
towel, argued earnestly against weekend absenteeism, in-
differentism, *laisser aller*, capitulation to the status quo.

They knew that at bottom the inert majority felt as they
did: the girls' rooms they visited were decorated with the
same rag-dolls and teddy-bears, pink kewpies won at shoot-
ing-ranges, poufs and taffeta comforters, Mickey Mouse
lamps, pictures of Mummy and Daddy in silver frames;

the boys still had their lariats and bridles, souvenirs of the
rodeo, autographed baseballs, bird-books—often, on the
athletic field, on a clear fall afternoon, a boy would be
seen flying a pale-blue kite into the blue sky. And yet
agreement, they sorrowfully learned to recognize, was not
tantamount to active adherence. In principle, most would
admit that what Jocelyn needed in its social life was a
certain modicum of formality and supervision. In practice, few, it seemed, were convinced by the assertion that
Dr. and Mrs. Mulcahy had put new life into the dances
by taking their chaperonage *seriously*. The majority would
not consent to try out, even once, in action what it gladly
conceded in talk, and, tendering promises of "another
time," "ask me later," "give me a rain-check" (male),
would follow the crowd as usual down to Gus's roadhouse
or off and away altogether. What disturbed the advocates
of the dances most profoundly was the discovery of a
fathomless paradox at the bottom of their friends' thinking: in following the crowd, against their own will and
judgment, they were following themselves, i.e., nobody.

Moreover, the claim that the Mulcahys took their
chaperonage seriously, queer as this sounded as an in-
ducement to youth in a progressive college, actually
touched on a vital issue. The tolerance of other chaperons
had been the subject of much student dispute. Certain
younger teachers had been courting popularity by winking at gross infringements of the rules, allowing the punch
to be spiked, hip-flasks to be produced on the dance-floor,
necking to go on unchecked; on one occasion, even, mari-
juana had been smoked on the steps of the gymnasium
during intermissions, with the tacit, shrugging knowledge

of the faculty-member present. More responsible teachers, asked to serve as chaperons, irritably refused to give their time. Others treated the affair condescendingly, as a lark, coming in late, wearing ski-clothes or rough tweeds patched at the elbows, dancing close with their favorites or with members of their own party—moist-eyed strangers out of the night, wrapped in bright scarves and smelling of liquor. To such teachers, who appeared to live for the pleasure-principle, chaperonage, plainly, was a vast jest or a tiresome imposition; progressive education was a jest, which you winked at and made your living off; the students were comic archetypes, fantastic humors, butts of an educational ideology or else simply fair game, trophies of an impersonal venery—every year there were rumors of seduction, homosexuality, abortion, lesbian attachments, and what shocked the students about these stories, some of them very circumstantial, was the fact that they appeared to take place in a moral vacuum, to leave no trace the morning after; the teacher was at his desk, unchanged, smiling, impassive, and the student's grade, a C usually in these cases, showed no improvement for the encounter.

Dr. Mulcahy, of course, was not the only instructor whose domestic life was regular, but he was the only one of the modernists who had a real sympathy for youth. He respected it in its integrity, its conservatism, its quest for forms, laws, definitions, ruling principles. Over his charges on the dance-floor, he exercised a jealous surveillance; woe to those intruders, Baal-worshipers, who tried to spike the punch when he was present. He did not dance, but his eye noted any disorder among the dancers; his plump finger signed; his head beckoned, vigorously nodded with

approval when a jitterbugging pair desisted. Jingling a
coin in his pocket against his wife's compact and lipstick,
he tested the beat of the music, relayed requests to the
band or to the boy in charge of the records.

To his wife, Catherine, he frequently called out, in his
soft, caressive voice, which always sounded coaxing as if
it were calling a kitten, to ask whether she were tired,
whether he could get her something, obviously for the
purpose of receiving her radiant negative, the shake of the
white mantilla proclaiming to all present her unquench-
able, dauntless vitality. A certain element of tender pre-
arrangement seemed to enter into their public relation, as
though she were a film-star and he her discreet devoted
manager. The girls loved this, as a sort of testimonial or
advertisement of the permanence of romance in marriage.
They clustered about the coatroom early to get a glimpse
of him on his knees, fumbling with the clasps of her
overshoes, while she waited, complacent, tapping her free
foot, brightly waving and signaling, powdering her pointed
nose. She would kick the overshoes off one by one, with a
deft arch of her satined foot and then, with an imperious
gesture, slip her old black daytime coat with its fox collar from her strong, full, lotioned shoulders and toss it to
him at the coatroom window, with a cry, "Catch, Hen,"
clear, bell-like, commanding, and a flash of the even teeth.
The conspicuous whiteness and evenness of those teeth gave
her beauty an incisory quality.

Dressed in their "date-dresses" or "semi-formals," jew-
eled barrettes in their new-washed hair, the girls gazed
at the pair with nudging, sympathetic smiles, like grand-
mothers watching babies in a play-pen, while the boys,

garroted in neckties, their oiled hair striated with comb-
marks, stood by with board-like faces, declining to see the
meaning the girls squeezed out of this byplay; a few of
the taller ones exchanged shrugs of irony that remarked
on the married condition and on how the mighty had
fallen.

And yet to the Jocelyn boy who suffered himself to
attend these dances the Mulcahys were both "regular"
guys. These youths, for the most part, were still squirming
in the straitjacket of puberty; their hands trembled when
they lit a cigarette; their wrists protruded from their coat-
sleeves; they lived in an existential extremity; every instant of communication was anguish. Besides the beer-and-
convertible crowd—the ex-bootleggers' and racketeers'
sons, movie-agents' sons, the heavy-walleted incorrigible
sons of advertising geniuses who had been advised to try
Jocelyn as a last resort—the male part of the college
included an unusual number of child prodigies, mathematical wizards of fourteen, as well as some spastics and
paraplegics, cripples of various sorts, boys with tics, polio
victims. There were a deaf boy, a dumb boy, boys with
several kinds of speech-defects; there were two boys who
had fits, boys with unusual skin diseases, with ordinary
acne, with glasses, with poor teeth, a boy with a religious
complex, boys who had grown too fast, with long, chickeny
necks and quivering Adam's apples. The girls, by comparison, were blooming, healthy, often pretty specimens,
with the usual desires and values, daughters of commercial artists, commercial writers, radio-singers, insurance-
salesmen, dermatologists, girls who had failed to get
into Smith or nearby Swarthmore, girls from the surround-

ing region, narcissistic, indolent girls wanting a good time
and not choosey, girls who sculpted or did ceramics of
animals or fashion-drawing, hard-driving, liverish girls,
older than the rest, on scholarships.

This disparity between boys and girls created an awk-
wardness at the dances that made them seem like children's
parties, an enforced or legislated pleasure—the girls con-
sciously exercised charity; the boys yielded to coercion.
Under the Mulcahys' auspices, however, all this took on a
positive character. Those who were recruited came back
again with a growing confidence that such wholesome pastimes were licit, superior, in fact, to the brute pastimes
of the majority. The division of labor between husband
and wife provided reassurance both to the boys who danced
badly and the girls whose feet they stepped on; it gave an
authoritative precedent for the differences between the
sexes. With Dr. Mulcahy as a model, appearances lost their
terrors. A stammer, a cast in the eye invested a cheese-
faced boy with clerkly functions—he squinted on his part-
ner from a knot-hole of male assurance.

Catherine Mulcahy, moreover, had a womanly, Irish
way with her that put the boys at their ease. She was only
thirty-one and light on her feet; she had a low, warm
encouraging laugh; she remembered first names and nick-
names, parents' occupations, where one had gone to school,
what one thought of it, where one went for the summer;
she was the sort of person who was interested in your
birthday, and who could tell you what sign you were born
under, your birthstone, and the patron saint of the day.
Like the hefty, bantering nurses who helped you undress
in the family doctor's office and knew your weight and how

much you had grown in a year and your favorite movie-
star, she had a sort of *expertise* in the gross data of your
history that both made you uncomfortable and vaguely
stimulated you, as though a cool hand, plumping your
biography, patted the secret tissue of your being.

Henry Mulcahy, on the contrary, had no humor or
small talk. He impressed the group of boys present with
his indefatigable seriousness. Standing by the buffet, he
allowed himself to be bombarded with questions, like a
pitcher emerging from a ball-park or a great man arriving on the *Queen Mary:* "Dr. Mulcahy, what do you think
of Whitehead? Do you accept Vico's cyclical theory? Do
you follow Freud or Jung? How do you stand on the veto?"
He dispatched each query in turn, coolly, methodologi-
cally, meting out his thought in measured lengths, his
reddish head bent attentively sideward to his questioner,
as though to catch the precise phrasing of the order. Only
the athletic coach, speaking of batting averages, winning
infield combinations, end-runs, had an exactitude as tire-
less and considered as Dr. Mulcahy's, a willingness to
be tapped by all comers, as he sat crouched in the shed
in his windbreaker. Like the coach, Dr. Mulcahy was sometimes tetchy, irritable with flim-flam and trifling; his mind
was on twenty-four-hour patrol against incursions of the
vague and the unformulated—women's talk. In this touch
of paranoia, the boys recognized themselves: the masculine
principle. Here, while the music played, drifts of boys
surrounded him; partners edged off the dance-floor—
"Come on, I want to hear this"—listened, and danced
again. A senior girl's voice, plaintive, "Dr. Mulcahy,
really, do we have to believe in orgones?" A racketeer's

son, guffawing, pulling his girl forward, *"This,* I gotta
know." But such questions and such auditors displeased
him. He drew himself up; his fists clenched; his moon-
pale face darkened; in or out of the classroom, he declined
to discuss sex with adolescents. "Take your bull-session to
the social room; I refuse to be baited and you know it."

He made enemies thus and he welcomed it, welcomed
it all the more because those who at one time or another
he had to exclude from the dance-floor belonged almost
always to the wealthier classes or to one of the powerful
factions that ran the campus newspaper or the student-
government association. Following such an outburst, the
concise smile that hovered on his lips would grow more
effulgent as his eye traced the offender out of the hall to
the coatroom. His voice, resuming the conversation, was
breathy with satisfaction, as though he had been running
for a train and caught it. A messenger was sent to Catherine with a bulletin of reassurance: "Tell her, 'don't
worry, Dr. Mulcahy says; everything has been taken care
of.' " The boys left behind in the circle eyed each other
embarrassed; they observed in the teacher a demand for
congratulation that left them cold and stony—sufficiency
was what they expected of adults. Yet in the long run
the blame, they felt, lay more with those who provoked
him than with Dr. Mulcahy himself. He was a good scout,
they reasoned out later huskily among themselves, if you
knew how to handle him, and, having pointed this out to
each other, with recourse to many examples, they vaunted
themselves on having found the knack.

Reports of such incidents naturally circulated. The
younger group who attended the dances knew that it was

said that Mulcahy wantonly tyrannized over them, that his caprices interfered with their normal pleasures and outlets. This flattered them, whenever they heard it, by making them feel "bigger" than the people who took their cause up, so that their denials had a certain unction: "Don't worry about us, Mr. Fraenkel, Mr. Furness; we love it; really we do." The effect was to draw together a little band of truth-seekers who met to tell each *the latest*, viz., the newest stupidity or distortion. Such slanders or crazy conjectures, the students noted, were especially rife in the Social Sciences Division. Mr. Fraenkel, for example, in Contemporary History, who tutored one of Sheila's roommates, Lilia Jones, had gone so far as to wonder in conference whether Mulcahy might not have some sort of "hold" on the dance-committee—"a threat, conceivably, Lilia, to lower somebody's grade?"

Pink Lilia recounting this interview to her fellow-committee-members spoke in a tense whisper; her fat ringed fingers gripped the conference table of the little room in Students' basement. "I *told* him," she protested, wailing, "that we wanted Dr. Mulcahy, that we loved Mrs. Mulcahy and liked to see her get away from the children. But he *just wouldn't believe me*. 'I can understand, Lilia, that you wouldn't want to hurt their feelings.' " "Fraenkel's got it in for Mulcahy," hoarsely summed up a boy's voice. But Lilia would not allow her tutor to be reduced to a motive; a staunch Social Science major, she saw both sides of every question. "No," she said, thoughtfully, relinquishing her babyish manner. "I think you simplify. I believe he was trying to help us. He's a younger man himself, a product of the Roosevelt years, and so he doesn't understand, just because he's so close to us, that our generation wants something different, more guidance, more control. Dr. Mulcahy," she concluded, somewhat primly, "is far enough away from us to see us as we are." "A-a-ah, what a raw deal, though!" cried another boy, wearily, making a face of disgust. "What's the guy done that they're always after him, hounding him, grilling you about him in conference? It stinks." The committee looked at each other, feeling that something definite was called for. "Do you think we should tell him?" ventured a second girl. "No!" exploded the boy. " 'All so eager to make trouble,' " he mimicked them. "Leave him alone!"

Thus it happened that without his knowledge, a silent and even expectant cordon of sympathy had been drawn around Mulcahy and his family. The students had no way of guessing that he would or could be fired; they simply feared the worst, hopelessly, without denominating what it was. The sight of his old gray Plymouth sedan plying the icy back roads at all hours of the day and night, fetching groceries and drugs from the village, sitters from the college, laundry from a Mrs. Schmittlap in a farmhouse, affected his sympathizers with a sort of helpless consternation and humorous wry affection. The very weather, it seemed, was against him. Everything conspired. They heard rumors of unpaid bills, importunate tradesmen, radiators that had burst from the cold, sickness. The old car was a cartoon of man's afflictions, out of Job by Laurel and Hardy. The roof leaked; the front window was missing; the windshield wiper was broken; the fuel-pump coughed; he was obliged to park on a hill to be sure of getting started. In town, coming out of the movies, four or five students would turn to and push him from the parking-lot where he was stalled. The tires were worn smooth, and the boys who sometimes accompanied him home to fix the furnace or shovel out the driveway could not teach him that the proper thing was to keep your foot off the brake and steer *into* the skid, so that in consequence he was dependent on the tow-truck and a surly garage-proprietor to whom he already owed money. Walking through the snow to telephone, he continually caught cold. His classes were accustomed to broken appointments, to the typed notice on the door, "Dr. Mulcahy will not be able to meet his students today. See assignment notice in the library."

And yet in the darkening afternoons, when he chugged up to the Co-op with Mrs. Mulcahy and the children, leaving the motor running while he hurried them in to the counter for an after-school treat, ice-cream cones and Nabs all around, he and his wife, their noses white-tipped from the cold, were always brisk and merry. The Co-op's prices, a current campus scandal, meant nothing to him at such moments; he paid festively, without demur, whispering in a child's ear to offer the temptation of seconds, an Oreo, Necco wafers. In the smoky, crowded room his children whined a great deal, had the ball of ice-cream knocked from their cones, screamed, stamped their feet, clutched the crotch of their snowsuits and cried to go to the bathroom, but he, who flew off the handle so readily in his classes, was in this aspect unfailingly soothing and remedial. "Daddy will spank," he chastised in his honeyed, wheedling voice, but he did not mean it; he would tap a sticky hand lightly with his fingers. The worn, scolding

formulae of parenthood were frequently on his lips, but
speciously, almost sycophantically, as an exudation of
love: Nora was "naughty," he coddled; Mary Margaret,
"a bad girl," and Daddy would "tell" Mummy on her,
while his freckled hand strayed over the pigtails and his
mouth puckered for a kiss. If a child cried, he "punished"
whatever had offended it (*"bad* table," *"bad rough* boy,
did he jostle her?") or else discovered "a sore place"
and promised to have Mummy kiss it and "make it all
well again." The little girls thus formed the habit of striking him whenever they were angry with him, a thing that
caused child-study majors and potential sitters to quirk
their eyebrows telegraphically over their cokes or coffee,
yet even they, watching him play hurt in turn ("acting out
the inner tensions") were moved to marvel aloud at his
extraordinary patience and selflessness; not many fathers
of this era would suffer children so cheerfully.

Mulcahy himself, just now, in speaking as he had to
Sheila McKay, had slowly become aware of the sentimental
appeal of his four children, four motherless children, he
absently fancied them, so orphaned did he see them in her
eyes. He had not fully appreciated, until he began to
improvise, what a responsibility he had to his family. He
had been speaking thoughtlessly, at random, out of the
welter of gloomy associations induced by the President's
letter. The girl's response brought him to his senses. He
saw at once that to any normal onlooker the central point
of interest in his dismissal would be the effect on Catherine and the children.

This obliged him to rearrange his emotions; he would

not deny that, man-like, he had been laggard in marital
feeling; an adolescent had set him to rights. Catherine's
health, always a matter of concern to him, now abruptly
became paramount. He had no right, he remorsefully acknowledged, to inflict a new worry on her at a time when
her strength was depleted. *On no account must Catherine
know;* he rehearsed the prescription to himself, until he
felt it inhere in him, like a natural, spontaneous anxiety.
No worry, rest, light exercise—the warnings of doctors,
reactivated, chorused sedulously in his ears. As if in deference to her condition, he lowered the pitch of his feeling;
his thoughts went on tiptoe, gently, circling round her as
he had seen her last that morning, milk-pale, dangling a
toy over the sick child in its makeshift crib. The term, heart
murmur, tumbled at him out of a disordered memory—
was it herself or young Stephen she had been speaking of?

"I will not answer for the consequences"—his thought
grimly fastened on this phrase which he had heard in so
many movies that he could not recall whether it had actually been pronounced to him by one of the family's many
physicians or whether it was simply the gist, the hard core
of what they had kept telling him. And to think, he said
to himself, parenthetically, that he had once called this
"meddling," "interference between man and wife." He
brought his fist quietly down on the desk. He had known
for the last five minutes, ever since the door had shut on
Sheila, leaving, that he had Hoar on the griddle: he held
him *personally responsible* for the life of his wife and/or
child. He repeated the words with considered savagery,
biting them off one by one, as though to say, Play *that* on
your guitar.

He felt convinced, all at once, that Hoar had chosen, deliberately, to strike at him through Catherine. The letter was a mere move in a game designed to bring him to heel. Hoar knew very well what the shock might do to a woman with her kidney condition; to know such things, in fact, was his business as an administrator. Hoar had no real plan of firing him (that, actually, had been clear from the beginning); he wished simply to hear him plead, promise good behavior, *learn his lesson.* Mulcahy's jaw set. Was he to come before this Pharisee as a petitioner, pleading for a woman's life? For a moment his soul clearly countenanced the idea of killing wife and child, or, rather, of letting wife and child perish for the sake of an illimitable freedom. He knew himself capable of it and then gave way with a short laugh. " 'Springes to catch woodcocks,' " he remarked, lightly aspersing the old conflict between love and duty. The lethal decision, he perceived, was not his but the President's, and Hoar was not equal to it. Smiling sharply, he locked his desk, opened the door into the corridor, found it empty, locked his door and, dropping the key into his pocket, hurried on tiptoe down to the little wing at the end, where his two friends and also Catherine's friends, Mrs. Fortune and Miss Rejnev, had their offices.

CHAPTER III

Mea Culpa

"MAY I SPEAK to you, Domna, for a moment?" Cautiously, like the emissary of his body, Henry Mulcahy's head protruded into the Russian girl's office, around the edge of the door, which had opened noiselessly to admit it, while Miss Rejnev and her boy-tutee, forewarned by a slight creaking in the hall a moment earlier, sat transfixed, as in a horror-film, watching the knob turn. Domna frowned and looked at her wrist-watch; she was new enough to teaching to have a puritan sense of duty to her students; she disapproved of interruptions during the tutorial hour; yet Henry Mulcahy for her was invariably a special case, precisely because he was contemned, despised, importunate, and a clever man withal. She hesitated. "I can come back a little later," he vouchsafed, twirling the doorknob and swinging the door on its hinges. "*I* can come back, Miss Rejnev," put in the boy-student, eagerly resolving the difficulty. But this munificence, in its turn, annoyed her; the better Jocelyn student, like this one, was all too accommodating, ready to be put off, to anticipate faculty weakness and serve it sedulously, like a cause. "Could you wait five minutes, please, in the corridor?" she said to

Henry abruptly, in a voice that mixed apology with severity. In exactly six minutes, she reopened the door, and
the tall student passed through it, smiling. "Next!" he
said to Mulcahy, with a wink.

Domna Rejnev was the youngest member of the Literature department, a Radcliffe B.A., twenty-three years old,
teaching Russian literature and French. To deter familiarities, she wore a plain smock in her office that gave her
something of the look of a young woman scientist or in-
terne. Her grandfather had been a famous Liberal, one of
the leaders of the Cadet party in the Duma; her father, a
well-educated man, a friend of Cocteau and Diaghileff,
sold jewelry for a firm in Paris. She herself was a smoldering anachronism, a throwback to one of those ardent young
women of the Sixties, Turgenev's heroines, who cut their
curls short, studied Hegel, crossed their mammas and
papas, reproved their suitors, and dreamed resolutely of
"a new day" for peasants, workers, and technicians. Like
her prototypes, she gave the appearance of stifling in
conventional surroundings; her finely cut, mobile nostrils
quivered during a banal conversation as though, literally,
seeking air. Her dark, straight, glossy hair was worn
short and loose, without so much as a bobby-pin; she kept
ruffling an impatient hand through it to brush it back from
her eyes. She had a severe, beautiful, clear-cut profile, very
pure ivory skin, the color of old piano-keys; her lips, also,
were finely drawn and a true natural pink or rose. Her
very beauty had the quality, not of radiance or softness,
but of incorruptibility; it was the beauty of an absolute
or a political theorem. Unlike most advanced young women,
she dressed quietly, without tendentiousness—no ballet-

slippers, bangles, dirndls, flowers in the hair. She wore
dark suits of rather heavy, good material, cut somewhat
full in the coat-skirts: the European tailor-made. Only her
eyes were an exception to this restraint and muted gravity
of person; they were grey and queerly lit from within, as
by some dangerous electricity; she had a startling intensity
of gaze that never wavered from its object, like that of a
palmist or a seer. Her voice, on the contrary, was low, concise, and even; a slight English boarding-school accent
overlaid a Russian harshness.

As Mulcahy had more than once said of her, she had
the temperament and vocation of a *narodnika*. This was a
girl, he estimated, who could very easily throw herself
away. He had marked her out for his friendship at the
beginning of the term, having watched her go through
her paces at a departmental meeting, and sped straight
home to describe her, like a man who knows horseflesh
who has just clocked a maiden filly at a morning run on
the track. His wife concurred in his judgment when he
brought her back to supper, approved the girl's bright
eyes, willingness to help with the dishes, aptitude for
mimicry of stuffy colleagues in the department, gratitude
for being initiated into the inside workings of faculty
politics, corroboration of Henry's assessments of various
key individuals, the librarian, the Gestalt psychologist,
the secretary of the faculty, the little *Four Quartets* boy
who squeaked "tradition" when you pressed him and
would cut your throat in an instant for the advancement
of Number One. It was not only the incisiveness of the
girl's mind that impressed both Mulcahys so forcibly but
the directness of her heart and the current of vitality that

ran through her, rare enough in anybody, but perfectly
unbelievable at Jocelyn in one of "our" persuasion. Sound
her as they would, they had, up to this morning, found
nothing false or hollow in Domna; in politics, perhaps,
she tended to use somewhat too simplistic an approach,
following her compatriots, Tolstoy and Kropotkin; yet she
rang true as steel on every immediate issue. The fact that
the usual time-servers and trimmers on the campus, including even the wondrous Hoar, appeared to share their
admiration put them a little on their guard, but so far they
had seen nothing to indicate that these others knew the
real Domna; and they laughed to think of what Maynard
would think if he could guess what the real Domna thought
of him.

Henry, as he hurriedly closed the transom and bolted
the door behind him, while the girl's eyes slowly dilated
in wonder and misgiving, had no doubt, he told himself,
of Domna's immediate partisanship. The meals she had
eaten in his house, the Canadian Club whiskey he had
poured for her, in violation of his custom and budget (for
Domna, as he and Catherine had quickly observed, liked
to drink three little jiggers of neat whiskey before she
ate her dinner), the small presents she was in the habit
of bringing them—a dish of Russian kïssel with a white
napkin over it, french *chansons* with pictures for the
children, a small volume of Heine—the silver lent by
Cathy for a party, the Christmas tree with real candles
ordered by Domna from abroad, the movies seen, car borrowed, opinions matched, jokes shared, all reassured him
of her fealty; she *could* not go back on this. Still, he felt
a certain constraint and uneasiness as to where to begin,

whether to tackle her first on the academic freedom issue,
or to convince her at once of the imminent danger to
Cathy, a danger which, only a few moments before, he
had been so fuzzy-minded as to regard as merely hypo-
thetical but which, now that he had faced up to it, should
make everything else secondary.

And yet there were many, he thought vindictively, on
this "liberal" campus who would suppose that Cathy's
condition was something cooked up by himself to ward off
being dismissed without so much as a thank-you, many,
indeed, not so far off at this moment—he shot a quick barb
down the corridor in the direction of Howard Furness'
office—who would want a thorough medical report signed
by an "impartial" physician, in fact a coroner's inquest
certifying the cause of death, before they would believe
the simple clinical truth, just as, he presumed, they would
have to see a Communist Party membership-card (produced by an F.B.I. agent) made out to Henry Mulcahy,
before they would be willing to admit that his dismissal
was a part of a campaign of organized terror in the universities against men of independent mind. But Domna,
he reflected thankfully, was not one of these; she did not
require a statistical analysis to see what was under her
nose; moreover, as he happened to know, she had lost
her mother under circumstances horribly similar to those
in which Cathy now stood. That good lady, stigmatized by
her family as a *malade imaginaire,* had died of typhoid
on a freighter en route from Lisbon to Buenos Aires, so
Domna's aunt, her sister, had informed him, while he
drove her around the campus to spell Domna, who was
teaching a class; and the family, for a long time, she as-

sured him, held Domna very much responsible, both for
instigating the trip ("Why not put up with the Germans, I
ask you, Mr. Mulhall?") and for not calling the ship's
doctor sooner ("A girl of fifteen is for us already a woman,
Mr. Mullaly, especially when she mixes in politics"). It
did not need Freud's insights or Madame Repina's inti-
mation ("A little nervous breakdown, you understand
what I mean, eh?") to sympathize with the youngster who
carried such a memory about with her, a veritable night-
mare of fantasied aggression and punishment, and to cal-
culate that of all things in the world that Domna would not
risk again, the death of an older woman would surely figure
first.

Indeed, had there been anybody else to turn to whom
he could count on as he could count on Domna, he would
gladly have spared her these next moments, which might
very well reactivate the traumatic experience; for, desperate and harried as he was, he did not deceive himself
as to what Catherine meant to her, what their long morning talks and endless cups of black coffee had done to
make Jocelyn habitable for this lonely, affection-starved
child. (And the fact that Cathy had given herself always
without stint, not ever letting Domna guess that her health
was not up to such demands on it, would no doubt add a
belated remorse to the poor girl's other feelings.)

Silently, he took the letter from his breast pocket and
handed it across the desk. While she unfolded it, he
dropped into the side-chair still warm from the student's
bottom and affected to study his fingernails while watching her beneath his granulated lashes. Truth to tell, he
was quite curious to trap her first reaction, not because

he doubted her at all, but merely from professional interest: would Hoar's move come as a surprise to a fellow-member of the teaching caste or had they all been quietly anticipating it while only he had been gulled? But the girl's eyes, moving across the typescript, betrayed nothing, really. She turned white, he thought, for an instant, and then a light flush that might have been anger reddened her pointed cheekbones. "No!" she finally whispered in a shocked and scarified voice, as she passed the letter back to him—from which he was able to glean that rumors of his debts and generally poor prospects had reached her; she knew, then, that this was the end for Henry Mulcahy and Co. They sat and stared at each other without a word. Mechanically, she took a package of cigarettes from her smock pocket and offered it to him, as a warden offers a smoke to a condemned prisoner, and he silently waved it aside.

They heard the bell ring for the next class before she roused herself to speak and then she only said, absently, "When did you get it? This morning?" That she made no other inquiry struck him at once as peculiar. Was her mind already busy with the next step, with remedies and recourses, or had she somehow known all along? Had the department been consulted? *Was* it a departmental decision, taken without his knowledge? Could she, even, have concurred in it? "But appointments are not made until spring," she suddenly objected, just as he was giving up hope of any spontaneous response from her. He drew a quick breath of satisfaction; she too, then, like himself, was simply stunned by the irregularity of these proceedings. Relieved, he decided to take the bull by the horns.

"Domna," he said, hurriedly, "I have something to tell you, in confidence. But first I must be able to trust you. Answer me honestly, is this the first word you have heard of this dismissal?" She nodded swiftly twice. "On my word of honor." "There's been no criticism of me in the department?" "Absolutely not. I swear it." Her tone had grown very positive, yet he thought he had heard, deep down, a little wavering in it, as of some qualification quickly overridden. . . . He waited. A faint, lurking smile appeared at the corners of her lips. "Some think you go too far," she murmured, "on the Buildings and Grounds question. Your scrambled eggs. . . ." A crinkle of laughter was in her voice, half-apologetic, as if inviting him to join in this belittling view of his activities. He stiffened. "Who thinks this?" he demanded, eyes narrowing. Domna flushed. "All of us. No one in particular. I, if you want, for one." Having made this confession, Domna obviously grew confused and began to let out more than she had intended. "But nobody," she explained, "takes a strict view of it, not even Maynard." Henry raised his eyebrows. "You've discussed it with him?" he cried. "Of course," she answered, self-justificatory, and would plainly have said more but he raised his hand to forestall it— it was evident that the girl had betrayed him, but the point was academic now. He got up, thoughtfully, from his chair and strolled over to the window, his hands plunged into his pockets, and stared out over the snow.

"Domna," he said, turning suddenly, "there's something I have to tell you. Cathy is ill, dangerously ill. She doesn't know it herself; nobody knows it but the doctor and myself and two other persons—Esther and Maynard

Hoar." The girl gave a frightened gasp and her hand flew
out in sympathy; she half rose from her seat, as though
to comfort him. But he held her off and commenced to
pace rapidly up and down. "It's a heart and kidney condition brought about by Stephen's birth. Nothing that she
won't recover from, given freedom from worry. There's
low blood pressure too and a secondary anemia, a syndrome, as they call it, embracing the whole system." Her
lips moved tensely, following him; plainly, she was trying
to relate the fearsome clinical terminology to the handsome, flesh-and-blood woman who was her friend, always
eager to lay down mop or carpet-sweeper for a cosy cigarette or a final mid-morning cup of coffee. "The doctors
agree," he consoled her, "that a normal life, in the circumstances, is the very best thing for her. Recreation, fresh
air, light housework, even driving the car—the point is
to spare her knowledge of her condition, which might af-
fect her like any other sudden shock, that is, induce a
coma or syncope that might or might not prove fatal." The
effort of pronouncing the last words in a tone of detached
objectivity brought tears unexpectedly to his eyes; with
a strangled sound and wry gesture, he sank into the chair,
removed his bifocals, and sobbed into his handkerchief,
while Domna stroked his frayed sleeve and uttered words
of comfort and hope. "What am I to do, Domna?" he
suddenly cried, from the depths of his extremity, pulling
himself bolt upright in his chair and transfixing her with
his eyes, half blind and crazily staring. "You tell me,"
he demanded. "What am I to do?"

Truly, he realized with astonishment, he had lost all
control of himself. To cry brokenly before a girl nearly

twenty years his junior had been no part of his intention; the utter misery of his situation had sprung on him, as he was speaking, from cover, like an animal at the throat. He wept hopelessly from sheer hatred of the universe, including the girl who was watching him and who could do nothing, of course, to help him, as he now for the first time clearly saw and admitted to himself. To his surprise, in the midst of his tears, Domna got up and left the room, locking the door behind her, coming back in a few minutes with an aspirin, a benzedrine tablet, a glass of water, and a clean handkerchief wrung out in cold water. "I've phoned Cathy," she said, "to tell her you're staying to lunch at the college. If you'd like a drink of whiskey, I'll take you home to my house in my car." Henry shook his head. He accepted the pills and put on his glasses, carefully, adjusting the wires over his ears. "Now," she said, "what did you mean when you said that Esther and Maynard knew that Cathy was dangerously ill?"

Henry bit his lips. He had added this detail on impulse and now he must make up his mind to tell her the whole squalid story, sparing neither the Hoars or himself, or forfeit the support she could give him; no half-measures would do. If Domna were satisfied that Maynard, knowing of Cathy's condition, had determined in cold blood to fire him for shabby political motives, she would fight for his reinstatement straight up to the board of trustees; even so, he frankly hesitated, being sharp enough to see that the knife cut two ways. If Cathy's condition or the knowledge of it imposed on Maynard Hoar the moral obligation not to fire him, should it not have imposed on her husband an even stronger obligation not to behave in such a way as to get himself fired? A man with a sick wife did not receive *carte blanche* to abuse the responsibilities of his position, but if a man with a sick wife was *unreasonably* discharged from his position, then the wife's health could become a significant factor in arguing for his retention. In short, the more he pondered on it, leaving his own feelings aside, the more clearly he saw that the case was and must be one of academic freedom. In which event, it behooved him to tread warily with Domna, who was capable of subordinating all other issues, dramatically, to the single life-or-death issue, in the manner of Dostoievsky and other Russian sentimentalists who opposed capital punishment and were fond of asserting categorically the absolute sacredness of the individual life. There was no question but that this would alienate from him certain older men on the faculty who, disliking Hoar, would probably be open to conviction on a purely professional argument. On the other hand, there was no doubt that Domna, pleading for another woman's life, would have behind her many of the women of the faculty who would not dream of enlisting their sympathies in an academic freedom case.

And the more he envisioned this prospect, the more he was of two minds about it: could Domna be trusted to keep this side of the affair in perspective? "I told Esther," he answered wearily, "a long time ago, under circumstances I don't like to remember." He rested his cheek in his palm. "Before your day, little Domna." Memories of that epoch disturbed him; he had almost forgotten the time when he and the Hoars had been like a single family, before Maynard unaccountably—yes, even now unaccountably, for all that he now knew of Maynard—showed him

the cold shoulder. "Yes?" Domna urged with a little whet
of curiosity. Henry. suddenly laughed. "Very funny,
Domna. Last spring, less than a year ago, when I brought
Cathy and the children here, I had Maynard's word that
the appointment was to run for two years, at the minimum.
Nothing on paper, of course. A gentlemen's agreement.
" 'Jocelyn doesn't part with good men, Hen; frankly, between ourselves, she can't afford to.' " He laughed again,
more harshly. Domna frowned. "A pity you didn't get it
on paper," she murmured.

This remark moved him to merriment. He laughed once
again, but now genuinely, intellectually, till the tears
rolled from his eyes. "Precisely," he cried. "You have it.
Proceed to the head of the class. A pity it is, indeed." But
as she commenced to laugh also, his mien immediately
sobered. "Domna," he confessed, "you won't believe it,
but I did try to get it on paper and at that moment my
friendship with the Hoars evaporated. Overnight. From
that moment, Maynard has hated me without respite." He
spoke with force and impressiveness, bringing his hand
down on the chair-arm; yet he thought he saw an inner
doubt or reservation shadow the girl's brow. "Listen,
Domna," he said earnestly. "Forget whatever you may
have picked up or whatever Maynard has told you and
hear my version first. It does me no credit, I promise
you, and you can judge for yourself how it leaves our
friend, Maynard." He began to pace the room. "Last
spring, as the campus gossip may have told you, my status
here was rather irregular. After the ruckus out West had
made all the papers and figured in the *Nation* and the
Witch Hunt book, as well as in a report of the A.A.U.P.,

several anonymous friends of the college got up a little purse and turned it over to Maynard, to use as he saw fit for victims of the purge in the universities. At that time, there was no vacancy in Literature and he used this grant to appoint me visiting lecturer in humanities—a special creation—with the understanding that I would be fitted into the Literature department at the first opportunity. However, as it happened, no vacancy did occur and I was unwilling to bring Cathy and the children on from her mother's without some assurance of tenure; Stephen had just been born. Maynard was very good about this; I was allowed certain traveling expenses to commute back and forth every month and free quarters in Barracks C, since it would be an obvious hardship for me to keep up two establishments on my salary. Once or twice I used this expense account to bring Cathy on to Jocelyn for a week or so; another time, say two times at most, I met her in Pittsburgh for a long weekend. I had my schedule arranged, so as to be free Mondays and Fridays. Well, as could have been predicted, someone—they say a student —carried the tale to Hoar: I alone on the faculty was teaching a three-day week! Maynard had me on the carpet, very firm, and, to do him justice, sympathetic. He foresaw an opening in Literature, but if my appointment were to be put on a regular, permanent basis, a new living arrangement would have to be stipulated. As an official member of the department, I would be expected to conform to the Jocelyn principle of *communitas!*"

Domna nodded, warmly. "I too!" she exclaimed. " 'The fully resident faculty. . . . we don't punch a time-clock here, Miss Rejnev, but we must ask you, in all conscience, not to emulate Bard and Sarah Lawrence and treat us as though you were a commuter.' " The vagaries of the President's diction seemed to evoke nostalgia from both of them, for a time when they had merely laughed over Maynard. Henry swiftly cut into this mood.

"Naturally, I insisted on a two-year contract to compensate me for the expenses of moving. Maynard perfectly saw my position, agreed with it, but unfortunately the policy of the trustees gave him no leeway. Contracts at the instructor level ran for the single year only. No exception to be made without establishing a precedent, and tradition only permitted three professorial salaries in the Division, one full professor in Languages, two associates in Literature. He could give me his word, of course, that the appointment would be continued, if I, on my side, would give evidence of my own commitment by bringing on Cathy and the children and taking a house in the neighborhood." He came to an abrupt stop in his pacing, folded his arms, and stood looking down at her, measuringly, while he tilted the tip of his tongue against the sharp edges of his teeth. "At that point," he said. "I did a very foolish thing."

"You told Esther," she suggested, in her low, consolatory voice. This divination of his conduct rather startled him; he had intended to take her by surprise. "About Cathy's condition? Yes," he acknowledged. "It was a question of paying the movers to get the furniture out of storage. My mother-in-law, who *could* pay, was understandably against the move. I didn't know where else to turn. It appeared to me that Esther, if she knew how serious things were with Cathy, how necessary security was for her, might stir Maynard up to give me a letter, something on paper, you know, to show the old lady. In fact," he admitted apologetically, "I'd already wired Cathy that such a letter was in existence."

Domna turned white. "Oh, no, Henry!" she protested, as if to deter him from continuing with a tale that harrowed him too much. "Wait!" He raised a finger and moved a little nearer to her. He experienced a strange, confident exhilaration in forcing her to know him at his worst. "Exactly fourteen hours after I spoke to Esther, Maynard called me to his office." He paused. Domna caught her breath. "To assure me that the ultimate decision rested with my own conscience. The college would exercise no pressure." He spread his freckled hands expressively. "By that time, the van was crossing the Alleghenies."

Domna's whole body stiffened, while Henry watched her curiously. This, he was aware, was the real crisis in her loyalty; yet he felt no impulse to press her, but rather a pleasure in waiting while she worked out her own course. She was too intelligent not to see that Hoar had put himself in the clear, that there was not the shadow of a claim on him, technically speaking: his hands were as clean as Pilate's, ceremonially laved on his balcony; his wife doubtless had had a dream and sent to him, saying, "Have nothing to do, Maynard, with this just man." Yet did not this precisely make the point? Would Domna be wise enough to know that this very avoidance of a claim on him was in Maynard the measure of an atrocious guilt, a refusal of responsibility, of jointness in the Mystic Body ("We are members, one of another")?

Domna's rose-colored lips curled. "Monster," she spat

out calmly. "Monsters, both of them. Do they think then that *that* absolves them?" She made a rather theatrical gesture of drawing her skirt aside. Henry was filled with amazement. He felt himself catching fire, quite impersonally, from her, as if his own paler responses blushed beside this defiance. What marvelous contempt, he inwardly exclaimed, and puckered his own lip sourly in imitation of this sublime disdain. "Still, Domna," he expostulated, in an aggrieved and somewhat whining tone. "Maynard can plausibly contend that he has no responsibility for Cathy, in fact that he tried to deter me from making an imprudent commitment. We mustn't commit the error of putting Cathy's health too much in the foreground of the case." Domna, as he had feared, seemed to be genuinely astonished. "Why not?" she cried. "What else could be in the foreground?" Her dark brows arched in vivid semicircles as she swung around to face him. As always in moments of excitement, her accent became more marked. "What is complicated here?" she protested. "It is all very simple. One does not undertake actions that will lead to the death of other people, short of war at any rate. Does Maynard Hoar accept himself as a murderer? Will you accept him so?" Her strange, intent eyes were shining; she tossed her head angrily and the dark, clean hair bobbed; she clicked her pocket-lighter and drew in on a cigarette. "This cannot be permitted to happen," she declared quickly, amid puffs of smoke. "One simply refuses it and tells Maynard Hoar so." She jumped up, knocking a book off the desk, and seized her polo coat from the coatrack. "I shall do it myself at once to set an example."

Henry moistened his lips, half tempted by this rashness.

"You forget that it must be kept from Cathy," he said peevishly. "If you go to Maynard in this mood, the whole campus will hear of it." Domna stood holding her coat. "Come," he said, "sit down. Do you think that you will convince Maynard by moral arguments when he has already come to this decision fully knowing of Cathy's condition? Let me tell you something more. In the desk at home, there is a forged letter purporting to be from Maynard, promising me a permanent appointment. Cathy believes in that letter. Do you see now that we must be quiet?" Domna slowly put her coat back and leaned against the desk, lacing and unlacing her fingers. "What's to be done then?" she asked in a toneless voice. "What's to become of you, Henry?" Her eyes, wide and frightened, ransacked him as though seeking his destiny. He shrugged. This new admission, he saw with relief and a certain misanthropy, had put her altogether in his hands; his malfeasance would make her submit to his better judgment as to ways and means, as she would submit to the superior knowledge of a criminal whom she was concealing in her house. At bottom, he reminded himself, she was conventional, believing in a conventional moral order and shocked by deviations from it into a sense of helpless guilt toward the deviator. In other words, she was a true liberal, as he had always suspected, who could not tolerate in her well-modulated heart that others should be wickeder than she, any more than she could bear that she should be richer, better born, better looking than some statistical median.

And now, lo and behold, she was proceeding to give him a perfect example of these mental processes, even when one would have thought that her eyes would have been opened to a darker truth about human nature than her philosophy admitted. "Henry," she began, frowning, "is it possible, do you suppose that Cathy, unknown to you, has talked about this contract among the faculty wives?" "Cathy doesn't see the faculty wives," he answered with impatience. "In the nursery school? In the grocery store?" She pushed her feminine point home with typically feminine insistence. "Supposing she did mention it?" she persisted. "It would be a perfectly natural and harmless thing to do, if one were talking about next year or plans for the children. Yet mention of a two-year contract could give rise to all sorts of jealousies and resentments, even on the upper levels. Suppose then some husband carried the story to Maynard and demanded to know whether it was true or not? Can't you then imagine Maynard's getting very angry and giving you notice straight off, simply to show you who was master, who wrote the contracts at Jocelyn?" She had moved along the desk till she was close to him and could look up softly into his face, like a pleading sweetheart urging her boy to reform—with no idea that she had offended him and was offending him more with every irrelevant word she uttered. "I don't mean to exculpate Maynard, but if this *should* be so, it at least makes him understandable. Perhaps, if I were to talk to him, he would tell me and I could explain it to him . . . ?" She stole another glance into his face and broke off, suddenly irresolute.

Without answering, he strode over to the window and looked out at a truck which was unloading some crates onto the platform of the maintenance building on which Domna's office faced. The blank brick walls of the maintenance building, the smoking chimneys of the incinerator, the heavy truck with its indubitably dubious cargo—how many crates short was this order, what was the kickback today?—all perfectly suited his humor. He and Domna were getting nowhere; she refused to see, as if it were deliberately, the real dynamite in the case.

"Domna," he said wearily, turning around from the window. "Can't you see that what you are suggesting means dismissal for cause, blacklisting? Have you ever read the morals clause in the code on faculty tenure? You mustn't ever mention this letter or even think of it again, even if you should come to hate me like the others. As for Cathy, she has been told that the letter is not to be spoken of—for the very reasons you cite. Perhaps, even, she knows me well enough to have half guessed the truth behind it—and to keep her guess to herself, a lesson to all wives." He paced in silence for a moment, with a musing, deliberative air. "What you're after, of course, is motive. Hoar's motive, naturally—how has he been tempted to do this, knowing Cathy's condition? I can enlighten you if you want, at the cost of losing your sympathy." He stood smiling down at the girl, who had dropped without a word into her swivel-chair; nothing moved in her but her eyes, which looked up at him, mesmerized with instinctive fear, like an animal's. "But first let me hint this, Domna—you are somewhat too *bornée* in your thinking. There is something in you, perhaps an upper-class habit, that keeps you, with your excellent mind and remarkable analytic powers, from making what one might define as the necessary metaphysical leap, the two plus two making five that Dostoievsky speaks of." The girl nodded, almost joyously; she understood what he meant. "For example," he proceeded, in a style that was purposefully leisured, "your very search for motive lacks creative imagination. You are looking in private places, while the answer is staring you in the face, from the newspapers, the radio, the forum. Domna, we are at war, though apparently you only realize it when you are reading your morning newspaper. You imagine that the war is located in the dispatches of correspondents, but it is also here, on this campus."

The girl's eyes flew wide open; did she begin at last to see what he was driving at? How much, he asked himself, was it necessary to tell her to send the point home irrefutably? "But leave that for the moment. Let us return to your thinking. As an intellectual exercise, the broad jump we've been speaking of, try putting the question that is bothering you in the form of a declarative statement: 'Knowing of Cathy's condition, Hoar has been tempted to do this.' "

Domna caught her breath. He moved closer to her and slipped into the chair by her side, feeling a curious, reckless excitement as his full intention became clear to him. He picked up the hem of her smock and played with it in his fingers, rubbing the grain of the raw silk against the whorls of his flesh. Then he began to speak very rapidly. "There's another aspect of the case that I ought to have told you about. Something you may have guessed or may not have. You may not want any part of me when you hear the truth." He could see her pointed breasts rise and fall with her quickened breathing; she moved slightly away from him, but he maintained his hold on her smock. "Does your Russian second sight tell you?" he murmured. She shook her head stubbornly, and the dark, shining hair, as usual, fell into her eyes. "Well, then," he declared, squaring his stooped shoulders, "I must tell you that I am and have been for ten years a member of the Communist Party."

A low cry escaped her. "You!" she protested, and when he nodded gravely she burst out, all a-frenzied. "I can't believe it. I shan't believe it. I refuse. It's not like you. You are not political. You are a-political, the last man I have known of whom this could be true." Henry sat smiling through this tantrum. "You think, then, that Maynard is right to fire me?" he inquired in a satiny voice. Domna recovered herself. "No," she said slowly, "no." She straightened herself thoughtfully and brushed the lock of hair back from her eyes. "No," she reiterated yet another time. "I will stand by what I have always said. No one should be fired for mere belief; indoctrination is another matter." She had the air of reciting a lesson to firm it mechanically in her memory, and her gaze distantly rested on him as though to firm him in it too. "But I cannot feel the same to you," she appended in a formal tone. "Am I another man, then, than I was five minutes ago?" "Yes," she promptly answered. "You have lied to me and to everyone." Henry tugged a little on the smock, as if to recall his need to her; her downrightness had impressed him very favorably. He coughed.

"Once again you are too hasty, my dear. I would not have confessed to you if I were not at this moment an arch-enemy of the Party, one of those unfortunate prisoners of the Party you have read about in your newspaper who lack the courage to break, who live in fear of denunciation by some comrade who suspects us of backsliding, who are forced to perjure themselves on the witness-stand or see their families starve. Fifteen years ago, in a momentary enthusiasm, I joined the Party and since then I've had no rest, no respite, no night's unbroken sleep; I've been fired from five universities on various academic pretexts, never knowing who was responsible, the jealous head of the department, a student I've awarded an E to, or a comrade teacher to whom I'd spoken too frankly my real opinion of the Party.

"Looking back on it now, I see that I might have gotten out quietly during the Yalta period, as many others did, but I feared exposure too much, teaching in a conservative college with a Catholic president and dean. Had I broken at that time, I could not know that I would not be expelled and my name printed in the *Daily Worker;* this actually happened to many teachers in my unit. At any rate, I was afraid. Very possibly, I am a coward. In any event, once I had lied to my superiors as to my affiliations—under orders, of course, but also for my own skin—I was done for, the Party had me. I have been useful to them from time to time in various little undercover jobs, and they content themselves with merely terrorizing me in the interests of some future big job, if they are driven underground, say, and they need a respectable front or merely a letter-drop." His lips tightened in a short, bitter smile. "So, Domnatchka, you see, I have taken refuge in my irony, in the peculiarity of my position, a Communist in name only, like a wife of the same brand, allowed to go my own way, so long as I keep up the observances and pay my protection-money to the Bridges Defense Committee, the Committee for the Hollywood Ten (there but for the grace of God), the Trenton Six, and so forth. A unique life in No Man's Land, a target for both sides." Domna impulsively took his hand. "But you are not a Communist," she reassured him. "It is all very simple. You have only to get up and say so, here in a progressive college, and we will all protect you."

Henry shook his head. "Too late," he insisted. "Too late for anyone to break today who will not play the role of stool-pigeon or police-informer. You forget that I have perjured myself before my superiors and before a state legislature—an indictable offense. No one will protect us exes in America unless we also become antis, unless we are willing to wear the shoes of a Budenz or a Miss Bentley and denounce former comrades, many of whom, my dear, are very likely in my own position. No, thank you, Domna." He rose from his chair and stretched himself. "*Ite missa est*, or in Church Slavonic, *get out, Mulcahy, you're finished*." Domna took a swift breath and put out a hand to detain him. "You feel certain that Maynard knows?" she said with a troubled face. "You feel sure that that is the reason?" "What else?" he remarked lightly. "As is common knowledge on the campus, two gentlemen from the F.B.I. paid a call to Jocelyn last week. A purely social visit, you think?" Wheeling suddenly, he approached the desk with a complete change of mien. "You see it all now, don't you?" he demanded in a breathy, sibilant voice. "The heat is on Maynard to get rid of me. I have become a political liability, and he will use any pretext to get rid of me before my name appears in a congressional investigation. And I myself—what a superb irony—have furnished him with just the lever he needs to slide me out quietly, without controversy—Cathy's heart condition. Very considerately, he notifies me well in advance of the termination of my contract, smoothly bypasses the department, and leaves it up to me to find other employment before I dare tell Cathy that we're moving on to pastures new." In the mounting excitement of the last words, he felt his head exultantly whirling; speed and the impediment of his lisp made him salivate copiously as he spoke. "What would you think now," he brought out, "if I put it to you: 'knowing of Cathy's condition, Hoar has been tempted to do this'?" Domna slowly raised her eyes. "I would think as you do," she acceded in a low, unwilling voice.

She rose from her desk summarily and tore a slip of paper from her memo pad, on which from time to time during the last five minutes she had been scribbling a list of some kind which his eyes had been mistrustfully glancing toward without being able to read. Now, with bated breath, he watched her take off the smock and put on her coat; she looked very smart, trim, and handsome, and he scarcely dared ask her what she was planning to do. "You're going to see Maynard?" he finally ventured. Domna shook her head. "Too early for that. As you say, this is not a private matter. Maynard must be faced with it in the open, insofar as we can do that and protect you and Cathy at the same time. You don't mind, do you, if I date your last active membership back a few years, say, *before* you were investigated by the legislature?" "Whatever you think best," he acquiesced gratefully; their roles, he perceived, had changed again, and it was better so for the moment. "But what?" he nevertheless queried, in some real mystification. She flashed the list before his eyes, rather gaily, and he was able to read on it the names of six colleagues, with notes and questions opposite each, written in violet ink in her large European hand.

"Your sympathizers," she tersely remarked.

CHAPTER IV

Ancient History

JOCELYN COLLEGE, on this mid-morning in January, as Henry Mulcahy trod softly through its corridors, had a faculty of forty-one persons and a student-body of two hundred and eighty-three—a ratio of one teacher to every 6.9 students, which made possible the practice of "individual instruction" as carried on at Bennington (6:1), Sarah Lawrence (6.4:1), Bard (6.9:1), and St. John's (7.7:1). It had been founded in the late Thirties by an experimental educator and lecturer, backed by a group of society-women in Cleveland, Pittsburgh, and Cincinnati who wished to strike a middle course between the existing extremes, between Aquinas and Dewey, the modern dance and the labor movement. Its students were neither to till the soil as at Antioch nor weave on looms as at Black Mountain; they were to be grounded neither in the grass-roots present as at Sarah Lawrence nor in the great-books past as at St. John's or Chicago; they were to specialize neither in verse-writing, nor in the poetic theatre, nor in the techniques of co-operative living—they were simply to be free, spontaneous, and coeducational.

What the founder had had in mind was a utopian ex-

periment in so-called "scientific" education; by the use of
aptitude tests, psychological questionnaires, even blood-
sampling and cranial measurements, he hoped to discover
a method of gauging student-potential and directing it into
the proper channels for maximum self-realization—he saw
himself as an engineer and the college as a reclamation
project along the lines of the Grand Coulee or the TVA.
The women behind him, however, regarded the matter
more simply, in the usual fashion of trustees. What they
wanted to introduce into their region was a center of "per-
sonalized" education, with courses tailored to the individual need, like their own foundation-garments, and a staff
of experts and consultants, each with a little "name" in his
field, like the Michels and Antoines of Fifth Avenue, to
interpret the student's personality. In the long run, these
views, seemingly so harmonious, were found to be far
apart. The founder had the sincere idea of running his
college as a laboratory; failure in an individual case he
found as interesting as success. Under his permissive system, the students were free to study or not as they chose;
he believed that the healthy organism would elect, like an
animal, what was best for it. If the student failed to go in
the direction indicated by the results of his testing, or in
any direction at all, this was noted down and in time
communicated to his parents, merely as a matter of interest—to push him in any way would be a violation of the
neutrality of the experiment. The high percentage of failure was taken to be significant of the failures of secondary
education; any serious reform in methodology must reach
down to the kindergarten and the nursery school, through
the whole preparatory system, and it was noteworthy, in

this connection, that the progressive schools were doing their job no better than the old-fashioned classical ones. Indeed, comparative studies showed the graduates of progressive schools to be *more* dependent on outside initiative, on an authoritarian leader-pattern, than any other group in the community.

This finding convinced the trustees, who included the heads of two progressive schools, that the founder was ahead of his time, a stimulating man in the tradition of Pasteur and the early vivisectionists, whom history would give his due. He left the college the legacy of a strong scientific bent and a reputation for enthusiasm and crankishness that reflected itself in budgetary difficulties and in the prevalence of an "undesirable" type of student. Despite a high tuition and other screening devices (a geographical quota, interviews with the applicant and with the applicant's parents, submission of a photograph when this was not practicable, solicitation of private schools), despite a picturesque campus—a group of long, thick-walled, mansarded, white-shuttered stone dwellings arranged around a cupolaed chapel with a planting of hemlocks, the remains of a small, old German Reformed denominational college that had imparted to the secluded ridge a Calvinistic sweetness of worship and election— something, perhaps the coeducational factor, perhaps the once-advertised freedom, had worked to give the college a peculiarly plebeian and subversive tone, like that of a big-city high-school.

It was the mixture of the sexes, some thought, that had introduced a crude and predatory bravado into the campus life; the glamour was rubbed off sex by the daily jostle in soda-shop and barroom and the nightly necking in the social rooms, and this, in its turn, had its effect on all ideals and absolutes. Differences were leveled; courses were regarded with a cynical, practical eye; students of both sexes had the wary disillusionment and aimlessness of battle-hardened Marines. After six months at Jocelyn, they felt that they had "seen through" life, through all attempts to educate and improve them, through love, poetry, philosophy, fame, and were here, it would seem, through some sort of coercion, like a drafted army. Thronging into store or classroom, in jeans, old sweaters, caps, visors, strewing cigarette-butts and candy-wrappers, they gave a mass impression that transcended their individual personalities, which were often soft, perturbed, uncertain, innocent; yet the very sight of an individual face, plunged deep in its own introspection, as in a blanket, heightened the crowd-sense they communicated, like soldiers in a truck, subway riders on their straps, serried but isolated, each in his stubborn dream, resistant to waking fully—at whatever time of day, the Jocelyn students were always sleepy, yawning, and rather gummy-eyed, as though it were seven in the morning and they unwillingly on the street.

Yet this very rawness and formlessness in the students made them interesting to teach. Badly prepared, sleepy, and evasive, they *could* nevertheless be stirred to wonder and pent admiration at the discovery of form and pattern in history or a work of art or a laboratory experiment, though ceding this admiration grudgingly and by degrees, like primitive peoples who must see an act performed over and over again before they can be convinced that some magic is not behind it, that they are not the dupes of an illusionist. To teachers with some experience of the ordinary class-bound private college student, of the quiet lecture-hall with the fair duteous heads bent over the notebooks, Jocelyn's hard-eyed watchers signified the real. Seeing them come year after year, the stiff-spined, angry only children with inhibitions about the opposite sex, being entrained here remedially by their parents, as they had been routed to the dentist for braces, the wild-haired progressive-school rejects, offspring of broken homes, the sexually adventurous youths looking to meet their opposite numbers in the women's dormitories, without the social complications of fraternities and sororities or the restraints of grades, examinations, compulsory athletics, R.O.T.C., the single well-dressed Adonis from Sewickley with a private plane and a neurosis, the fourteen-year-old mathematical Russian Jewish boys on scholarships, with their violin cases and timorous, old-country parents, hovering humbly outside the Registrar's door as at a consular office, the cold peroxided beauties who had once done modeling for Powers and were here while waiting for a screen-test, the girls from Honolulu or Taos who could "sit on" their hair and wore it down their backs, Godiva-style, and were named Rina or Blanca or Snow-White, the conventional Allysons and Pattys whose favorite book was *Winnie-the-Pooh*— seeing them, the old-timers shook their heads and marveled at how the college could continue but in the same style that they marveled at the survival of the race itself. Among these students, they knew, there would be a large percentage of trouble-makers and a handful of gifted creatures who would redeem the whole; four out of five of these would be, predictably, the scholarship students, and the fifth a riddle and an anomaly, coming forward at the last moment, from the ranks of Allysons or Blancas, like the tortoise in the fable, or the sleeper in the horse-race, a term which at Jocelyn had a peculiar nicety of meaning.

And over the management of these students, the faculty, equally heterogeneous, would, within the year, become embroiled, with each other, with the student-body, or with the President or trustees. A scandal could be counted on that would cause a liberal lady somewhere to strike the college from her will: a pregnant girl, the pilfering of reserve books from the library, the usual plagiarism case, alleged racial discrimination, charges of alcoholism or homosexuality, a strike against the food in the dining-room, the prices in the college store, suppression of the student paper, alleged use of a course in myth to proselytize for religion, a student demand that a rule be laid down, in the handbook, governing sexual intercourse, if disciplinary action was to be taken against those who made love *off* the college premises and were observed by faculty-snoopers. No truly great question had ever agitated the campus since the original days of the founder, but the ordinary trivia of college life were here blown up, according to critics, out of all proportion. There had been no loyalty oath, no violation of academic freedom, but problems of freedom and fealty were discovered in the smallest issue, in whether, for example, students in the dining-hall, when surrendering their plates to the waiters, should pass them to the right or the left, clockwise or counterclockwise; at an all-college meeting, held in December of this year, compulsory for all students, faculty, and administrative staff,

President Maynard Hoar had come within an ace of resigning when his appeal for moderation in the discussion had met with open cat-calls from the counterclockwise faction.

Thus the college faced every year an insurrectionary situation; in the course of twelve years it had had five presidents, including the founder, who was unseated after only eleven months of service. During the War, it had nearly foundered and been saved by the influx of veterans studying under the GI bill and by the new plutocracy of five-percenters, car-dealers, black-market slaughterers, tire-salesmen, and retail merchants who seemed to Jocelyn's presidents to have been specially enriched by Providence, working mysteriously, with the interests of the small college in mind. These new recruits to the capitalist classes had no educational prejudices, were extremely respectful of the faculty, to whom they sent bulky presents of liquor or perfume, as to valuable clients at Christmas-time; they came to the college seldom, sometimes only once, for Commencement, passed out cigars and invitations to use the shack at Miami or Coral Gables *any time at all*—this benign and preoccupied gratitude, tactfully conscious of services rendered, extended also to friends and roommates of the poorer sort. Several years after graduation, little shoals of Jocelyn students would still be found living together co-operatively, in Malibu or St. Augustine—occasionally with an ex-teacher—sharing a single allowance under the bamboo tree.

Hence, though the college was in continual hot water financially, it had inevitably grown accustomed to close shaves and miraculous windfalls. Only the bursar seriously worried about balancing the budget, and his worries were accepted tolerantly—this was his *métier*. The faculty now took it for granted that fresh students would appear every fall out of nowhere, from the blue sky of promoters' ventures, a strange new race, or stock issued by a wildcat bank, spending what would appear to be stage-money; and the yearly advent of these registrants in defiance of the laws of probability created in the staff a certain sense of displacement or of nonchalance or autarchic license, depending on the individual character. Careless of the future, fractious, oblivious of the past, believing that the industrial revolution was an actual armed uprising of the nineteenth century, that oranges grew in Norway and fir-trees on the Nile, these sons of shortages and rationing seemed to have sprung from no human ancestry but from War, like the dragon's teeth sown in the Theban meadow. And the faculty which was teaching them their Cadmean alphabet fell to some extent under their influence; they too became indifferent to the morrow and forgetful of past incentives. There was a whiff of paganism in the air, of freedom from material cares that evoked the South Sea islands even in the Pennsylvania winter; more than one faculty-member, washed up on this coral strand, came to resemble, in dress and habits, the traditional beachcomber of fiction.

But the absence of pressure from without, the unconcern of parents and inertia of alumni groups, produced at the same time an opposite and corrective tendency. The faculty contained a strong and permanent minority of principled dissenters, men and women whose personal austerities and ethical drives had made them unacceptable to the run of college presidents and who had found the freedom of Jocelyn both congenial and inspiriting. If beachcombers had come to rest here, so had a sect of missionaries, carrying the progressive doctrine from Bennington, Bard, or Reed, and splitting here at once, like the original Calvinist college, into a new group of sects and factions. From its inception, the college had been rent by fierce doctrinal disputes of a quasi-liturgical character. Unlike the more established progressive colleges, which lived, so to speak, on the fat of their original formula, without questioning its content, Jocelyn had attracted to itself a whole series of irreconcilables, to whom questioning was a passion, who, in the words of Tolstoy, *could not be silent.* Beginning with the founder's time, Jocelyn had served as a haven, like the early Pennsylvania country itself, with its Moravian and Mennonite and Hutterite and United Brethren chapels, its Quakers and Shakers and Anabaptists, for the persecuted of all tendencies within the fold of educational reform, and each new wave of migrants from the centers of progressive orthodoxy wished to perpetuate at Jocelyn the very conditions from which they had fled—thus the Bennington group assailed the Sarah Lawrence group and both assailed Dewey and Columbia, i.e., the parent-movement. Those who did not subscribe to any item of the progressive creed tended nevertheless to take sides with one faction or another for temperamental reasons; Aristotelians in philosophy joined with the Theatre myth-group to fight the Social Sciences.

An unresolved quarrel between the sciences and the humanities was at the bottom of every controversy, each claiming against the other the truer progressive orthodoxy, the words, *scholastic, formalistic, scientism, positivistic,* being hurled back and forth in the same timbered hall that had shivered to *Petrine, pseudo-Protestant, Johannean, Romanizing* in the days of the Mercersburg controversy, when a schism in the Lancaster synod had broken the old college asunder. It was the perennial quarrel, in short, between Geneva and Heidelberg, between Heidelburg and Augsburg, none the less passionate for the smallness of the arena and the fact that nobody cared, beyond the immediate disputants, how the issues were resolved. To whom did it matter, certainly not to the students, whether the college were to drop the term *progressive* and substitute *experimental* on page three of the catalogue? Yet to these men of conscience and consistency the point was just as cardinal as the spelling of *catalogue* (*catalog?*). Under the pretense of objectivity was a fighting word or spelling to be lowered from the masthead and a flag of truce run up? The defenders of the progressive citadel were always on the lookout for a semantic Trojan horse in any seemingly harmless resolution introduced by the enemy. And quite correctly so, for the enemy was cunning. Who would have suspected that a motion to drop the old engraved Latin diploma and replace it with a simple printed certificate, in English, announcing that the holder had completed the course of studies, concealed an entering wedge for a movement to bring Latin back into the curriculum? Many of the ultra-reform party had voted Aye to this suggestion, not seeing the infernal conservative logic behind it, which was that the college had no right to bestow a Latin diploma on a student incapable of reading it, and hence did not really rank with the old conferrers of the sheepskin but in a separate class, along, it was suavely argued, with the

trade schools and hairdressing colleges, which made no pre-
tenses to Roman universality, to the *nihil humani a me
alienum* implicit in the traditional scroll.

Blandness and a false show of co-operation, discovered
the ultras, were the characteristic revisionist subtleties—
agreement and a *reductio ad absurdum,* the dangerous
methods of the Greeks. Your true classicist would not
argue in favor of the spelling, *catalogue;* rather, he would
concur with the simplified spelling and move that the
whole catalogue be revised in this spirit, with *night* becoming *nite, right, rite,* and so on, merely for the sake of
consistency, at which point some burning-eyed and long-
repressed progressive fanatic would pop up to agree with
him, wholeheartedly, enthusiastically ("Let us break, in
one stroke, with the past"), and the fat would be in the
fire; the faculty, that is, exhausted by these shifts and
reversals, would vote to leave things as they were. The
experienced parliamentarians quickly learned the trick of
party regularity, that is, to vote the opposite of the enemy,
whatever the merits of a motion, but this rule was not
foolproof against a devious opponent, who could suddenly
change his position and throw the whole meeting into
confusion. And despite a great deal of coaching, the honest
and sincere doctrinaires of both sides tended, in the heat
of debate, to take individualistic stands and even, in moments of great excitement, to make common cause with
each other.

Nowhere did Jocelyn's faculty show its coat of many
colors more bewilderingly than in the discussion, which
took place every fall, of the winter field-period. According
to the orthodox view, which had been carried here from

Bennington, the field-period was the crux of the whole progressive system: the four weeks spent by the student *away* from the college in factory, laboratory, newspaper plant, publishing firm or settlement-house were the test of his self-reliance and his ability to learn through *doing;* the measure of the success of the field-period was the measure of the success of the college. The ideas of the founder and of Dewey, Pestalozzi, and Montessori here coalesced. However, in the course of years, modifications of the original program had been permitted to creep in, concessions to practicality or to humanitarian sentiment. Some employers were steadily enthusiastic about hiring Jocelyn students for the allotted four weeks in February, others not so much so, owing to certain dire experiences which had created an unfortunate "stereotype" in the employer mind. Volunteer work, of course, was usually available, either in the social-service agencies, or in the wrapping department of commercial firms, but for poor students on scholarships, counting on a warm college room, and a regular job waiting on tables or running the college switchboard, it was often a cruel hardship to be turned out in February to work, gratis, in a strange city and pay for meals and a furnished room. Moreover, volunteer work was open to two objections: either it was "made" work, answering the telephone, running errands, taking notes at rehearsals, and hence of no social utility; or it involved scabbing—some employers, it was discovered, actually laid off workers in the February slack season, counting on the yearly migration of progressive students to keep the wheels turning at a slower pace. Thus the practice of allowing the student, under certain circumstances, to write an aca-

demic paper or note-topic and even in rare cases to be
housed in a college dormitory during the free month
slowly grew to be tolerated, and with tolerance came
abuses, so that the "pure scholarship" or "regressive" party
could claim that the field-period had ceased to fulfill its
function and therefore ought to be abolished.

The extremists of the progressive side found nothing to
criticize in this statement; either a return to first principles
or no field-period at all was the slogan that governed their
voting, and here they were in conflict with the moderates
of their own tendency, who felt obliged to defend the field-
period as it had actually evolved, abuses, academic papers
and all, against this two-pronged attack, to show how, in
certain circumstances, the preparation of a note-topic
might contribute to self-development, in short, to invoke
the arguments of traditionalist education and disparage
the very axioms on which Jocelyn was founded. The whole
question was further complicated by a material factor: one
of Jocelyn's great attractions for its faculty was precisely
the winter field-period, the four free recuperative weeks
in deadly February which could be spent in travel, literary
composition, private research, or simply in rest and enjoyment. The less scrupulous of both sides, therefore, making
up every year a plurality, voted shamelessly for any motion that would save their precious vacation. Those who
went so far as to admit that the student got nothing from
the field-period justified it on the grounds that *some* hiatus
was necessary for a faculty drained to the lees by the
exactions of individual instruction. "I don't care what you
call it," declared Ivy Legendre of the Theatre (Theater?)
Department, in her deep, bellicose, lesbian voice. "Call

it Faculty Rest or Florida Special, if you want, but get the little bastards out of my yellow hair." Mrs. Masterson of the Psychology Department, a spinsterish, anxious little widow with a high, thin voice, had compiled some very interesting figures on the relation of rest-periods to efficiency in factory work which she proffered to the faculty as relevant to the "vital discussion we are having"—it was this same little lady who had made a comparative study of the wages of teachers and garage-attendants in her busy Hudson coupé.

Henry Mulcahy, naturally, had electioneered for the field-period with white, bitter, tight-drawn lips, smiles of commendation for its supporters, glances of hatred for its enemies. Though he did not believe at all in learning through doing or the instrumental approach, he felt the issue as an extremely personal one and quarreled with his friend, Alma Fortune, who deprecated the field-period on principle; he was persuaded that she was trying maliciously to snatch from him a long-held, inalienable possession. To him it was an issue of immediate loyalty or disloyalty, and when he spoke, hissingly, of "the enemies of the field-period," it was as though the vacation were a person under threat of physical attack. He was everywhere at once during the crucial period, behind the scenes caucusing with the scientists whom he had despised but with whom he now discovered more than one common aim, in corridors buttonholing middle-of-the-roaders, on the telephone, in a sibilant whisper, lest the party-wire be listening, at the door of the faculty meeting, adjuring, fortifying, counting the number present in the chamber and how they were likely to vote. When it was over and the faculty voted, as usual, for the field-period loosely construed, he had an exalted sense of public service, as if by superhuman effort and by not counting the cost to self, he had averted from the college a danger of which it was largely unconscious.

In the same way, but on the opposite side of the fence, he had been busy in the undercover campaign against individual instruction, which just at this time was becoming the subject of complaint. On the virtue of small classes, everyone was agreed, but the more controversial part of the Jocelyn program, the so-called major project, or trial major project, had not worked out in practice quite according to Hoyle and was open, in fact, to the same kind of objections that had been made against the winter field-period. In brief, the system was this: the student was supposed to spend one hour a week with a tutor in his major field, this tutorial hour being the center of his education, accounting, theoretically, for one-fourth of his academic work and requiring a minimum of eight hours of preparation. This latter provision, the student, like all students everywhere, interpreted very freely: he put in as few hours as he could get away with. But the practicality of hoodwinking the tutor varied with different departments and thus gave rise to inequalities. For example, in sculpture, music, painting, or drama, and to some extent in physics and chemistry and zoology, the student was obliged to check in with the instructor for the requisite hours of studio or laboratory work and risked academic failure if he were not at least physically on the premises and engaged in a show of work. With the so-called "heavy" reading subjects, the situation was altogether different. A tutor carrying anywhere from six to eleven tutees—for the concentration varied from department to department—was in no position really to check up on how much reading was done, since each advisee or tutee was working, supposedly, in a different corner of a very wide field, a corner chosen by himself in accordance with his special interests. Thus a teacher of philosophy could not keep up with Heraclitus, Popper, Freddy Ayer, Pascal, Heidegger, Kierkegaard, and James, say, all in a single week, nor a teacher of literature with Richardson, James T. Farrell, Ben Jonson, Dos Passos, Horace, Zola, Gogol, Longinus on the Sublime. However well or little he had known these authors once, he was simply not up to the detailed questioning and discussion required to keep a student half-way up to scratch. The same was true of history and, to a lesser extent, of economics and political science, whose bibliographies were somewhat shorter. What happened, therefore, in practice was that students with applied art or science majors tended to gold-brick on their reading courses, and students with reading majors neglected their major project in favor of time spent in studio or laboratory in connection with an ordinary course. This difficulty appeared to be inherent in the system and provoked many departmental jealousies, with the scientists and applied-art people taking a superior line ("We can get work from our majors; why not you?"), so that irritation with individual instruction was concentrated largely in the humanistic studies and was tinctured with a sense of being misprized. The students, it was angrily noted, had been made to feel by the whole muscular progressive approach that reading was somehow bad for them and put on very touching and pathetic airs when a solid assignment in history or the novel was set before them.

But this was only one aspect of the question. In principle, the choice of subject within the field was left entirely up to the student. Within the realm of his major interest, he was at liberty to select any writer, period, movement, or phenomenon that struck his personal fancy. He could concentrate narrowly on a single exemplar or range over a whole epoch; he could study monotheism, Egyptian burial customs, Marx, Roman coins, land enclosure, English town life in the sixteenth century, the Maccabeean movement, the treatment of animals in primitive society, the history of absolutism, the phenomenological philosophers, war novels, Polynesian culture-heroes, Kafka, symbolism, naturalism, the rise of mercantilism, Steinbeck—anything he chose. The catalogue, which in some respects had not been altered since the founder's day, contained an alluring account of this freedom and its practical effects on hitherto unresponsive clay, written up rather in the manner of the old dynamic advertisement, "They laughed at me when I sat down to the piano." The classic case cited was that of a boy of religious temperament who was sent to Jocelyn after he had flunked out of two other colleges; his only interest was playing the organ in the chapel; after four years at Jocelyn, he was able to graduate, well up toward the middle of his class, having devoted his major project to a study of the influence of organ-music on eighteenth-century poetry. This manuscript, three times rewritten with the help of his tutor, was preserved in the library, together with the thesis of the girl who had come to Jocelyn unwillingly, wanting only to become a vet, and had finally made a niche for herself by comparing the role of the animal-as-magic-helper in Russian and German fairy-tales. Another boy (in this case a highly gifted student), fifteen years old, having an affair with a twenty-year-old girl, did a legendary paper not mentioned in the catalogue on the Older Woman in Stendhal and Benjamin Constant. A girl with a prostitute complex, so she maintained, had been helped to marry by studying her type in *Manon.*

Other examples, less curious, convinced the average entrant that he was not only going to be encouraged to express his individual bent, but that if he did not already have some personality-defining interest he had better work one up fast. Yet within the first few weeks he discovered that actuality did not jibe with these fancies—to his bewilderment he found himself pursuing a study, say, of Katherine Anne Porter instead of writing the radio serial he had come to college to do. Further and worse, when he went to the library to take out *Flowering Judas,* he learned from the librarian that all ten copies were out: Mr. Van Tour, his tutor, was giving it in Contemporary Literature, and several of his other tutees were making it their special interest. The librarian kindly offered to lend his personal Modern Library copy (he had done the same thing last year for several of Mr. Van Tour's students), and he also recommended an article by Mr. Van Tour in *Prairie Schooner* on "Regional Elements in the Work of K.A.P."

Were the boy to change to Mr. Furness, he might have the same experience with Kafka; to Dr. Mulcahy, with Joyce. If lucky, last year he might have got old Mr. Endicott, a veteran of the department, now retired, who would let him study anything he pleased and report on it, while the old man smoked his pipe in comfort, with his hearing-aid turned off. Except for certain younger teachers, like Miss Rejnev, who made much of being conscientious, the faculty, in practice, had arrived at a quiet gentlemen's agreement whereby each teacher offered two or three specialties, a limited choice, or else let the student roam, unsupervised, to some salt-lick of his own choosing. A student who did the latter was likely to get a high mark in Spontaneity but to rank low in Effort, Ability to Use the Tools of the Discipline, and Lack of Prejudice. The better students, in general, adjusted themselves without repining to what the faculty had to offer, pointing out to their juniors that it was better to allow Mr. Van Tour to teach you what he knew than what he didn't, patently; but the poorer students complained constantly of having to study things in which they were not "interested," i.e., those who had no real interests and no capacity for absorption but only passing whims with which they quickly grew bored felt genuinely deprived and disenfranchised at having to study a subject which someone else also was studying. They viewed the course of studies as a tray of sweetmeats held out before their greedy and yet suspicious eyes and cried out in fury when the tray was whisked away from them, still gluttonously hesitating, or when they were forced to accept a piece that another child had nibbled.

The effect of these sulky accusations was to make a section of the faculty wish to withdraw from the catalogue all claims to individual instruction and to have advisees in the reading courses double up in the tutorial hour, as they were already doing in sciences and languages, without anybody's saying anything to forbid it. But this proposal, though practical in one way, was in another sense, as everybody ought to have known, totally fanciful and heedless, since it was obvious that only individual instruction could justify the high tuition, which alone kept the college going. Hence the President and those close to the budgetary problem felt a real choler rise in them when anyone had the temerity to broach such a suggestion. To the men at the helm, in this hour of peril (the President, like all heads of institutions, was addicted to the nautical comparison), this was not a matter for free discussion, but savored, rather, of willfulness or mutiny on the high seas. And his face darkened as he said it; he would entertain no argument on the point. For he not only believed with all his heart in the merits of individual instruction but knew this belief to be necessary to his own and the college's survival, so that those who questioned it seemed to him true destroyers. The perfect college they hinted at might exist on paper but it would never attract students, for it would have no selling-point, no gimmick, as they said in advertising, which for the unendowed or virtually unendowed college was the very heart, the pump, the ticker.

Therefore, despite personal friendship, President Hoar experienced a nettled impatience with Miss Rejnev and other teachers of her ilk who were too stubbornly principled, on the one hand, and too eager for self-improvement, on the other, not to allow their tutees an absolutely free hand and indulge their own intellectual curiosity on the college time. He would not listen to criticism of the system from people who had no sense of proportion in the application of it; Miss Rejnev, Mrs. Fortune, and certain other members of the Literature department drove them-

selves too hard out of sheer whimsicality and caprice—
some might even call it perversity—and then put the blame
on the method, which others could handle with ease. And
to a certain extent, President Hoar's appraisal was correct.

Although it was true that these critics of individual instruction were among the few who practiced it literally,
their motives were somewhat dubious—did they really
wish to make individual instruction succeed or to show
that it could not do so? Second, did they really dislike it as
much as they pretended? The fact was, that much as they
decried the Jocelyn system as "intolerable" and "intellectually dishonest," these people were, in their own fashion, extremely happy at Jocelyn, like all people everywhere
who are working a little too hard on materials that are
new to them. To be allowed, under the cover of duty, to
pursue the world's history down its recondite byways was,
for Domna Rejnev, a pure nightly joy, a passion of legiti-
mate conquest, and her students were quick to discover
that they could not please Miss Rejnev better than by discovering a wish to study an author she had not read, prefer-
ably an old author, in some forgotten cranny of culture.
Thus, though she and others like her, themselves trained
in the classical order, protested on behalf of the student
Jocelyn's disorganized ways, it was the very lack of or-
ganization, the sense of teaching as a joint voyage of discovery or pleasure-trip, that made the college, despite
everything that could be said against it, a happy place for
its faculty. It was the faculty, paradoxically, that profited
most from Jocelyn's untrammeled and individualistic arrangements, the students being on the whole too disorderly

or lazy or ill-trained to carry anything very far without the spur of discipline.

For the faculty, as has been indicated, Jocelyn was by and large lotos-land. Those continuous factional disputes and ideological scandals were a form of spiritual luxury that satisfied the higher cravings for polemic, gossip, and backbiting without taking the baser shape, so noticeable in the larger universities, of personal competition and envy. Here, living was cheap and the salary-range was not great. The headships of departments were nominal, falling, by common consent, to the member with the greatest taste for paper-work. Such competition as there was centered around the tutees. The more ambitious teachers, as everywhere, vied for the better students, partly because these were more interesting and also easier to teach, partly because of vanity, and partly from the more insidious egotism of the Potter's Hand, the desire to shape and mold the better-than-common clay and breathe one's own ghostly life into it—the teacher's besetting temptation, God's sin, which Christ perhaps redeemed. Yet here, where such proclivities abounded, on account of the creative emphasis and the personal character of the tutorial relation, the danger was so manifest that defenses were erected against it. Strong influences were frowned on, academically, and those who wished to exert them were expected to do so off the premises, to the tinkle of the teacups or the cocktail shaker. In the assignment of tutees, impartiality was the order: anyone who wanted an A student agreed to accept two or three duds into the bargain. Since there were never enough A students to go around, inequities might have resulted, but for the fact that there were certain good-natured and easy-going

teachers who, from long habit, preferred the inferior student, like a broken-in pair of shoes, and hence righted the
balance—in fact, that diversity of tastes counted on by
utopian social theorists to take care in an ideal society of
the inevitable shortages of certain consumers' goods, such
as Rolls Royces, rubies, or good women, here operated in
practice, so that the majority of teachers were personally
content and just enough dissatisfied in conscience to make
life worth living. The intellectual scruple substituted for
the itch for gain by suggesting new incentives, opportunities
for reform and improvement, second chances, either for
the self or for the college, reasons, in short, to get up in
the morning that seemed to be lacking to the student.

The salary-scale here was significant. It ranged from
three thousand to five thousand a year, not much, one would
have said, by worldly standards, but adequate to the
needs of the "creative" people who, as in most progressive
colleges, made up a considerable part of the faculty and
had another string to their bow. Most of the instructors
were young and unmarried and did not grudge the few
settled family men their professorial stipend, which went
into bringing up children and not into conspicuous entertaining. Among the older married teachers, there were a
number of those husband-and-wife "teams" that progressive colleges like to hire and others, for some reason,
do not—for them the double income made a low salary
practicable. And even such an instructor as Henry Mulcahy, tortured by debt, doctor bills, coal bills, small personal loans never paid back, four children outgrowing
their clothes, patches, darns, tears, the threatening letters
of a collection-agency, knew himself well off here in com-

parison to many an instructor at state university or en-
dowed private college, where a stipend of twenty-five hundred would not be considered too low. Jocelyn, in this respect, followed the progressive pattern of offering a reasonable security to those in its lowest rank, while holding
out few prospects of advancement or of juicy plums at the
top of the tree. In this way, it had been able to recruit a
faculty of poets, sculptors, critics, composers, painters,
scene-designers, and so on, without academic experience
and without, also, academic ambitions of the careerist
sort—as well as beginners in history, science, or philosophy fired with the love of a subject and impatient of
graduate-school norms; plus a certain number of seasoned
non-conformists and dissenters, sexual deviants, feather-
bedders, alcoholics, impostors.

All these, on the instructorial or assistant-professor level,
constituted the bulk of Jocelyn's faculty, which included
many transients and floaters, here one year and gone the
next. Behind them, on the associate- or full-professor level,
was the staple minority of family men, Fathers of the
progressive republic, kindly, genial, older statesmen
wedded to pipe and tobacco-pouch, steeped in a beneficent
content, rather in the Swiss style, fond of *bierstube, lieder,*
mountain-climbing, ice-skating, aperitifs on the plaza of a
well-loved foreign town, chary of commitment, generous of
praise, prudent, thrifty, foresighted—the best type, in
short, of bourgeois summer-wandering scholar who saw
events, as it were, three-dimensional, through the broaden-
ing stereopticon of travel. Such men had been drawn into
the progressive life more or less by accident, through a
chance recommendation, a meeting on a promenade deck,

a college friendship kept up, and stayed in it partly from habit and partly from that taste for a foreign yet familiar environment that governed their vacation schedules: the scandals and oddities of the successive years at Jocelyn were preserved in their reminiscences like views of the Bay of Naples or, more appropriately, like the *graffiti* at Pompeii. Unlike their younger colleagues, they were able to find extenuating circumstances for any piece of rascality; seasoning had made them tolerant. Like all long-time residents in an alien environment, they used a double standard, one for themselves and another, more lenient, for the native folkways.

Such a man was Aristide Poncy, professor of French and German, head of the Languages department of the Literature and Languages Division, a Swiss in actual derivation as well as in temperament, brought to America by his parents when he was six years old, educated at Zurich and the University of North Dakota—a middle-aged, fatherly man with large, smooth chaps and an outing taste in dress that suggested Sherlock Holmes. He had been at Jocelyn from the beginning without making an enemy; he taught his pupils, by preference, out of secondary-school textbooks and was himself engaged in a lifelong study of Amiel, on whom he had already published an admirable bibliography and two pertinent articles. None of his students, alas, could be got to share this interest; they preferred to read Sartre and Camus or, rather, to hear about them—he himself had lost patience with the French novel about the time of Maurice Dekobra. Under his multilingual auspices a variety of rather curious younger people had come to teach at Jocelyn. He had perhaps a cantonal prejudice (unconscious) against the French of Paris or even that of Marseilles, so that he had introduced into his division a veritable babel of accents. As assistants and colleagues in French, he had had at various times a Belgian, a German, a Corsican, another Swiss, an Egyptian (who, as he confided to Mrs. Fortune, spoke French "like a native"); this year, under him, were Domna Rejnev, a Russian, and a half-American Turk whom he had met in Istanbul, a Mr. Mahmoud Ali Jones, a tall, stiff, bearded man with a queer rigid gait who resembled a flat Christ in a primitive, under Byzantine influence, and who was thought by some, for this reason, to be an international criminal. Aristide's taste for colonial or, as it were, secondary sources of a language extended also to German, which was taught by himself and an Austrian, and to Spanish, by a girl from Peru.

The fact was, Aristide Poncy was a good and innocent man—the father of three little Poncys who all took piano-lessons—whose shrewdness and knowledge of the world applied only to money-matters at home and to the exchange of currency in foreign countries. He had been guilty, as he once confessed to Domna in an undertone, "of many grave mistakes in the judgment of character." Whenever, during the summer, he took a party of students abroad under his genial wing, catastrophic events attended him. As he sat sipping his vermouth and introducing himself to tourists at the Flore or the Deux Magots, the boys and girls under his guidance were being robbed, eloping to Italy, losing their passports, slipping off to Monte Carlo, seeking out an abortionist, deciding to turn queer, cabling the decision to their parents, while he took out his watch

and wondered why they were late in meeting him for the
expedition to Saint-Germain-en-Laye. Returning home, usually minus one student at the very least, he always deprecated what had happened, remarking that there had been
"a little mix-up" or that the Métro was confusing to for-
eigners.

Was it, Domna Rejnev wondered, as she rapped sharply
on the door of his office, this fatal gullibility that had
drawn her to him now to unfold Mulcahy's story, or was
it rather his fatherly qualities, his tolerance, experience,
and human kindness that made her fear him less at such
a moment than she would have feared Howard Furness or
Alma Fortune, both friends of the Mulcahys, where Aristide was not? Already, as she hurried through the building, she had begun to have the feeling that the tale she
bore was incredible (which, of course, her training reassured her, did not make it any the less true), and she had
commenced to rehearse in her own mind, her lips moving
swiftly as she climbed the narrow stairs, certain little modifications and additions that would make the President's
guilt more evident to an a-political audience. For there
was no doubt that, of all persons she could have chosen,
Aristide Poncy was the least qualified to appreciate the
nuances of the affair, so that even as she knocked, she
hesitated, hearing her superior trill out, *"Entrez,"* with a
wonderful, exhibition *r* that made her see already his large
pink tongue soloing against his red mouth-roof and his
large clean white teeth (Aristide spoke French virtuoso-
style, like a demonstrator in a department store or a professional diver in slow motion, holding his mouth open to
illustrate the mechanics of the production of the various

dentals and alveolars). He rose from his desk to welcome her, a busy, energetic man as his office showed, book-lined from floor to ceiling, with a special section for magazines, French, Swiss, and German, and for journals of the trade, yet he was evidently, as he said, *très content* to see her, eager to show her a new volume on M. de Vogüé which he had just procured from his bookseller with the idea that it might interest her, *très content,* and, as always, full of restrained anticipation for the good gossip that would follow.

Domna, shown to a chair, assuring him that his pipe did not bother her, felt at the same time a reluctance to begin on her narrative and a queer conviction that with this eager listener she had an absolutely free hand; owing to his personal security and remoteness from political conspiracy, he would accept whatever she told him as an attested marvel. "You don't say?" he would interject from time to time and sit back to be regaled with the details. This prediction, she remarked to herself parenthetically, while clearing her throat to commence, would hold good for the greater part of the Jocelyn faculty—with two or three exceptions, they would believe anything you told them touching political entanglements. And with this a terrible temptation came to her, who was a model of honesty: why not involve Maynard Hoar? As even Aristide knew, Jocelyn's "liberal" spokesman had tuned his guitar more than once to the Russian balalaika and was far more guilty, really, than the misled and hapless Mulcahy, who had not known how to disengage himself from an embarrassing commitment. Why not say that Henry, just now, in confessing his Party membership had also implicated

Maynard in the Party tie? Easy to assert, in confidence, and no more, in a sense, than the truth. As soon as this devilish idea reached her full consciousness, she expelled it as wicked and useless—it could only end in ineffectuality or in *both* men's losing their jobs. Yet the fact that it could have proposed itself to her so readily, easily, and naturally gave her a disturbing shock. What had happened to make her so ready to embark on a course of opportunistic lying? Are we less scrupulous when we plead for others than when we work for ourselves? And how in the course of a few minutes had she come to hate Maynard to the point where she would see him ruined, gladly, and think it a just desert? These questions remained troublingly in her mind, as she began to relate to Aristide, as truthfully as possible, and yet with great anger and conviction, the story of Henry's dismissal. "You don't say!" he presently ejaculated. *"Incroyable!"*

CHAPTER V

In Camera

AT ONE O'CLOCK in Mr. Poncy's office, Domna was tensely retelling the story to a group which now consisted of Mr. Poncy himself, Mrs. Fortune, young Mr. Bentkoop of Comparative Religion, Mr. Kantorowitz of Art, Mr. Van Tour, who had put his round head in, crying, "*Here* you all are!" and Mrs. Legendre of the Theatre. Sympathy and shock were instant; a sense of vicarious outrage—the vocational endowment of all educators—fused them like a Greek chorus behind their colleague as protagonist; strophic interjections of pity and disgust broke into the narrative before it was halfway finished. Even Mr. Poncy, who had thought to hold aloof from the affair, found himself with a capital stake in it by sheer virtue of seniority; as the first to have heard the story, he automatically assumed charge of it and kept interrupting Domna to underscore a point or add a detail which had made a strong impression on his own imagination, and very often, in doing so, he slightly altered the original, which in turn had been colored by Domna with the dye of her own temperament. Thus, in the telling and the response, the story became a living thing—the joint possession of the group—

and was to some extent already alienated from its hero, of whom everyone agreed that, whatever was to be done (and on this there was great disagreement), he must be kept in the background, lest he do damage to his own case as they saw fit to administer it. In short, as usually happens in such affairs, the Mulcahy cause was immediately expropriated from its owner and taken over by a group which viewed it somewhat in the light of a property or a trust to be handled by an inner circle in accordance with its own best judgment; the element of secrecy enhanced this proprietary illusion; by common consent, lines were drawn between those who could be trusted and those who could not, between those in the office and those outside. And even within the office, certain discriminations began to be felt; Aristide in a low voice was emphasizing to Alma Fortune a departmental aspect of the case too little, he felt, taken into consideration by Domna, while Kantorowitz and Bentkoop, in the window-seat, exchanged a series of cryptic signs and voiceless words, indicating that Van Tour ought never to have been admitted to the conclave, and Ivy Legendre, whose empty stomach had set up its own growl, lazily urged Domna to call the meeting to order.

Everyone, that is, felt called upon to stipulate, like a lawyer, his own degree of interest in the case, and to distinguish his own area of human solidarity from that of his neighbor, carefully set up boundaries and limits, eminent domain. To Aristide, it was the *manner* of the dismissal, the irregularity of it, that was unsettling, while Alma felt for Catherine and the children, Kantorowitz for the Humanities, Bentkoop for theism, Ivy for all rebels and bohemians, irrespectively; only poor Van Tour appreciated the politics of the case, having once in his early struggles as a regionalist short-story writer and would-be contributor to *Anvil* joined the League of American Writers and the League for Peace and Democracy, in the same spirit, as he now protested, that a small-town doctor, hanging out his shingle, joined the Rotary or Kiwanis or roared every Tuesday with the Lions. For everyone but the plaintive Van Tour, in fact, Mulcahy's confessed Communist past and the President's right to fire him for it became immediately subordinated to some collateral issue; thus Bentkoop, on the strength of a number of conversations about grace and theological despair which he had enjoyed with Mulcahy was impelled to state, categorically, speaking as a neo-Protestant, that his support for Mulcahy rested, very simply, on his belief that it was important to have at least one theist in the Literature department.

On any other occasion, this avowal would have provoked a clamor, since it laid bare a view of education-as-indoctrination that was as shocking to the liberals and pluralists present as would have been the sight of an imported serpent rearing up on Aristide's Coptic rug. But this morning such a response was held in abeyance, as it were, for the duration of Henry's emergency; the notion, in fact, of a working alliance with God produced an agreeable sensation of jesuitry in everyone, as though it were a pact with the dark Plutonic powers. They felt heartened and stimulated by the very novelty of it and by a sense of mysterious big battalions moving up to support them from the rear. What impressed them about Henry's case, as presented by Domna, was precisely the mixture of the commonplace and the bizarre. On the one hand, there was the family man and fellow-teacher; on the other, the arcanum of Communism, which excited their curiosity and at the same time relieved it. They saw themselves plunged into the adventurous and already looked on their colleagues, who were not to be made privy to this secret, as so many insensitive pharisees, incapable of understanding the motives that could have influenced a high-strung, conscientious individual to immolate himself in the mass. And the fact was, of course, that they did not understand it either, but forebore from asking embarrassing questions out of shame and a kind of shyness in the presence of the equivocal. Like so many gingerly Thomases, they contented themselves with fingering the wounds held out to them and attesting their intellectual superiority by their readiness to believe the incredible. When Van Tour cried out, for the third time, in his wailing, womanish voice. "What *I* don't see, Domna, is why doesn't he come *right out* and confess it," everyone sighed aloud, and Aristide got up and, leading him into a corner, took him over by rote the whole history of the case, of Senator McCarthy, the Hiss trial, the crisis of liberalism in American universities, though in reality Van Tour's question had more than once visited his own mind.

Meanwhile, in the faculty dining-room, Howard Furness, head of the Literature department, who had had an appointment with Alma Fortune at twelve forty-five sharp to discuss a certain student who was coming up for Sophomore Orals, was glancing at his Cartier wrist-watch, a gift from one of last year's parents, and straightening his knitted tie from sheer uneasiness. His sharp, dapper mind was extremely sensitive to any disarray in the outer garment of reality, and the empty places at table wounded him, like missing buttons on a coat. He had been quick, in fact, to see that those who were absent belonged to his chosen circle; something was up, he perceived, from which he was being excluded—a judgment was being passed on him. He was not so stupid, however, as to think, after the first bad moment, that they had met to discuss him directly; rather, he scented a crisis, having learned to detect a crisis by the fact that people avoided him during its early stages. Deeply mistrustful himself, he had learned to know that he was mistrusted and could not think why; the longing for intimacy he felt seemed to him a plain guaranty of the openness and simplicity of his character; it did not occur to him that he was gregarious out of suspicion.

When the vegetable soup had been removed and the napkins still lay rolled in their napkin rings before the empty places, he slipped out into the hall to telephone, pausing to glance at himself in the men's room mirror, where he saw only bright delft-blue eyes, flat, rather wooden features with a certain set of resolve to the jaw, and a Bermuda Christmas tan that gave a "finish" to the whole, like a wax stain on floorboards. This simulacrum reassured him; he caulked his face for the inquiry. "Give me the Co-op," he murmured, legato, to Switchboard, with a sliding determination in his voice. The store phone was finally answered by Mrs. Tryk, the Co-op or soda-shop manageress, who shouted into it as usual in a surly, contumelious tone. "This is Mr. Furness," he said lightly. "I had an appointment with Mrs. Fortune. I wondered if she could have mistaken it and be waiting for me in the store." "Not here now," called Mrs. Tryk. Howard sent his smile over the wire. "Would you mind looking around for me and seeing if any of the other people from my department are there? Or Mr. Bentkoop or Mrs. Legendre? They might be able to tell me where she is." "Nobody here but Fraenkel of History and Mulcahy. Do you want to talk to them?" Having obtained this much information, Furness lifted an eyebrow—so Mulcahy, who regularly went home to lunch, was eating in the Co-op! But where, in that case, were the others? He felt this violation of the established pattern to be an offense first against himself and second against common decency. "Don't trouble to get Dr. Mulcahy to the phone," he said hastily. "Just ask him if he has seen Mrs. Fortune." He added this latter merely for form's sake; he felt a sudden unwillingness to know where any of them were.

"Hello, Howard." Mulcahy's rather ectoplasmic voice effused itself into Furness' ear. Both men disliked each other intensely, under cover of departmental solidarity and a joint sponsorship of the same canon of authors. The Proust-Joyce-Mann course, in which they alternated from year to year, had been a buffer between them, Furness making it a point to stress Proust by innuendo over Joyce, for whom he felt no great sympathy, and Mulcahy vice versa. "Alma's not here. Can I help you?" Furness, who combined crudeness with the sensitivity of the princess of the pea—in short, a raw man, well polished, a bright, country-green apple—distinctly heard an ooze of satisfaction percolate through the voice of his subordinate. Wherever she is, he knows, he said to himself with bitterness.

The vindictive thought that this egregious fellow might
at long last have been fired had more than once darted
through his mind, yet the voice on the other end of the
wire sounded more as if it had received a promotion. "No
thanks, Hen," he said shortly and moved to put up the receiver; the line, however, remained open—Henry was
waiting, like an encouragement. "Are you through?" inquired the operator. "You haven't seen Domna, have you,
or Ivy?" Furness burst out, thickly, despite himself. His
tone suddenly grew querulous, as when he had been drinking, and a wild feeling of loneliness drove him to abase
himself. "Where is everybody, anyway? What's up?" "Perhaps they've gone to Gus's for a drink," suggested Henry,
too helpful. "Probably," assented Furness, hanging up.

Mulcahy made his way back to his table, where the
small scoop of chocolate ice-cream he had ordered was
melting into the plastic and waxed paper chalice. He was,
in fact, waiting for Domna, who had promised to fetch
him for lunch some fifteen minutes ago and who had
neither come nor telephoned. Yet he felt no particular
apprehension; the fat was in the fire, and he had only to
wait on the outcome; his fate and he had separated.
Furness' telephone call assured him, at any rate, that all
was going according to schedule: six empty chairs in the
faculty dining-room must be testifying, like a vacant jury-
box, to a discussion of his peers still in progress. Here, in
the near-empty shop, with Mrs. Tryk and her assistant
engorging their noonday sandwiches at the table in the
corner and Bill Fraenkel correcting some papers for an
afternoon class, he had a sense of having crossed a Rubi-
con and of belonging no longer to himself but to history,

a strange and yet restful experience, as though one part of him sat in a stage-box, watching with folded arms for the rise of the curtain, oblivious to the groundlings and their noise.

What interested him retrospectively, and just precisely, he thought, as an onlooker, was the question of how and when the risky inspiration had come to him. That Maynard considered him a Communist must have been a strong factor from the outset, yet as he had paused in the hall outside Domna's door, listening thoughtfully to her and her student, he had not yet (he was certain) felt the metonymic urge that would prompt him, once in her office, to substitute the effect for the cause, the sign for the thing signified, the container for the thing contained. It was the artist in him, he presumed, that had taken control and fashioned from newspaper stories and the usual disjunct fragments of personal experience a persuasive whole which had a figurative truth more impressive than the data of reality, and hence, he thought, with satisfaction, truer in the final analysis, more universal in Aristotle's sense. Evidently so, to judge by first results; there could be no doubt that Domna, just now, had experienced an instant *recognition:* of himself as the embodiment of a universal, the *eidos,* as it were, of the Communist, Lazarus to their Dives, the underground man appointed to rise from the mold and confront society in his cerements. That he had never, as it happened, chanced to join the Communist Party organizationally did not diminish the truth of this revelation.

Sitting here in the soda-shop, licking his little wooden spoon, he tried deliberately to re-imagine himself as a Communist, as the man he had just described to Domna,

and perceived that, just as he had thought, very little
adaptation was required. To *them*, he opined, glancing at
the manageress and her assistant, who were conversing
sotto voce over their pot of tea, he was a Communist
already or worse, just as to Maynard Hoar he was a Communist or worse, i.e., an honest doubter who went to what
meetings he chose, irrespective of the Attorney General's
list and the hue and cry in the colleges. And if they in
their own minds and deeds equated him with a Communist,
what more had he done just now than appropriate the
label they dared not attach to him in their public pro-
nouncements? By a faultless instinct, it would seem, he
had been led to obey the eternal law of the artist, *Objectify*,
or as James had put it and he himself was always urging
his students, *Dramatize, dramatize!* Contemplating what
he had done he felt a justified workman's pride, which became tinctured, as he waited, with a drop or two of bitterness: he could imagine the hostile critics, the derogators,
and detractors, finding flaws, carping, correcting, and
above all minimizing, cutting him down to scale. Easy
enough, he assured them, by hindsight to demonstrate the
logic of the process, which was that of a simple reversal
or transfer; anybody, having been shown, could do it a
second time; yet the fact remained that he was the first,
the very first, so far as he knew, in all history to expose
the existence of a frame-up by framing himself first.

Naturally, he acknowledged, shrugging, there were holes
in the story. Maynard, he dared say, would pretend to
have had no previous knowledge of this "alleged" membership; trust dear Maynard to feign bewilderment, innocence, injury. But in the adage of the martyred President,

which he heartily recommended to Maynard, you can fool some of the people all of the time, all of the people some of the time, but you can't fool all of the people all of the time. The gullible public, he promised Maynard, would find that denial a mite hard to swallow when it put it together with the F.B.I.'s visit, the swift, peremptory dismissal, the victim's open confession. . . .

A little, secure smile glinted from his eyes and faded as, inadvertently, he caught sight of the clock. Fear suddenly reduced him; they had had time, and more than time, to come to a decision. Supposing they were asking for some piece of tangible evidence? He had not thought of this. Was it likely, he swiftly countered, that he would have kept his Party card in his desk at home for a student-sitter to discover? Or in a bank vault rented for the purpose? Nonsense, he remarked, crisply, turning his impatience on himself. What was proof in these days that anybody dreamed of looking for it? Who asked Miss Bentley for proof in a far more weighty context? In these days, it would be a work of supererogation to show that one had been a Communist; the rub was to show one had not been.

The idea that a man in his right mind would run the risk of proclaiming himself a Communist when the facts were the other way would simply occur to no one. *That* he could safely vouch for; the ordinary liberal imagination, he affirmed with a side glance at young Fraenkel, busy as a bee with his papers, could not encompass such a possibility. And it *was* of course a fantastic hazard—to that extent one should not blame Fraenkel and the others —one that few men alive would take and that he himself would not have risked this morning at many colleges outside of Jocelyn. In the present state of public opinion, all his advisers would tell him, he was inviting an academic lynching bee by such a gratuitous admission; if news of it percolated out West, thanks to some indiscretion of Domna's, he would be open to prosecution for perjury. But this prospect, he observed with interest, did not daunt him; the choice he had just made in accepting himself as a Communist was having, he discovered, an extraordinary effect on his prejudices, as of liberation, such as a man might have in accepting himself as a homosexual. In fact, he could trace in himself a certain detached interest in the experience of being imprisoned, so that he felt rather defrauded by a vague recollection of having heard somewhere that perjury was not an extraditable offense.

On the other hand, he assured himself, the risk was not really so great as lesser minds would assume. He was gambling, as he had already pointed out to himself, on Maynard's reputation as a liberal, which meant something to Maynard that the worldly would not understand, but, over and above this, on the element of fantasy in Jocelyn, which nobody would understand who had not witnessed the freakish character of its tides of opinion, the anomalies of its personnel, the madness of its methodology which had produced here a world like a child's idea of China, with everything upside down. And as if to illustrate the point, the door now slowly opened to admit a blast of wind and Mr. Mahmoud Ali Jones in galoshes and turban. "Good morning," intoned Mr. Jones, inclining his long body from the hips, like an idol being bowed in a parade. "Are these ladies serving us, dear colleague?" he inquired in a deep, "cultured" voice, rhythmically unwrapping the turban, which proved to be an Argyle scarf. He made his way stiffly to the counter; the manageress paid him no heed. "May I implore a western sandwich?" he asked in a sonorous tone, addressing the room at large; his elongated, hanging-Christ profile was turned toward Mulcahy; one drooping brown eye slowly winked. "The kitchen's closed," shot out the manageress, addressing no one, in her turn, but stating this as a generalization. Henry bit his lips. "By whose authority?" he quietly challenged. Fraenkel's Eversharp suddenly paused in its scribbling; there was a pregnant silence, till the manageress slammed down the teapot and pounded over to the counter. "I can give you ham-on-rye, Swiss-on-rye," she cannonaded. "Swiss, if you please. A thousand thanks," said Mr. Jones, bowing to Henry. "I was perishing for a bite to eat. May I join you?"

He took the plate which the manageress pushed toward him and balanced it on a cup of coffee. "This *is* a pleasure," he announced, in that curious, careful voice that appeared to have an echo in it, like a *double entendre*. "May I tell you how much I enjoyed your performance at last Tuesday's faculty meeting?" The notion that this Byzantine lay-figure was capable of factional feeling alerted Henry's interest and made him conscious of a moral law behind the smallest actions, as though a stone had spoken up or a fish in a German fairy-tale. "What points especially struck you?" he queried, in a disengaged and considerate tone, which nevertheless had a little feeler behind it. "The scrambled eggs, my dear fellow. Delicious!" Jones uttered a two-note musical laugh. "I

am very fond of a pun, though my friends tell me it is
the lowest form of wit. Do you agree with that?" Henry
was aware of a great disappointment. "Our two greatest
writers, Shakespeare and Joyce, were accomplished pun-
sters," he said shortly. Mr. Jones took a bite of his sandwich. "Domestic, of course," he sighed. "My wife tells
me that our President would be more sympathetic with
your protest if he were obliged to eat, like ourselves, from
the commissary. My wife is a Corsican, you know; from
Ajaccio." He offered these credentials in a definitive tone,
quite bewildering to Mulcahy, who did not understand
what they were supposed to signify—that his wife was an
expert on cookery or a woman of implacable passions?
Nevertheless, Henry's interest cautiously revived; strange
bedfellows, he reflected; and yet an unexpected ally, discovered thus casually, deserved, he thought, generosity,
like the prodigal son returning. "We are both under medical orders," pursued Mr. Jones. "We neither smoke nor
drink nor permit ourselves any gassy foods—hot breads,
of course, foods fried in deep fat, fatty meats, commercial
cakes made with baking powder. . . . Quite a hardship,
we've found it, dining in commons. In our apartment, of
course, there is a little hot plate, but my wife does not
think it economical to purchase for two in your stores here.
But if you will do us the honor . . . ?" Henry's pale eyes
shifted; he felt his integrity compromised; yet he did not
wish to offend. "My wife is not well," he explained in a
lowered voice. The idea of binding Mr. Jones to him
privately, without yielding the social *quid pro quo* that
Mr. Jones was angling for, gained a foothold in his mind,
though experience bade him dislodge it: nothing in life

was free, as he had learned to his bitter cost; the Joneses of this world, foiled of their pound of flesh, could become the most dangerous enemies. "It's a heart and kidney condition brought about by the birth of our boy," he quickly amplified, lest Jones begin to execute a withdrawal. "Nothing she won't recover from, given complete rest. These extra-curricular activities required by the college have put too much of a strain on her; there's low blood pressure too and a retroverted uterus. Our doctor privately tells me that those Saturday night dances might have killed her." He was tempted now to go on, go the whole hog, but the door opened again, and it was Domna. He got up in haste from his chair and began to tie his muffler. "It's been good to have this talk with you," he murmured. "Let's see each other again." "By all means," declared Mr. Mahmoud Ali Jones, still seated. "I've been wanting such a time to ask you—do you know that delicious little thing of Maurice Baring's . . . ?" Domna was faintly smiling and dancing a little on her toes. "Ah, good morning, Miss Rejnev!" Mr. Jones began slowly to rise, like a fountain in the gardens of Allah. Henry turned up his overcoat collar and hurriedly took Domna's arm; he had gone pale and his lips were bluish, as though he were already out of doors. "Another time," he muttered. "An appointment. . . ." His mittened hand agitated the door. "Your check, Mr. Mulcahy," called the manageress, an accusing finger pointing to the table where the evidence, the ice-cream calyx, still remained. Trembling, he began to search his pockets; Domna paid, from her purse.

"It is all right," she called to him, as they ran through the wind, arms interlocked, to her car, a blustering old

Buick touring model, unpainted, without a muffler, and buttoned up now, with torn celluloid and canvas curtains in the old-fashioned style. She turned on the ignition, threw a robe over him, and began to work the choke. "It's all right," she reiterated, maternally, over the throbbing of the juggernaut. "They've voted to support you. You wish to go to Gus's or to town?" "Town," said Henry faintly. The car started off down the hill, with bravura; behind the curtains, in the deafening noise, he had a sense of being kidnapped; even the snowy landscape looked unfamiliar. This captive feeling was intensified by the fact that he could hear what she said only in snatches; she did not turn her head; the car roared; the wind whistled; he shivered, forlorn, in the rug. The names, Alma, John, Ivy, and so on, came to him from a distance, repeated in a tone of authority, as if, he glumly felt, they belonged to her; she knew them now better than he. Nevertheless, he endeavored to feel grateful for what she had apparently done for him; he gave her full credit in advance. A certain feeling of jealousy, brought about by the repetition of those names, made him prefer, for the moment, to depreciate the others and think of it all as *her* doing, *her* spontaneous mediation, as though she were a divine goddess; his eyes moistened obediently, as he choked out his formula of thanks; humility made gratitude more fulsome, as he had discovered in the past.

Yet she, on her side, seemed girlishly determined that he should appreciate them all. Alma, he heard, was "wonderful," Milton Kantorowitz was "wonderful"; even Aristide was "wonderful, so unexpectedly staunch," as though, Mulcahy thought, grimly, the simple performance of one's duty deserved a medal for heroism. Van Tour was "absolutely amazing." "Who would have thought," she cried gaily, "that the young man had so much blood in him?" It was clear, reflected Henry, watching her assured profile, that a meeting of the mutual admiration society had just concluded its business. And he could not help being nettled by the knowledge that they were all exploiting him, making him a pretext for the discovery of each other's virtues: in this business, he remarked to himself sourly, *he* seemed to be the forgotten man. Every one of them had his own ax to grind here, a thing Domna made abundantly clear, but joyously, as though self-interest were a newly discovered cardinal virtue. "It means that each one has a real stake in it," she cried, like some Hobbesian Miranda. "Only a really *interested* act is worth anything." "Your view has the merit of paradox, at any rate," commented Henry, non-committal. And he was the more resentful of Domna's shining eyes, wind-whipped bright cheeks, with their flags of pride and accomplishment, when he discovered, toward the end of the ride, that the glorious little group had decided nothing whatsoever, so far as he could see.

They had decided to use "the existing machinery"— the very phrase set his teeth on edge. "It's Aristide's counsel we're following," she elected to inform him, while backing into the parking-space before the red-brick restaurant. "Just look behind and see if I am too close," she interposed, as he started to protest, a typically feminine maneuver, he thought bitterly, seeing that it was as he had thought, his instinct had not misled him: he *had* been taken for a ride. He obeyed, however, with a shrug—"All right here." "Aristide thinks it best," she calmly pursued, shifting into first and letting out the clutch, "that we leave the political thing dormant for the moment." "Look out!" shouted Henry involuntarily, as she hit the bumper of the car ahead. "Oh, how stupid of me! He thinks it best that we handle it departmentally and simply, as I say, get the department to accord you a vote of confidence which he, as head of the division, will carry to Maynard as a protest. Would you pass me my pocketbook, please?" "Domna!" His cry finally arrested this "normative" flow of words. "You must be mad! Don't you see that that means working through Furness?" He gripped her arm to restrain her, lest she evade the issue by getting out of the car. "My dear girl, this is serious business. Furness, as you ought to know, is the classic type of informer, an academic police-spy. He's already got the wind up; he called up the store just now, spying out the land. I told him nothing, naturally, but he's got the bee in his bonnet. We shall have to work fast to circumvent him." Domna's face wore an expression of childish, crestfallen disappointment; she looked ready to cry from sheer defeated altruism, the vanity of good intentions. "We thought . . ." she jerked out, "Aristide . . . Milton . . . we all thought. . . ." Henry stretched his legs. "You thought," he told her calmly, "of your own skins, procedural safeguards, and all the rest of it." Domna's lips quivered; tears stood on her thick lashes. "Not you, Domna," he said, more kindly. "I exempt you from such intentions. At worst, you have been thoughtless. Didn't it occur to you, after all we have said together about Furness, that you might, just possibly might, be endangering Cathy's life if you followed the method you approve of? What a temptation to malice to let her know, by a slip of the tongue, what was happening to her husband!" She stiffened, as if in disagreement, and stole a look at her watch. "I must hurry," she muttered. "I have a class." "Or an anonymous denunciation, posted to the F.B.I.?" He smiled to see that she was shocked by these possibilities he was suggesting, shocked, of course, more by him than by Furness, and, truth to tell, he enjoyed shocking her: it reinstated him at the tiller of his fate.

Actually, after his first revulsion, he was inclined to let them have their way, but not without unsettling them a little, for future policy's sake. If he yielded now, as he proposed to do in a few moments, and Furness proved obdurate to their entreaties (as he almost certainly would), then the next step in the dance, he could promise himself, would be called by Henry Mulcahy. He himself, through a natural impatience, common in quick minds, tended to prefer the short cut, but he had sufficient experience with faculty parliamentarians to know that, in every instance, it was necessary to exhaust legal means first, "employ the existing machinery," etcetera, before they could be brought to an action that common sense would have dictated in the first place.

"You misunderstand Furness, I think," answered Domna in a low, serious voice. "He likes you but fears you don't like him. He has a bad character and longs to be loved. As to whether he would tell Cathy"—she shrugged, rather dispiritedly—"what is the use of arguing? I think not, but how shall I prove it?" She shrugged again. "Naturally, if you don't wish it, we won't do it that way." She spoke in a flat, stubborn voice, but her breast rose in a sigh, in memory of the work lost. "But I must tell you frankly," she added, as if compelled by conscience, "that if you refuse to do it our way, you will probably be out on a limb. Many people who will support you humanly will not involve themselves gratuitously in a political mess." "And if I do it your way?" he insinuated. Domna suddenly looked blank; she had not, plainly, thought ahead beyond her conviction of easy victory. "What do you people offer me in exchange for the risk I shall be running?" His tone was perfectly pleasant, but the question seemed to disturb her. "*Offer* you?" she repeated, vaguely knitting her brows. "What do you mean, Henry? That seems a most odd conception." "What will you do," he said, waspishly, "when Furness turns you down in the department? Does your solidarity regretfully stop there?"

Domna once again looked hurt. "Alma and I spoke of resigning," she finally let out, in a whisper. "Wonderful," he absently assented, but his mind was elsewhere immediately. That was the sad thing about a confederacy: nothing was ever enough. "Just you and Alma?" he queried in a wistful tone, for already he was thinking in terms of a whole department. Domna flushed, which recalled him to the present and to the gratitude he was supposed to be showing. "Overlook my behavior," he begged her. "I'm half crazy. I hardly know what I'm saying. Anything you want to do, of course, will be right because *you* decide to do it. Forgive me for questioning you at all. The defendant or victim in such cases as mine ought to be held incommunicado till his well-wishers have concluded their efforts. To be a victim or a defendant is simply inhuman. It brings out all one's paranoia. Do whatever you think best and ignore me." He spoke swiftly, bobbing his head in contrition, and then scrambled out of the car and hurried around to the other side to help her alight. Howard Furness, who had stopped for gas down the street, watched, behind the pump, while Mulcahy guided her solicitously into the restaurant.

CHAPTER VI

Lucubrations

"LOOK HERE, Alma," countered Howard Furness, with a light rasp in his tenor voice, "how do we know any of this is true?" The teacup on his saucer lurched and slopped as he spoke; they were drinking tea in her apartment in Linden Hall; a meeting of the full department was scheduled to begin here in a few moments, and Howard had arrived first, by design. Already, he felt captious and stubborn. "You take too much for granted," he decreed roughly, thrusting a cigarette into his holder; like everything he did when he was jarred, this ordinary action seemed brutal and personal, a violation of frontiers. In silence, Alma passed him a little box of Vulcan matches. She was a widow of forty, small, dark, wiry, energetic, with a passion for Jane Austen and Goethe, the poles of an unusual temperament, which was at once rough-hewn and fanciful, delicate and dynamic. Twenty years ago, she had been a New Woman, of the *femme savante* school, and she had not been altered either by marriage or by the death of her life-companion—it was as though she had lost a congenial sister or a woman colleague with whom she had shared a flat and a small collection of books,

bibelots, and common habits; having lived together with
Mr. Fortune by a continuous stipulation of mutual consent, she had allowed him his independence in departing.
She dressed in jerseys and wool skirts and brogues, wore a
boyish haircut and necklaces of turquoise or Mexican silver, was fond of tea, little Cuban cheroots, Players, English Ovals, candied ginger, and so on. In the spring, she
picked the first violets; in the autumn, a bouquet of wild
grasses, which stood all winter on her mantel in a brass
container. She was both extremely outspoken and extremely reserved; her personality was posted with all sorts
of No Trespassing signs and crisscrossed with electric
fences, which repelled the intruder with a smart shock. To
men, in particular, the protocol of her nature was bewildering, like court etiquette; like a queen, too, she had
her favorites, who were permitted familiarities and in-
dulgences not granted to their superiors in rank or outward attainments—at Jocelyn, this footstool position was
occupied by Henry Mulcahy and his dependents.

Howard Furness was a friend of Alma's, but she pricked
him continually, like a nettle. Her black, wizened, pep-
percorn eyes regarded him with a permanent twinkle which
anticipated his weakness and shriveled his independence;
she would seldom speak to him seriously, except on department business, called him "Howie," or "little Howie,"
though he stood five feet nine, or even, when specially
humoring him, her "little manikin-minikin," which suggested, and not only to Howard's mind, a dressed depart-
ment-store dummy or a ventriloquist's puppet. In moments of peace, he endured this, but in moments of crisis,
like the present one, he was driven to take up with her

a peculiarly sidling and derogatory tone, full of insinua-
tion, as though he coarsely "saw through" her, like that
of a boy to his sister. And at bottom, he did murkily consider all attainment, idealism, and so forth, to be a sort of
speciousness; the upper world, for him, was divided into
admitted frauds, hypocritical frauds, unconscious frauds:
this fraudulence, in fact, to his glazed-pottery-blue eye,
constituted the human, and below it was only animal activity, which was of no interest or amusement to the observer. Every relationship, therefore, propelled itself for
him toward confession and mutual self-exposure; the slur-
rings and elisions of his voice conspired to this end; even
in his ingratiating mood, his talk had a sidelong motion,
suggestive of complicity. At the same time, he had a firm
sense of what was reasonable and proper, of the Palladian
façade of appearances and observances, a sense which
was at present aggrieved by the farrago of incoherent accusation which was being offered him in all earnestness by
a woman of supposedly critical temper; his jealousy of
Mulcahy was sharpened by creative envy—to what lengths
would sheer audacity carry the man?

Yet his natural envy, as of a fellow safe-cracker, together with a respect for the laws of slander, imposed on
him a code, if not of silence, at any rate of restraint. He
would do no more than restively hint his belief that Hen
was lying, and this made him irritable, since nobody, he
knew, would credit him with a voluntary act of absten-
tion, but, on the contrary, everyone would gladly misjudge
him and suppose that careerist motives kept him from
supporting a colleague whom actually he distrusted for
impersonal reasons and in the end from a sense of pro-

portion. He made a deft little grimace and pushed his
cup aside. "Let's try to keep our heads," he advised, with
a worldly flourish of the cigarette-holder. "We're all
sorry for Cathy, but that's the risk Hen has run. Frankly,"
he shrugged, "the human angle leaves me rather cold. We
all have our hard-luck stories, and Cathy was Hen's lookout." A peculiar, provocative smile had become affixed
to his features, and his voice had a ring of defiance; in
this atmosphere of coddling, he felt it his duty to vaunt
himself as a particularly hard-boiled egg, but he found a
cool pleasure in the role that outstripped his corrective
intention; the desire to be original passed, through justification, into a positive wish to offend.

"In Maynard's place," he rather airily announced, "I
should have acted sooner. For six months, at least, our
friend Hen has been asking to be fired, and today he finally
got what he was looking for. I'm not interested in his
Party membership, or the meetings he went to; the more
fool he, if he didn't break with the Party when the breaking was good." His voice had begun to rise, despite himself; Alma's assessing silence worked on him like a reproach. "What you fine people choose to ignore," he said,
curbing himself, "is the academic record. In the two years
he's been here, how many times has he turned in his
achievement sheets on schedule? Or reported class absences? Or filled in the field-period reports? How many conferences has Hen missed? Have you any idea?" In reply,
Alma slightly lifted her shoulders, as though to deprecate
all this as immaterial. There was a knock on the door, and
Aristide softly entered; with an air of great precaution,
like a late theatre-goer who fears to interrupt the per-

formance, he tiptoed across the room and lowered himself
onto the Empire sofa. As Howard's indictment continued,
his mild, smooth, benign face, like a Swiss weather-clock,
registered a variety of alarmed expressions, from administrative pain to total mystification; this recital of quotidian
misdemeanors affected him like a traveler's tale, an account of strange customs prevailing among unfathomable
peoples. "Last summer," Howard concluded, with a sweep
of the white cuff, "seven of Hen's students wrote me,
wanting their projects back. The others apparently didn't
care." He gave a little laugh, in tribute to his normal
skepticism. "We have *some* duty to the students, I assume.
Little Elmendorf, let me remind you, nearly didn't graduate last year when Hen mislaid her thesis and insisted,
in the department, that it had never been turned in." He
quirked an eyebrow. "We know enough elementary Freud
by this time to see the psychopathology of that. Little
Elmendorf's father, as we have cause to remember, was
a trustee."

He suddenly gave vent to a wholly unpremeditated and
rather concessive laugh. A truant sympathy for Hen made
his argument sway and topple, just as he reached to crown
it—his public positions were always unsteady, being built
up, block by wooden block, like a child's tower, out of
what he held to be correct and fitting; a mere stir in the
ambience or an inner restlessness could unbalance him.
In this case, it was the presence of Aristide, perturbedly
nodding and deploring, and the recollection of Elmendorf
Senior, a beetling kulak of the region, that brought a
glint of malice to his eye. The subversive he acknowledged
in himself was all at once irresistibly appealed to by

Hen's consistent vagaries of character. One side of Howard, his best, the side that drew his students, was an airy sybarite in the moral sphere and behaved as a sort of prodigious host, officiating, somewhat in the background, over the great banquet of life and letters, calling in the dancing-girls and the poets, drunken Alcibiades and simple Agathon, applauding each turn without invidious distinction; in this mood, he wore a garland perpetually round his neck; his collar was loosened, his blue stare moist with afflatus; he cried, Encore, encore; and his methodology was simply reductive: he considered Socrates to be a man and mortal. The indignation he had felt, just now, with Mulcahy, tacked as it neared the ethical and sought another route for its expression. He took a more pacific tone and, thrusting his rather undershot jaw out, said, "God knows, Alma, I don't enjoy playing the Christer. Minding Hen's p's and q's is not *my* idea of a picnic. But let's face up to the facts here. If you've got to champion Hen out of personal loyalty, that's your affair; each to his own taste. Take it up with Maynard; *I* won't stop you. But for God's sake, if you must go into it, do it *with your eyes open*."

There was a second knock on the door. Aristide leaned forward. "Excuse me, Alma," he interjected, "Ellison asked me to tell you that he was sick in bed." Alma gave a snort; Herbert Ellison, the young poet of the department, who taught verse-writing and modern poetry, was never on hand when needed; she suspected him of moral cowardice or of an intellectual superiority to the mundane, which amounted to the same thing. Domna Rejnev and Van Tour came into the room together and without a word took seats, side by side, as if pledged to a common intransigence. "Let's not kid ourselves," Furness exclaimed, paying no attention to them and continuing, deliberately, from where he had left off, "Hen's appointment is not being terminated for political misbehavior. If Hen was ever a Party member, this is the first Maynard or anybody else ever knew of it." He paused to let this sink in, together with its implications, and his eye inadvertently met Domna's; she was staring at him with an expression of such cold ferocity that he shivered and lost track of what he had meant to say. He had been steeling himself for the last half-hour against just this look of hers, which he had precisely anticipated, but which nevertheless made him quail. His soul, however, stiffened obstinately; he was half in love with Domna, or so he kept telling himself, and this drove him, tactically, to resist her. "I don't delude myself," he cried, with a certain resolved desperation that brought all eyes but Domna's curiously to rest on him, as if for once he spoke directly from the heart, "I know what you're thinking!" Domna turned him her profile in a gesture of contempt. "That I'm behind this dismissal, that I'm jealous of Hen, that I'm a trimmer"—he made a slight ironic bow to Alma, who was fond of using this word. "Believe me," he glanced at Domna, who kept her head averted, "Maynard didn't consult me. If he had consulted me . . ." He shrugged. "What would you have had me say? What would you have said in my place if you had been nearly two years acting as a buffer, between Hen and the bursar and the registrar, between Hen and his tutees, between Hen and the *Jocund*, between Hen and the student council?

If other departments had complained to you about Hen's raids on their students?"

Aristide cleared his throat; Domna's pink lips parted and swiftly closed again; she took out a pencil and began to draw, indifferently, in her notebook; Alma coughed, a quick, shrill, peppery cough that at once earned her the right to answer. "No need to quarrel," she said tersely, and the room came to order. Her voice was like a pointer, moving sharply on a map or blackboard, which gave her an air of authoritative impersonality, though as a matter of fact she was congenitally nervous and suffered from intermittent eczema, asthma, shingles, and all the usual disorders of the repressed female brain-worker. Her neck, as she spoke, reddened and she coughed, from time to time, awkwardly. "We have a simple difference of opinion. We differ, apparently, as to Henry's professional qualifications. We indorse him; you do not. That's the nub of the matter. The political question is secondary. Nobody has the right to teach merely because he is or was a Communist—on that we can all surely agree?" All heads promptly nodded but Domna's. "You disagree?" swiftly asked Alma. " 'Nobody has the right to be a policeman,' " quoted Domna, rather slowly. "I am not sure. In principle . . . yes . . . no. I am not sure." A heavy frown appeared on her forehead; everyone turned to look at her in perplexity. Domna's thought-processes, as they all knew, were rather lengthy and tortuous; Van Tour heaved a sigh. "Let's say you temporarily abstain," put in Alma, kindly. "The point need not come up unless Howie persuades us that Henry is unfit to teach on academic grounds. I think we would all say, however, that membership in the Communist Party, past or present, does not in itself establish unfitness to teach." Aristide revolved this statement. "Well now, Alma," he allowed, "I am not sure you have the correct formulation. Intellectual freedom—that is the usual point, isn't it? Can a Communist under discipline have intellectual freedom? We hear that they cannot, that they are under strict orders to promote their infamous doctrine; their minds are not free as ours are." Van Tour interrupted, excitedly. "Catholics are not free either," he protested with heat. Like many teachers of English, he was not able to think very clearly and responded, like a conditioned watch-dog, to certain sets of words which he found vaguely inimical; in an argument he was seldom able to discriminate between a friend and a foe, the main contention and a side-issue. With a person of his temperament, a statement of preliminary axioms, such as Alma had been attempting, was fatal. He was now under the impression that Aristide was slurring Mulcahy; a mid-western distrust of foreign languages, moreover, led him to associate Aristide, who was a Protestant, with the ukases of the Vatican. "Catholics believe in a single truth, too," he cried, warming. "They only tolerate opposition in countries where they haven't taken over the government. Look at Spain! Why should we let *them* teach when we won't allow it to Communists?" "Hear, hear!" remarked Howard, amused. "No one has intellectual freedom," asserted Domna suddenly, in a vicious, smoldering tone.

Alma coughed and resumed control of the discussion. "Let me re-frame the point. *Past* membership in the Communist Party does not in itself establish unfitness to teach."

"Aye, aye," cried Van Tour. Aristide nodded. "Hence," pursued Alma, "if we can agree that Henry possesses the necessary academic qualifications, we will be in a position to argue that his dismissal be reconsidered, (a) in view of the present discriminatory practices in the colleges, which will make him, if fired, virtually unemployable, (b) in view of his own admission of former membership in the Communist Party, which, in the absence of direct evidence of his incompetence, *suggests* at any rate that political discrimination may have been exercised here against him." Howard withdrew his tongue from his cheek and whistled. "Very discreet, Alma," he commended. "You make no concrete charges, bring forward no evidence, and merely counsel Maynard to avoid the *appearance* of evil. I take my hat off. May you mediate for me when my hour comes." He blew her a congratulatory kiss. "Agreed," retorted Alma, absently. "Alma," put in Aristide, "a single correction, if I may. Strictly speaking, Henry is not being fired. His contract is not being renewed, a rather different thing where future employment is concerned. I presume that you are using the expression loosely, as a sort of shorthand, and, so long as we all understand that, it may be convenient to do so."

Alma nodded. "Now, whatever we think ourselves, Maynard will undoubtedly tell us that Henry is not being fired, as you say, Aristide, but being let out for routine administrative reasons. What's more, he will mean it, I assure you. If Maynard has fired Henry for political activities, he has no conscious idea he has done so. Therefore, it devolves on us to give him our opinion that Henry is professionally competent and deprive him of the psy-

chological basis for treating the problem as a purely routine incident. And, as Howie points out, it is possible that
Maynard has been acting in good faith and knows nothing
of the Party membership. In which case, the vigorous
protest of Henry's department ought to open his eyes
to what appears to be a flagrant injustice. Now, Howard,"
she said pleasantly, with an air of "drawing him out,"
"you are in disagreement with the rest of us. You do
not think Henry competent for a number of reasons which
you have cited and which, so far as they go, we are prepared to accept, I think, without further question. The
head of the department, we will all agree, is in a position
to have a certain kind of knowledge of a teacher's routine work and routine failures which the rest of us, hap-
pily, are spared. We will all admit, I think, that Henry
has been lax, but which of us here, I wonder, is in
a position to cast the first stone?" Her shot-like eyes
peppered them; she folded her muscular hands in her
lap. "Not I," said Van Tour eagerly. "I'm *always* late
with my achievement sheets. My students are *forever* after
me to return their little term papers." He flapped a white
hand in the air. "And the complaints I've had from the
registrar's office!" He heaved his shoulders in their suede
jacket and sent his eyes to heaven. "Nor I," exclaimed
Domna. "You know yourself, Howard," she chided him,
"that I forget to record class absences. And my library
history is shocking. I never remember," she earnestly told
them, "to put the books on reserve." "We all have our
peccadilloes," warmly declared Aristide, "I remember one
of my students—do you recall the case, Alma?—Hyslop,
I believe the name was, who was doing a paper for me

on Victor Hugo or was it Dumas *fils?*" His large flat
lips stretched and tightened around the proper names,
like a rubber band contracting; he had never anglicized
a French word in all his professional history, with the
single considered exception of *Paris.*

Howard broke in with a jerky laugh. *"Et tu,* Aristide?"
he reproached him. "I should never have thought it." The
malicious smile returned to his face. "Shall we all confess and take our hair down? I could unfold a tale or
two myself." Every face, he noted, showed alarm—what
tales, he asked himself, were they thinking of? Alma, he
knew, privately censured him for "too close a relation
with the students." It was believed, also, that he had written certain well-to-do students' term papers. Moreover, he
kept a trot in his office, of the plots of the world's famous
novels, which he had once pressed on Domna in an
emergency. For a moment, scanning their faces, he felt a
lurching desire to rock the boat of their conventions by
some untoward and scandalous revelation; he steadied
himself with a jolt. "We've all of us let our work pile
up on us from time to time," he announced in a rather
cavalier and yet sententious tone. "But in Hen's case,
there's a point where quantity became quality. The quality
of his work has been affected."

"How do you know?" cried Van Tour. "You don't
know the quality of a man's work from the memos you
get from the registrar!" He spoke quickly and bellig-
erently, from what everyone recognized to be a job-inse-
curity of his own. He was a well-intentioned, fat, youngish
man with a sentimental devotion to literature and a belief
in its "improving" qualities, but chronically vague and

disoriented; like many sentimental people, he really felt
things more deeply than those who characterized him as
sentimental; he was truly moved by a beautiful passage
and truly warmed to indignation by injustice to man or
animal, yet there was always something in his feeling
that seemed wide of the mark or of too literal or personal
an application—in this case, his defense of Mulcahy
had, in the embarrassed ears of his colleagues, an overtone
of personal defensiveness; he was unable to distinguish
between Mulcahy and himself, and he plopped into Mulcahy's ambience like a whitefish into a sea-full of sharks.
"How do you know," he demanded, "the quality of a
man's relation with his students from these two-by-four
official complaints? A teacher's relation with his students
is something very private and sacred; yes, sacred!" he
cried. "I'm not afraid of using the word. I've heard
Domna's students beef about those reserve books, but
that doesn't mean they don't adore Domna." Domna, somewhat offended by this direct and unexpected criticism,
even though she had just confessed herself guilty, moved
uneasily on her straight chair. "And the same goes for
Hen," Van Tour added, settling back in his seat with an
air of virtue and finality.

"But in that case, Consy"—Mr. Van Tour's name was
Considine—"how are we to assess anyone?" inquired Furness, soothing; folly in another made him considerate, like
a nurse. "We can't quiz each and every student on his
instructor without setting up a spy-system; teaching would
become intolerable." He gave a slight shake of his straight
shoulders. "And we can't let the students have a veto-
power over the faculty; that would be frightful. Teaching,

like all the arts, can't be democratic or subject to referendum; it must be run from within, by an autonomous guild, according to guild standards." "Exactly, Howard!" exclaimed Mrs. Fortune. "You've put your finger on the point. Now what are these standards to be? Are they to be administrative or internal, like the standards of a poem? Within certain limits, isn't it possible for each teacher to make his own, as a poem makes its own laws? Isn't that what we have here at Jocelyn that all of us treasure, whatever we may say about it? A certain autarchy, a rule of equals, without mutual interference?" Her small, dark-complected face had flushed; she leaned forward, hands folded between her knees, her skirt stretched tight, exposing round garters. Domna's forehead puckered. "But a poem," she objected, "justifies itself in the long run by referring back to life. . . ." "Tolstoyan!" retorted Alma playfully, "be silent." Seizing the pacific opportunity, Howard winked at Domna. "Somebody—I believe Orwell—" he lightly divagated, "says that you can't *prove* that a poem is good. A piece of news we must keep from the students at all costs or we should *all* be out of a job." "You can't prove that a poem is good, but you can *know* it," said Domna, suddenly, with conviction. "There's an act of faith involved, in each step of the esthetic initiation, a kind of new and quite arbitrary decision made when we choose to replace Turgenev with Tolstoy, or Lydgate with Chaucer. We make these choices in accordance with our own life-purposes; knowledge is not fortuitous but the fruit of a conscious decision, a turning toward, as Eliot says. In general, we submit ourselves to the judgment of the poets in these matters; we allow our poets to tell us that Donne is superior to Milton, and here perhaps we are wrong, but we cannot *know* that we are wrong until we also become poets. Tolstoy was wrong, in my belief, about Shakespeare, but his wrongness has a certain authority; we pause to listen to him because he was a poet. In the same way, it is only we teachers who have earned the right to be listened to on the question of another teacher's competence, who have earned," she finished, somewhat defiantly, "the right, if you want, to be wrong."

Howard nodded, soberly. He had followed Domna's argument to the end, unlike most of the others, because he knew her to be honest and presumed that therefore, before she finished, a doubt would suddenly dart out of her, like a mouse from its hole. In general, he agreed with what she had said, though with certain practical reservations. He was quite well aware that he knew nothing empirically about the quality of Hen's teaching; but neither, he was certain, did the others, and he would have liked to get this admission on the table. "Fitness to teach" was an imponderable which he had no intention of pretending to weigh; administratively, however, Hen was a nuisance, and while he himself would have done nothing to dislodge him, he thought it obtuse to pretend that no reason for dislodging him existed. Domna's "right to be wrong," he thought, smiling, he did not contest, especially since the phrasing seemed calculated to disturb the certainties of the others, those of Aristide, in particular, whose face, bent in consultation now with Domna, wore a thoroughly anxious look, as though he had abruptly discovered that he had been exposed to some contagious disease. "You think it possible, then, that we are mistaken in Hen?" he gravely queried, accepting a piece of ginger from Alma and sinking his large, white teeth into it cautiously, as his big pale gray eyes probed Domna's bright ones.

"Unlikely," declared Alma, plumping down the silver dish. "Domna is right, of course, abstractly. Some sort of act of faith is probably involved for all of us here. But it's not the unreasoning faith of a savage; it's the accumulation of a lifetime of observation and inference. I can't say, of course, from my own direct knowledge, that Henry is a good teacher. I go partly by hearsay and mainly by inference. I know, from our talks together, just as you all do, that Henry is a man with a brain, a big brain. The finest brain, if I may say so, on our faculty. I can't think that our students can find anything but profit in being exposed to that brain, whatever happens to their projects or their ridiculous achievement sheets. I've profited myself, I can promise you. The man thinks rings around me." She blew out a puff of smoke and mechanically all looked upward for the ring to form. The definiteness of her tone produced in every mind a concrete and haunting image. Mulcahy's brain seemed to materialize before them, under Alma's pointer, like a slide in a medical lecture, a cranium in profile or cross-section, with the tissue of veins and arteries, the soft gray matter, the cerebrum and cerebellum, all of unusual size and preternatural activity. Aristide's eyes protruded. "You don't say?" he exclaimed. "I should not have rated him quite so high. Where would you place him, Alma, on our friend Grünthal's scale?" Van Tour giggled. "How about the Rorschach?" he whispered to Domna. "I agree with Alma," she proclaimed, silencing him with a jab of the elbow. "Henry is the only man in the department who has standing outside of Jocelyn. I knew his early articles in the *Kenyon* when I was still a student. The synthesis he tried to make between Marx and Joyce was an important critical effort of the Thirties. You may pretend, Howard, that Joyce is a dead end," she went on, excitably, though this was what she thought herself, "an interesting molehill in which certain pedants have tunneled till they buried themselves alive, that all this is pseudo-modernism, neo-orthodoxy, but what else, please tell me, is there that you find so un-sterile and fructifying? Where has your Proust led us? What you consider modern, your new decadence, is simply the latest billow of the Gothic Revival—Petrus Borel, my God!" Her accent had become more marked, as she felt herself moving along sure ground; like most European women when they argue, she was both angry and zestful. "You may say that these Joyce excavations of Henry's are like some labor of the Pyramids, a monument of waste in the desert! Yes, in a certain sense, I agree, but it is at any rate a monument, a work requiring patience, study, the knowledge of seven foreign languages—a human sacrifice! What have you or I or any of us here to compare with it? Which of us has learned Italian or studies Hebrew at night with the Bible?"

Domna stopped, breathless, scornfully conscious that she was probably giving offense to the feelings of the others. Whenever she saw, or thought she saw, excellence, she had a summary impulse to make others bow the knee to it, as she did. Generosity in all things was a point of pride with her, but she had no pity for those too lowly placed to dispense it. Thus, in the little speech she had just made, she had been driven by the demon of arrogance to wound Furness' vanity and incidentally, for all she knew, the separate vanities of the other three. But for the moment she felt perfectly reckless of such matters and did not care whether the effect of what she had said would be a net reduction of the sympathy that had hitherto been extended to her idol. Indeed, she rather enjoyed the idea that only she was sufficiently spendthrift (that is, sufficiently rich in resources) to pay Mulcahy full homage.

A constrained silence followed her outburst. "Grant Hen everything you say," remarked Furness at length, "none of all that really touches on the question of whether he's the right man for Jocelyn or for this particular department. God knows," he interjected, laughing, "I don't want to put myself in the position of robbing the poor-box or taking the widow's mite. Let's pretend that poor old Hen was a big figure in his time; let's allow him his few words of Hebrew and his quotation from Leopardi. What you're invoking, nevertheless, Domna, is a medieval standard of scholarship as an end in itself. Here at Jocelyn, I've been given to believe, we're after something different: an active, two-way relation between the student and the faculty-member. Great learning can be an impediment to this; it opens up too great a hiatus, as in Hen's case, between the student and the instructor. Hence we don't insist on the Ph.D. or even the Master's; in fact, we regard advanced degrees as a liability, if anything. None of us, except you, excuse me, Aristide, would be

here if the college didn't have this policy. Quite apart
from other factors, Hen's appointment, from the beginning, was a regression from Jocelyn principles. Hen, to
speak frankly, has never subscribed to our methods, and
I think a great deal of the trouble we've had with him
can be laid to an unconscious resistance on his part to
the experimental ideology. This refusal to fill out the
achievement sheets and the field-period reports isn't the
result of mere inefficiency—it's an act of obstructionism,
or sabotage of the experimental machinery, unconscious,
as I say, and very likely irrational; I think it very prob-
able that Hen literally *cannot* fill out our achievement
sheet. More power to him, in a way; one can't help but
respect an integrity that buckles at putting a check beside 'prejudiced but genial' or 'truly liberal.' " The mock-
ing smile played over his lips, but at bottom he was
powerfully in earnest. For all his derogation, he truly
believed in the modern, as subversive of established values,
a mine or fuse laid under the terrain of the virtuous; the
words, *modern, secular, experimental,* were drawled out
by him in a seductive, blandishing tone, like a veiled erotic
invitation.

"Hence, Alma," he declared, "I can't join you in thinking that all Hen's sins of omission can be relegated to
the realm of mere technicalities. They're the expression
of a certain reactionary Schweikism which we've seen
also in faculty meetings." "Most interesting, Howard,"
exclaimed Aristide. "I've observed the same thing myself. Hen and I have had a number of discussions on
the question of relative grading, and he assures me that
he doesn't believe in it. He believes in absolute grading.

I had not myself drawn the inference that he subscribes to a belief in the Absolute." "I too believe in absolute grading," insisted Domna. Furness laughed. "My eye," he said. "How many Excellents did you give last term? You're a real fraud, Domna, when it comes to the achievement sheet. You grade them on their beauty or on a look in their eye. Your marks, take it from me, my dear, are an exercise in *sheer coquetry*." He laid a drawling stress on the last words; Domna colored. "As far as that goes," he continued, "our friend Hen is rather liberal with the Excellents when it serves his purpose. But seriously, the point is, Hen doesn't belong here, doesn't share our objectives. He came here—let's be frank—for asylum; we gave it to him. He ought, long since, discovering his hostility to us, to have looked for another connection. Instead, he's remained here on sufferance and treated his post as a sort of embassy, with extra-territorial rights, from which to attack our institutions. Why should Maynard stand for it? He's stood for it this long, I can assure you, out of simple kindheartedness and decency, in the hope that Hen would have the grace to move on, once he had re-established himself, to the kind of academic work he prefers. If Hen had made the slightest effort to find a post he liked better, during the two years he's been here, I should have more sympathy now for him *and* for Cathy. . . . After all, Alma," he argued, turning his persuasion on her, "Cathy is responsible, equally with Hen, not only for his hanging on here, but also for the attacks he's made on Maynard and the faculty as a whole. Having been married, you know very well that the woman can always control these choices. I've tried, more than

once, to get her to see that Hen was doing himself harm
with these continual rows over trivialities, and she's gra-
ciously informed me that Hen owes it to himself as a
pedagogue to correct misdoing wherever he sees it. That
Zeal-of-the-Land-Busy approach bores me, I must say.
She encourages Hen in these power-fantasies to keep her
hold on him as the one true and excellent wife; why, the
woman's a regular Maintenon. As it happens"—his eyes
narrowed—"the last time I went there, to offer a little
unwanted advice, my car wouldn't start when I left and
I was treated, through the picture-window, to an imitation
of myself. Cathy, wearing Hen's hat and muffler, was
prancing up and down the room—"

"Stop it," cried Alma, sharply. She and Domna exchanged a horrified look. These imitations of Cathy's were
well known to them; indeed they had laughed at them
heartily, but seen from Furness' side of the window, they
assumed another perspective. In this light, Mulcahy's
position at Jocelyn did in fact appear unjustified. Moreover, the two women could not help but feel to some
extent implicated in that rather dubious position; they
also had encouraged Hen to tilt against the local pieties
and abetted him in his sarcasms; for the first time, strangely
enough, it came home to them that Maynard Hoar *did* have
a sort of case against their friend, but at the same moment they discovered that it would be wiser not to see
this just now—any justice to Maynard would have to be
done hereafter. Yet a sense of complicity held them silent
in each other's presence; each read the other's thoughts
and did not wish to be the first to disavow them. But
Van Tour rushed in, colors flying, and saved them from a

moral predicament. " 'Why don't you go back where you came from?' " he hotly quoted, turning to Furness. "Isn't that what you're really saying, Howard? It's the old move-on-buddy line that we used to hear in the Hoover days when anybody got independent. 'Why don't you go back to Russia if you like it so well there?' I must say," he added, chastely, "I never thought I'd be listening to that old bull slung at Jocelyn." For a moment, every face wore a look of gratitude to the speaker for reviving the old militant simplicities, like a martial tune from long ago, but then a sigh went up; the inalienable right to "bore from within" was something they no longer believed in, though they felt a sort of pain where the belief had been, as a veteran does in an amputated limb. "It's no good, Consy," said Furness, regretfully. "Change that phonograph record. Maynard doesn't owe Hen a living just because Hen disagrees with him. How about it, Domna?" he pressed her. "Even you wouldn't allege that."

"I don't know," she admitted. "Candidly, I don't know. Logically, you are right, of course. Maynard *owes* Henry nothing as a college president; yet as a man I feel that he does. There's a certain *noblesse oblige* that we owe to people who criticize us and whom we have the power to harm. Strength ought to impose chivalry; we stay our hand against a disarmed opponent." Furness smiled, recognizing an echo from his own course in the Epic. "You think it's my feudal background?" averred Domna. "The code of the noble which is based on privilege? That is true, I think, but it is also the Christian ethic. What would you put in its place? A purely utilitarian view, which treats men as things in terms of their utility value?" Her voice had grown firmer as she moved into the field of rebuttal. "As long as we have a society of privilege, the code of the noble should restrain us against the exercise of an absolute power.

"What you charge Henry with, is an abuse of hospitality. All very fine, as if Maynard had treated him in the style of an Arab sheik, as an honored guest of the college! Then, if this were so"—her eyes had begun to flash —"I would say yes, by all means, Henry had the obligation to repay courtesy with courtesy. But this is not the case here. Far from it. Maynard has used Henry to advertise his own reputation as a liberal; he hires him to salve his own conscience and write an article for the paper on how much better conditions are at Jocelyn than behind the iron curtain of reaction in the big rich universities. He treats him as we treat the DP's, as a sort of testimonial to the paradise of freedom we have here, and then imposes on him all sorts of restrictions of what he can think and not think, do and not do. He is put to work at the lowest possible salary, housed in wretched conditions at an exorbitant rent, ordered to adapt his teaching methods to the progressive routine, expected to conform socially, to take advice and be grateful every day, like a refugee counting his blessings. When he shows signs ·of independence, it is time to get rid of him; out with him, out with the wife and children, accuse him of disloyalty to the Jocelyn way of life!"

Furness made a motion of ducking; he smiled uneasily. Domna, roused, he thought, was rather splendid, in the manner of a classic heroine; a chaste fire glowed from her; she had the air of a dragon-killer or an acrobatic virgin bringing the serpent to heel. He allowed his admiration for her person to neutralize the effect of what she was saying; that is, he evaded the task of considering it as either true or false. "Go on, Domna," urged Alma, sympathetically. Domna complied, but more modestly; she feared that once again she had yielded to the temptation to show off—was she herself not treating Henry as an occasion for the display of youthful virtue and high feeling? "Hospitality," she speculated, "is a mutual affair, as the French word *hôte* indicates. Here in America, I think, we tend to overemphasize the obligations of the guest, as though he entered a hotel where the rules were pasted over the wash-basin. It may be that Henry has infringed the house-rules of Jocelyn by treating himself, not as a visitor, but as a member of the family, with all the prerogatives of criticism that family membership implies. But if he is wrong, and he is not a member of the family, but a stranger in the house, must we not then treat him with *aidôs?* Does not his special situation make gratitude less incumbent on him than *aidôs* on Maynard and on us?"

Tears suddenly shone in her eyes; her voice trembled slightly; she was one of those romantic girls who are more moved and shaken by a concept, visiting their own lips, like an annunciation, than by poetry or visual art. Alma, who had a tenderness for youth and its sudden gusts of feeling, nodded quickly at her with sympathy and understanding. Furness folded his arms. "May I ask," ventured Aristide, "for a translation? At one time, I was fortunate enough to pick up a little modern Greek in the Peloponnesus but my classic Greek is rudimentary." "*Care* or *ruth*," threw out Furness, negligently. "At bot-

tom, untranslatable. The concept doesn't exist for us. See
Gilbert Murray." "It's another of those double words like
hôte," supplied Alma. "*Aidôs* is both that which inspires
horror and pity, and the feeling aroused in the bystander.
Aidôs applies to the wretchedness of a beggar or a sup-
pliant and to the sentiment of concern one is obliged to
show for him. A certain awe surrounds it. It is what
Achilles, the killer of his son, in the end feels for Priam
when he raises him up and weeps with him." "And what
the boy in the *Iliad* begs of Achilles," put in Domna, "who
is about to slay him. 'Have a care for me.' Greek logic
demands that whatever is full of horror should command
an appropriate response. 'The concept doesn't exist for
us.' " She fixed her stern bright gaze on Furness. Aristide
took out a little notebook and inscribed the word and the
definition with a flourish, like one taking down the address of a *pension*. He snapped the notebook shut.

"So," inquired Alma, whimsically smiling, "are we to
show *aidôs* for Henry?" She looked around her expectantly. Howard stroked his jaw. "*Aidôs*," he remarked,
"whatever it may be, and you girls can have it to play with,
is not an official quantity. In strict justice, there is no *aidôs*,
and I for one propose to deal justly. As a working member
of the department, I would be guilty of misconduct if I
signed a petition citing Hen for merit as a teacher. There
has to be *some* standard in these things, in fairness to the
students and the rest of us. You can do what you want
unofficially, Alma; appeal to Maynard for clemency; that's
your feminine privilege. But we can't let clemency become
the official business of the department." He lit a cigarette
and deliberately leaned his head back, exhaling; he

yawned. "But it's not a question of clemency," insisted Domna, abruptly shifting her ground. "I feel and I think we all feel—with the exception of you, of course—that Henry is a qualified teacher and more than that—as Alma says, a first-class mind. Added to that we feel that his rather desperate personal situation entitles him to more consideration than we would be entitled to ourselves and far outweighs what one might call the personality issue. Plus, to my mind, at any rate, a third factor: in the current political situation, a liberal college ought to lean over backward not to fire anybody who is suspected of Communism, just as a woman's college ought to lean over backward to hire women when they're discriminated against in the men's colleges. Where discrimination exists, protection of the out-group is mandatory, even where such a policy runs the risk of creating a new set of special privileges."

"I'm glad to hear you acknowledge the risk, Domna," remarked Furness on a rising note of irony. "You see where your policy would lead. To vying groups of separatist minorities organized for self-protection. We have something like this already in the Catholic and Jewish boycott groups, in the FEPC, which all you so-called liberals favor without seeing where it tends. I feel very little enthusiasm for the extension of this admirable principle to the universities. We're not yet relief organizations, you must admit. The time may come, of course, when it will be sufficient to show need to get any kind of a job that individual vanity suggests; a wife and four hungry children will entitle the holder to teach calculus or astronomy or whatever his little heart fancies, and a college will become a mere dispensary for cripples of the social order." He spoke roughly, with feeling, having come up the hard way himself; yet there was a certain sparring note in his voice suggestive of sport for sport's sake; he baited Domna for the whim of it.

"*Other things being equal,*" she retorted sharply. "Please don't distort what I say." The others sat back, with a certain sense of relief from responsibility, prepared to enjoy *le boxe;* none of them, including the participants, would know what they thought of this matter till the winner had been certified. "Many factors," declared Domna, "are involved in a decision to let an employee go. Professional competence; the so-called personal equation; the employee's need and future prospects; and finally what one might name the exemplary effects of such a decision. If Maynard lets Henry go, how many other college presidents, seeing what Maynard as a professional progressive has done, will cease to feel any qualms about proceeding against their own Communists, ex-Communists, quasi-Communists? This isn't a permanent situation in which to be a Communist will guarantee eternal *carte blanche* to teach and conduct oneself as one pleases, but an emergency in which any individual weakening of principle is likely to produce a landslide. Each of us knows from his own inner experience how tenuous are the restraints of conscience, how pliant to mass opinion and precedent, to the justification by numbers. If Maynard is permitted to fire Henry, without protest or challenge, fifty other heads will roll."

Furness made a light gesture of disparagement. "Those unfortunate cases," he said lazily, "will have to be decided on their merits. No action would ever be undertaken if one could envision all its consequences. Is Marx responsible for Stalin or Christ for the history of the Church? Very likely so, but the thought is a deterrent to virtue. Maynard's responsibility, I should say, began and ended here at Jocelyn. To cultivate his own garden here and maintain the teaching standard is to set a sufficient example. To debase the teaching standard—however low you may think it already—on behalf of some vague social need would be an act of malfeasance, like the watering of stock or the currency. The same principle might be extended to our students: how often have we heard the argument that a student *needs* to graduate?"

"I believe I've heard it from your lips, Howard," remarked Alma, smiling. Howard grinned. "Guilty," he agreed, "guilty. You will never hear it again. It betrays a certain contempt for our diploma, as I think you yourself have argued."

Domna twisted her hands. "I think I would not graduate an incompetent student merely because of his need to please his family." Aristide cleared his throat. "There have been cases, however, Domna, where we have done so, where we have taken into consideration an unfortunate family situation, a browbeating father or grandparent and a wholly dependent offspring. I believe only last term," he pursued, in an undertone, "you and I contrived to pass a certain student who was in danger of a nervous breakdown." Domna bit her lip. "Yes, I know," she murmured, "but that was really a marginal case. In general, the principle of need should not be governing, unless other factors are equal. Howard is trying to push us into a position where we will admit that our support of Henry rests on his incapacity. That isn't so, really. If he were honestly a poor teacher, we would be wrong to indorse him. We would try to find some other means of solving his family problems, help him with money or fit him into some other position, where he could use his capacities better. . . ." Her earnest voice faltered, as she saw the magnitude of the difficulty. Furness was smiling. "And if he didn't wish, Domna, to be 'fitted into some other position' but wished only to teach literature under our aegis?" His voice was triumphant; he had isolated what he believed to be the crux of Hen's position. "No teacher," replied Domna, flushing, "who wishes to teach can be totally bad, I suppose. . . ."

"Ah," exclaimed Furness, "so that if Henry were only *relatively* bad, you would still wish us to sign a petition for him?" "Not on the same basis," she said stoutly. "You keep distorting what I say, like a lawyer." Yet she knew that he had not distorted, but on the contrary clarified a thing she did not care to have clear. "In any case," she cried, "he is *not* relatively bad." "Supposing," suggested Furness, "there was no question of Cathy's health or of Communism, would you still defend him? Would you insist that the college keep him on his merits if he would have no difficulty in getting a job elsewhere?" "Yes!" she cried, emphatically, suddenly relaxing and pushing her hair back; this, she believed, was what she really thought; Furness himself had shown her a way out of the corner he had driven her into. "Yes, I would," she announced, "for the sake of the college, if not for his."

"In that case," argued Furness, "if you really believe

that, why don't you stick to your guns? Why bring in all this stuff about Cathy and Hen's being a prisoner of the Party, if you really think it's a straight case of merit going unrewarded? Have the courage of your convictions; go ahead and convince me that he's a wonderful teacher!" He looked around the room pleasantly.

Domna gritted her teeth. "*I* did not bring in this stuff, as you call it, about Cathy and Communism. It is there. It has to be reckoned with. If you want, it provides additional reason for not firing Henry. *Other things being equal.* There is nothing strange or unusual about what I'm saying. It's a rule we invoke every day in ordinary practice. If there are two candidates for a job, say, in a woman's college, and both applicants are of equal or near-equal merit, we take the woman, since she lacks the man's chance of being hired by a men's college. Or a Jewish college, like Brandeis, will naturally hire Jewish applicants, since most other colleges discriminate against them."

"And is that a cure for discrimination, Domna?" asked Furness, gently.

The friendliness of the tone troubled her. "I don't know," she admitted. "I see what you mean. You are trying to say that a merit system, honestly applied, is a better cure for these evils. That if Vassar were to hire men without discrimination, and Fisk or Howard to hire whites, this might provide a superior example for Harvard or Columbia. That, as it is, Harvard feels no moral pressure to hire women, since they have their own colleges, and the same is true of the Negroes and the Jews." Furness nodded. "A very profitable discussion," said

Aristide. "I often think we should keep minutes. However," he glanced at his pocket-watch, "I believe we have strayed from the point." "Domna doesn't think so," observed Howard, tenderly. "She's been driven to see that she is really asking Maynard to keep Hen on as a charity. This is all very well for Hen, but sets a poor precedent." He got up and stretched. "Let's all go to Gus's for a drink." "But nothing is settled," protested Van Tour. "It's settled between Domna and me," insisted Howard, winking, and putting an arm around her. Domna frowned and drew away. "No," she said coldly, "it is not. You have not persuaded me at all that I regard Henry as a charity or that I am asking Maynard to discriminate in favor of him on account of his Communist past. If I were, you might be right in principle that such a policy might be bad for the progressive colleges since it amounts to a political means test in reverse." She spoke very rapidly; her forte was not original thought but the ability to return someone else's suggestion fully made up and labeled, like a pharmacist's compound. "Certain colleges we could name have been subjected to a political deep-freeze by the fear of firing deserving Communists or fellow-travelers. But this is not the case here. I would argue, as I said, for Henry's retention if the political question had never been introduced. In fact—" she hurriedly broke off, for what she had been about to say was that she, for one, would accept Furness' challenge and narrow the issue, gladly, to one of intellectual merit.

Yet she checked herself, thinking of Henry. There were many here, like Van Tour, she assured herself, whose support for Henry must derive from a vicarious sense of

political outrage, who were not large-minded enough to
defend him if they did not suspect behind the scenes a
conspiracy to displace him, a conspiracy of powerful interests to which *they* might fall the next victims. She had
no right, she stoutly argued, to narrow the issues of the
case to suit her individual fastidiousness. Moreover, she
had been secretly struck by the perspicuity of Howard's
analysis and was wholeheartedly amazed and grateful that
the others had let themselves be diverted by her from
what was technically a very telling argument: *did* Mulcahy, after all, have an intellectual claim on a college
whose axioms he openly derided? Did she, for that matter, or Alma have the right to put themselves forward as
guardians of the college's interest, when, strictly speaking, the college's interest, as conceived by its President
and trustees, was daily contravened by the whole group
of them, who quite frankly preached to their classes the
necessity of intellectual discipline, order, historical background, and who, in certain cases, had gone so far as to
recommend to certain bright students that they transfer to
a traditional college, where they stood some chance of
getting a thoroughgoing formal education?

Humanly speaking, of course, she and Alma had the
same right as anybody else to interfere in what was none
of their business, the duty, in fact, of the bystander to
interfere between father and son, employer and employee,
state and subject, to protect elementary human rights and
secure fair treatment for the weaker. Yet today's fashion
was to disguise this moral feeling in an expedient garb,
to show Maynard Hoar that it was to the *interest* of the
college not to fire Mulcahy, that is, to attribute to oneself

a wholly specious sentiment of concern for the college's welfare, as certain labor leaders fondly presented themselves as capitalism's best friend, in short, to "sell" a moral argument in terms of a higher utility.

All this was quite repugnant to Domna, yet, having persuaded herself that it was necessary, on Henry's behalf, to use every available means, play on every chord of sympathy, she felt Cathy's contingent death hang over her, like a sword of judgment, if she permitted herself to reason in a matter that ought not to allow of reason but only of total adherence. And yet she no longer, she shamefacedly discovered, thought of Cathy as a person but as an opinion to be propitiated. It was only the spectacle of Furness, who stood before her, grinning, a horrid cautionary example of the consequences of cool logic and detachment, that encouraged her to push aside her doubts.

"What I am trying to say," she blurted out, "is that the case is complex. You can't reduce it to a single question of merit, but merit enters into it. Can't we agree, Howard, that Henry as a teacher has sufficient merit not to be let out when his wife may die of the shock of it?" Touching the simple verities of the case, she smiled at him, certain that he would at last give in. "Come on, Howard," urged Van Tour, "you can't quarrel with that. Let's give him our vote of confidence and get it over with, for God's sake." He pulled on his big overshoes and stamped impatiently on the floor. "Do you want a formal vote?" asked Alma. They all looked to Furness, expectantly. He stood, tying his blue muffler, surveying them with a queer, sad, impudent expression, teetering slightly on the balls of his feet, as though to hold the group on tenterhooks. "How about it?"

said Van Tour; for the first time, he divined that Furness might really vote against them. "Sorry, children," said Furness, with a little tightening of the voice, as he adjusted the folds of the muffler, "I can't do it. You'll have to count me out." The faces watching him slowly fell, in a graduated series; Domna's was the last to give up. "Oh, Howard," she softly remonstrated, looking him searchingly in the eyes. "Sorry to be an old fogey," he apologized. "A matter of principle, I'm afraid." He made a jerky half-bow.

"Well, come on, what are we waiting for? We can outvote him," proclaimed Van Tour, as everyone else hesitated. Aristide intervened. "I strongly advise, Alma," he said, "that you observe the principle of unanimity, as we've done in all cases touching personnel. In our own department, we've found it a source of discord to carry any personnel decision over the dissent of an individual member. The effects on teamwork have been quite disquieting." Alma nodded. "I move no vote," she suggested. Van Tour bristled. "What has Aristide got to do with this?" he complained. "I thought he was here as an observer to carry the sense of the meeting back to his own branch of the division." "I am not voting," Aristide pointed out. "And Domna, strictly speaking, has only half a vote, since she teaches only the one course in your department." Van Tour threw up his hands. "That cooks it," he declared, despondently. "What's the use of voting? Since Alma's gone over to the enemy, that leaves one and a half to two. What about Ellison?" he recalled. "Where is he anyway?" "In bed," replied Alma, shortly. "All in favor of no vote?" She and Furness promptly raised their

hands. "Opposed?" Van Tour waved his hand vigorously
and signaled to Domna, who, however, made no move
and merely stared at her fingers enlaced tightly in her
lap. She was too dispirited to vote and moreover agreed
with Aristide that unanimity was desirable, but a new
reluctance to offend Henry made her unwilling to put this
on record. "Carried," announced Alma.

"Good-bye, Hen," said Van Tour bitterly, jerking on
an Eskimo jacket with a big fur-lined hood. He glared at
Furness as though he wished to strike him. Alma lit a
cheroot. "Domna," she called. "Before you go, I have
something to show you." She hurried over to the desk
and picked up a long white envelope. "My letter to Maynard," she said proudly. "Penned this afternoon." The
men, on their way out, paused in uneasy curiosity. "What
do you mean, this afternoon?" demanded Furness loudly,
sensing some animadversion on himself. Domna had
opened the unsealed envelope; her eyes ran over the typed
lines and then rose to meet Alma's, a look of admiration
in them; Alma, whom she liked and somewhat feared,
was always a jump beyond her. "You knew how it would
come out?" she said, marveling. Alma nodded. "Of
course." She glanced at Furness. "What did you expect
of *him,* forsooth?" "Henry predicted it," Domna whispered. Van Tour was peering over Domna's shoulder.
"You want him to see it?" the girl asked. "Why not?"
said Alma, carelessly. She folded her arms and watched
them. Consy gave a cry of dismay. "Alma's resigned," he
exclaimed in horror. Aristide blanched. Furness utterly
lost his self-possession. "But you should have *told* me,"
he repeated in a peculiar tone of injury mingled with

placation, "you should have *told* me, Alma; you should have *told* me, darling." He swayed as he stood before her, as though he meant to fall down at her feet. Alma surveyed him coldly and put an arm around Domna. "I had no wish to coerce your decision, Howard, or to bargain with you. You voted as you saw best. And my own decision is final; whatever Maynard chooses to do, I shall not stay here any longer."

CHAPTER VII

Oh, What a Tangled Web We Weave

"But it's not fair to *me*, Alma," argued Mulcahy the following morning. He had hurried over to her office as soon as he got the news. He was in a mood to be angry with Domna, who ought to have told him at once, he contended, even though they had agreed not to communicate by telephone for fear of Cathy and her questions—"What did Domna want, dear?" The girl ought to have had the sense to realize that this was urgent and not waited to let him find out, via the campus mail, that Alma had taken a decision that imperiled his whole cause. Merely another illustration, he exclaimed savagely, as he flew across the campus, overcoat flapping, of the folly of entrusting one's destiny to the lax attentions of outsiders—what did it matter to Domna that a trump card had just been thrown away while she slept in her virgin bedstead the sleep of the just and the idiot? Alma's letter of resignation was by this time—he glanced despairingly at the chapel clock —waiting on Maynard's blotter for his eminence to read. Had he himself been informed on time, it might have been possible to go through the mail-sack and remove it.

Even now, he calculated, as he endeavored to drill reason into Alma's obstinate head, there was still a chance that Maynard might be late getting to his office or away on one of his eternal fund-raising tours or addressing a forum of educators on the Spirit of Free Inquiry, ha, ha. The prudence of an official, he thought limply, ought never to be underestimated; it would not be the first occasion on which this one had taken cover to let some tempest of criticism blow over, give tempers time to cool, the counsels of moderation to prevail, etc., etc. A great one was Mr. Hoar for "letting things shake down a bit till we can view them in their true perspective."

Even assuming that the damage was done, that this fool Draconic letter could not be retrieved, Alma herself, in all conscience, one would think, could do something to undo its effects. It was not unreasonable, certainly, to ask of her that she go to Maynard of her own accord and explain how things really stood: that she had written hastily, in the first shock of hearing of her friend's dismissal, but that she would be pleased to withdraw her resignation just as soon as Maynard, on his side, withdrew his own ill-considered letter of yesterday. Yet Alma, perversely, refused to see that this "final" resignation of hers was intrinsically selfish and seemed determined to persist in resigning no matter what amends Maynard made, a thing which was as unfair to Maynard as it was to himself and to the students, who had been given every reason to think that the old girl was a fixture at Jocelyn.

"Can't you see, Alma," he supplicated, "that such a stand is really un-Christian?" The necessity of taking this tone filled him with impatience; he had an innate

distaste for flattery, yet there seemed no other way of
making an unpleasant truth palatable to a woman accustomed to dictate in her own little circumscribed sphere of
fawning pupils and colleagues who feared her sharp
tongue, even, to tell the truth, as he himself did a little
at this moment, so that he kept going all around Robin
Hood's barn, he thought wearily, instead of coming to
the point and talking to her like a Dutch uncle, which,
God knows, she deserved. "You're bent," he gently chided,
"on punishing the whole college for one man's mistake,
and for all we know, Alma—let's be charitable—it may
have been simply a mistake, an error of judgment such as
all of us are liable to. Even I," he went on earnestly,
"who've been singled out for Maynard's persecution, even
I think it wrong to condemn Maynard unheard. It's very
Old Testament of you, like those jealous, feminine wraths
of Jehovah that wanted to wipe out a whole city in return
for a sin. You put me in the absurd position of the inter-
ceding prophet, pleading for our latter-day Sodom against
your terrible ire. Relent toward us, stay your hand!" But
this mock-heroic approach was a mistake; she merely
shook her black locks, smiling, as though he had paid
her a compliment, her berry-black eyes coruscating in
their eternal, indulgent twinkle. "I did what I had to do,"
she affirmed with a sudden faraway look, as though fixing
an appointment with her destiny.

"But what about *me?*" exclaimed Henry, nettled at
her opacity. She kept missing the point on purpose, he
thought furiously—did she want him to spell it out for
her in letters a foot high? *Very well,* he inwardly told
her, setting his teeth. *You force me to speak plainly; on*

your own head be it. "What you don't seem to realize, Alma," he expostulated, "is that this gesture of yours is a disservice to the very party you intend to benefit. Your resignation, offered provisionally, can be a deterrent to Maynard. His high opinion of you, the department's dependence on you, can be just the lever we need to force him to do what we want. But if you resign out and out like this, you present him with one reason less for doing the right thing. He has no incentive to rehire me if you tell him in so many words that you won't come back in any case. When you've got a pistol to a man's head, you don't pull the trigger until you get what you can out of him." The strain of speaking patiently such elementary truths was tiring him; his vocal cords ached as after a long tutorial with one of those exasperating students who kept their own counsel and allowed you to explain and explain what they had already learned from the textbook. From Alma's frowning brow, he could get no idea of whether he had already said enough or too much or too little to carry his message home. Her chin was sunk in her hand, and he had a suspicion that what he said depressed her in some way: did she think him venal, he wondered, for bringing the bald facts of barter to her attention? He suddenly felt the need of lifting the discussion to a higher plane. "I understand very well," he continued, "your reaction of moral revulsion, but you're behaving as though there were only yourself to consider. Once you go, Maynard's conscience goes; you must face that, Alma. To have a firm character like yours is a responsibility, which you mustn't and can't run away from. So long as you can play the part of Maynard's spiritual gadfly, you

have the obligation to do so. I won't speak of myself and
Cathy—I know that you wouldn't willingly harm us and
have done what you did in our interest as it appeared to
you—but beyond my own selfish concern, I can see something else: a weak man like Maynard in a position of
power has the right to expect others stronger than himself
to keep a watch on him and call him to task when he goes
wrong. It's a thankless job but you must keep it and not
run away, like Jonah, into the belly of the whale."

He moistened his lips and sat back, confident that he
had at last made an impression. Alma's voice, when she
spoke, was crestfallen; he supposed that the allusion to
Cathy had cut her. "My strategy," she said, "was different.
I know Maynard Hoar very well, Hen, and my feminine
instinct tells me that he responds only to the irrevocable,
to a *fait accompli*. It's a defect of imagination; you and
I have too much; Maynard has too little. Tomorrow is
never present to him until it becomes yesterday. My father
was such a man. I left home for good when I was fifteen
and went to work as a stack-girl in a library—my sisters
reaped the benefits of his repentance. I've never seen him
since." The cords in her neck tightened with her emphasis;
Henry regarded her thoughtfully; it was the first auto-
biographical word he had ever heard from her and her
intensity carried a certain conviction.

He remained, as yet, unpersuaded, but his mind had
opened to new possibilities. Unconsciously, he took a new
tone with her, as though he wished her to defeat him in
argument. "Look, Alma," he said, decisively. "You really
have no right to do this. I can't permit you to break your
career on Cathy's and my behalf. You think you'll have

no trouble getting another appointment, but let me tell you things aren't what they were when you first came to Jocelyn. You'll find conformity entrenched in every office, studying your dossier, asking questions, wondering 'what was the background of your decision to leave Jocelyn.'" His voice suddenly tautened as he cited the well-remembered formula. "Guilt by association. The amalgam. The smear. I know it too well, Alma. You'll be tarred by the same brush, I can promise you!" Tears sprang to his eyes as he relived his own experience, forgetting blindly, for the nonce, the purpose of what he was saying. "Naturally," he concluded, dully, "I'm grateful to you for your warm-heartedness, but there are things one cannot accept."

Despite himself, while he was speaking, a growing reverence for this woman began to mingle with his reprehension. Thought of detachedly, as a story, a tale to be told in the common rooms, her sacrifice had magnitude; it stirred him, like a legend heard in the distant future, on his own tongue. As he half-listened to her answer once again with the arguments she had just invoked, one part of his mind commenced to wonder how he *could* accept this sacrifice, having repudiated it so firmly, while another part still faintly protested at being sidetracked from its original object—how was it possible for her to have read Maynard and human nature better, as she kept averring, than he? "I learned long ago," she stoutly reiterated, "that one can't bargain in these affairs. If one wants to be effective, one hands in one's resignation and clears out. There's no other way for a man or an institution to learn that one is serious than to learn it too late."

His pale eyes watched her curiously: she had been

laying out her class notes, solitaire-wise, in a series of stacks, and now, with an abrupt gesture, she scooped them all up together, like a deck of cards when the hand is finished. The neatness of the desk, the small, tense, wiry hands, the old-fashioned pen-holder and pen-wiper, the silver paper-cutter (a legacy, surely, of Mr. Fortune, who was said to have left her well fixed), the worn briefcase stood in the corner all suddenly struck him as manifestations of a disciplined life-force; he became aware of reserves of certainty in her before which his own convictions prepared to abdicate. Not since graduate school, he dreamily realized, had he experienced this uncanny sensation, like an animal's, of the *otherness* of a separate being, with its own mysterious sources of propulsion; and that this epiphany should have been accorded him at this crisis in his affairs seemed to him instantly a Sign, which he obeyed with a sort of joy and altar-boy's punctilio.

"Very well," he acceded, with a sigh.

"In this instance," his Diotima continued, "we *must* let Maynard know that he is living in the real world, that if he takes certain actions certain consequences will irreparably follow. If I make my resignation contingent on concessions from him, he will never be sure that I would have gone through with it, that he couldn't have won me back in June or during the summer term. In fact, the whole tendency, Hen, of a conditional resignation would be to encourage Maynard to procrastinate, stave off any decision in the hope that I might exercise the proverbial woman's privilege and change my mind. And, oh my dear, who knows? Perhaps I would," she exclaimed on a more

sprightly note. "We're weak vessels, all of us, we thinking reeds. I hold it safer to burn my bridges."

She snapped a rubber band around her notes and stood
up, with a shake of her skirt. "I have a class," she apologized and rapped him with her knuckles sympathetically
on the arm. "Don't worry. One resignation will be enough
to give Maynard an idea of how the wind blows. He'll be
taking in sail soon. Wait and see if he doesn't. You have
other friends, you know. Even poor Howie is having some
second thoughts. He's afraid that Domna will be next,
and you know his little *penchant* there."

Henry made a sour face. "Domna will never resign,"
he asserted, not knowing why he said this. Now that Alma
was leaving him, he felt all at once abandoned, cheated,
misused; he picked on Domna, partly to vent his mis-
trustfulness on a convenient target, and partly to detain
Alma; yet the instant he had spoken he had a vicious certainty that he was right. "Domna is very young," pen-
sively observed Alma. "Moreover, she has a moral
problem. We talked it over together last night." Henry's
suspicions returned; he disliked the suggestion of "sharing" or "quiet time" that had come into Alma's voice
and felt like a carcass greedily picked between the two
of them—what *were* their relations anyway? No wonder
Domna had been too busy to telephone him with the news.
"She isn't altogether sure in her own mind," said Alma
thoughtfully, "whether she *wants* to stay at Jocelyn. If
she's going to resign in any case, she feels that it might
be dishonest for her to let Maynard think, by resigning
now, that she was doing it on your account. Or, conversely,
if she resigns now, she feels that she might be under an

obligation to stay if Maynard renews your contract."
Henry made a movement of impatience. "What infernal
jesuitry!" he exclaimed. Alma shook her head at him,
reproachfully. "No, my dear. You are quite wrong. Domna
must know what she wants herself before she can rush
into an action. There's a side of her—she confessed it—that
merely wants to emulate me. And another side, related
to it, that would like to take credit for a principled action
while suiting its own convenience. It was I, if you must
know, Hen, who warned her against this possibility."

"I see," said Henry, slowly, with a polite show of
being convinced; in one part of his intelligence, he was,
if not convinced, then impressed by this exercise of feminine scruples; he stored the lesson away in his memory
against the future. "But Alma," he interposed, as she
made again to leave, "I don't precisely follow how this
argument can apply to Domna and not to you. If Domna
must withdraw her resignation when Maynard renews my
contract, why not you? It would seem to me that the same
principle holds." Alma's eyes crinkled with laughter.
"That's a man for you," she cried. "It's not the same at
all. Domna, you see, would sacrifice herself by staying.
My sacrifice is to go. It's very important," she continued,
soberly, tapping him with a forefinger, "to play for real
stakes in these cases. You are worth something to us, my
dear friend, and we must show that we mean it. No flim-
flam or mere attitudinizing. Until Domna decides in her
own mind whether she would stay on at Jocelyn if this
unfortunate thing hadn't happened, she has no way of
knowing whether it would cost her anything to resign. And
she must *not* resign until she knows." In the peremptory

underscorings of that voice he heard the echo of many a formidable tutorial; Alma had what he had characterized as a sentimental severity that scared the girls stiff and left the boys stolid: many a soft lower lip had been sharply caught back and bitten, as Mrs. Fortune, leaning forward across her desk, eyes glistening and chin propped on her knuckles, lovingly impaled a moral weakness and squeezed it, like a pimple. "I see," he repeated.

And as he hurried off to telephone Cathy, he did indeed see, he believed, something which had not come under Alma's notice: the older woman, surely, was devoured by pride and watchful envy of the younger and wanted to have all the honors of a disinterested action to herself. She it was of course—how crudely she had given herself away!—who had talked the stupid Domna carefully out of the limelight. The girl had been all set to resign yesterday afternoon—she had told him so herself—and had simply let herself be bamboozled out of double billing. Yet it was clever of Alma, he had to admit, to have fixed on the typically Russian preoccupation with motive to divert the girl from her own rightful claims on celebrity; nothing would have served so well. The conceit of the "noble" action, he said to himself, chuckling, *l'acte gratuit*, the selfless, improvident, senseless, luxurious, spendthrift action, this had touched the soft spot of the little iron maiden, so resolved to distinguish herself from the others, the mere *canaille* of the faculty whose ancestors had had to work for a living, by the implacable purity of her motives. He was in no mood now to carp at this jousting of the two ladies for favor, which had a certain charm as well as a higher utility; all honors to Alma for carrying off the first round of the tourney. Yet even as he fancied them caparisoned for battle, another idea genially obtruded itself, like the gloss of a Marxist critic; he smiled sardonically as he walked.

In Domna, he was ready to wager, there was a *fond* of shrewdness, a sharp mother-wit, as there had been in old Tolstoy, that knew which side its bread was buttered on. The silken shirt under the peasant blouse—he had heard Domna hotly deny this story related of the old sinner, and then, characteristically, defend it by paradox. After all, the Marxians were not so wrong to look for the economic base—with Alma out, Domna would be the reigning *précieuse* of the department, with a step up in rank, very likely, and a nice little salary hike. He would not be surprised, for that matter, if Alma herself did not have another appointment tucked up her sleeve. More power to her, he thought succinctly; so long as she kept it dark. And yet, along with his relief, if this should be so, he admitted to a certain wry disappointment which made him dismiss the suspicion as if it had come from someone else.

Having been persuaded, *faute de mieux*, to accept Alma's resignation in its present and no doubt irrevocable form, he was free at last to take a satisfaction in it that had been coursing through him all along, like a subterranean rivulet which he had tried dutifully to hold within bounds but which now bubbled up in a freshet of joy and, yes, brotherhood. He longed to share with the incredulous, infidel world the glad news of what Alma had done for him, the splendid finality of the thing, a bursting of the bonds of materialism and selfishness that turned

the wintry morning, as he sped along, chin burrowed in
his coat-collar, into an Eastertide. And as he walked, he
argued *sotto voce* with an imaginary opponent, a devil's
advocate who tried, of course, to strip the act of its significance, reduce it to the level of things seen every day.
How many others, answered Henry, would have been equal
to it; how many cases could you name in recent academic
history where such solidarity has been manifested, straight
off, the first crack out of the box, without anybody's asking for it? He nodded to passing students, promising
himself that in time these too would hear what Cathy's
condition unfortunately now interdicted, and yet at the
some time he wondered whether everybody's well-meant
efforts at secrecy *could* keep the story, once it broke, from
spreading like wildfire on the campus. Howard Furness
would soon be talking and Miss Crewes, of course, Maynard's secretary—how could you hope at Jocelyn to keep
such a scandal under wraps?

"I told her," he said breathlessly to John Bentkoop,
whom he ran up against in the main building, in the mill-
ing, mid-morning crowd by the mail-safes, "I told her
that there were things one couldn't accept, that I was grateful to her for her warmheartedness, but that I couldn't willingly see her expose herself to the proscriptions of our
present era, which hasn't been surpassed, I assure you,
since the times of Sulla or Diocletian. After what I've
been through myself, I couldn't permit another human
being. . . ." He broke off as a few curious students began to collect at his elbow. Young John withdrew a long
hand from his mail-safe, glanced through his mail leisurely, and gripped Henry's shoulder. "Easy," he advised

in his cavernous and yet fraternal American voice. "That's Alma's affair, Hen; you must let her take care of it." Under his gaze, which warningly identified them, the students moved off. He was a follower of Niebuhr and Barth, a farm-boy of the region who had gone to Jocelyn on a scholarship, lost his faith and regained it through the medium of anthropology. Every word he uttered had a weight of great consideration, and his deep young voice creaked, like a pair of high shoes ascending a dark stairway with precaution. He had large, grave brown eyes, with a strange blackish glitter in their depths, a long face, lantern-jawed, but rather winsome, and a crew haircut. "The time may have come in Alma's life," he pontificated, "when a change may have great value. We don't make such decisions until we're inwardly prepared for them. You may have been merely the necessary stimulant for a fruition long overdue." A dim smile, touching his cheekbones, like a ray of light falling from a clerestory, indicated that this remark was illuminated by the comic spirit.

Mulcahy recognized, with discomfort, that he had begun on a false note. Nevertheless, he persisted. "No, John," he said apologetically, "you're all wrong. There's no need to pretend that everything is for the best in the best of all Leibnitzian worlds. This is going to be an awful wrench for Alma. Her whole life and her memories are here. She's made an extraordinary sacrifice. She doesn't pretend otherwise, and I'm grateful to her for not pretending. She said in so many words that she wished me to know what I was worth to her, what my continuance here was worth to her and to all my friends." Bentkoop's jaws flexed, but he said nothing. Mulcahy saw in a disillusioning flash

that none of these "friends" cared to hear of Alma's sacrifice, lest it be construed as a demand on themselves, like
those oral pledges made at charitable meetings. "Naturally," he went on, with a short laugh, "I don't expect
everybody to commit suttee for me. Though just between
ourselves, I have a suspicion that Domna and Alma are
vying for the honors of the widow's pyre. I really shouldn't
say that," he added, seeing a shade of interest cross the
young man's face. "It's all Alma's show and more credit
to her. Amazing woman, don't you think?" In his refusal
to be dislodged from his topic, he found himself beginning to babble. "But I must tell you, she had a wonderful formulation, quite in character for her, straight out
of the feminist movement, with the sound of the doors
slamming in the Doll's House. She said 'there's no other
way for a man or an institution to learn that one is
serious than to learn it too late.' " He looked at Bentkoop expectantly; Bentkoop gravely nodded. "I have a
tutee coming; how about you, Hen?" he interposed, with
just a hint of admonishment. Mulcahy had the unpleasant
feeling that all through this conversation there had been
pity for himself in the atmosphere. He had already missed
an appointment this morning and wondered if Bentkoop
knew it. Bentkoop had the office just across the hall and
often left his door open, as though to spy on his comings
and goings. "Very likely," he said shortly. "They keep
changing their hours. *I* can't keep track of them. Half the
time I wait there and they don't show up. Then they have
the hypocrisy to go and complain to the registrar."

"Come on, boy," said Bentkoop equably, with again
that nuance of understanding in his manner, as though,

thought Mulcahy spitefully, he were guiding a drunkard past a beckoning saloon door. They walked back across the campus together.

"I imagine Maynard is on the hot seat this morning," confidently remarked Mulcahy, as they came abreast the Administration Building; he could not resist a final allusion to Alma's *coup de foudre*. "Poor fellow," observed John, unexpectedly. Mulcahy's eyes dilated. "What do you mean, *poor fellow?*" he scornfully cried. "I should think I was more to be pitied. Or Alma." Bentkoop gripped his arm again; he wore a long dark back-belted coat of a cheap shaggy material much affected by priests and young existentialists. "Don't harrow yourself so, Hen," he murmured, with a moved note in his deep voice that touched and surprised Mulcahy. "Don't deliberately try to think we're all against you. I'm on your side, boy. Surely Domna told you. What I meant was simply that I shouldn't like to be in Maynard's shoes. A man who does a foolish thing is more to be pitied than his victim, provided the victim has recourses. How would you like to be opening Alma's letter, receiving petitions, listening to deputations. . . ?" Henry's heart gave a surge of happiness. "Deputations?" he ventured.

John kicked away a clinker on the walk. "So I understand," he said. "But who?" marveled Henry. "When?" "Domna and myself, I believe," answered John casually. "It's not been decided for certain yet. There's to be another meeting, I'm told, at lunch-time. You know, Hen, if I were you, I'd try to stay out of this thing as much as is humanly possible. Everything's being done that can be done, as they tell the patient's relatives. This is an operation; anesthetize yourself till it's over any way you know how. You'll only alienate sympathy if you don't keep your hand out of it. You have more at stake than we have, which makes you more eager, more fearful that we're not doing the right thing by you. *You* can't help it, but the public doesn't like it. That's the terrible thing about victims," he added thoughtfully. "In fact, you could define a victim as one who must be more concerned about himself than anybody else is for him. Even Christ on the cross had such a moment: 'My God, my God, why hast Thou forsaken me?' "

"You're right," exclaimed Henry. "You're right." For the second time that morning his heart was swollen with gratitude; tears came to his eyes at being understood, finally, after years of what he now understood to have been a mere fancied neglect. The idea that he had been at fault toward his colleagues entered his mind and was welcomed. "You don't know what it means to me to be set right when I need it. People seldom speak plainly to me; it must be my own fault. I repel it with my arrogance, I suppose. I'll try to do what you say, John; keep out of it till it's over. No more back-seat driving. And yet, truthfully, my nerves are so bad that I hardly know whether I'm up to it. What do you think I should do, John, go home and stay there for a day or so and let Domna run the show?" "How much can you keep from Cathy?" replied John, glancing at him sidelong, with a certain curiosity. "Very little, in the past," admitted Henry. "It's not as though I'd had side affairs and were a practiced deceiver. Sometimes I feel sure she'll smell it on me, like liquor or another woman." "Better not try to stay home then," advised Bentkoop, with what sounded like a slight loss of interest. "Stick it out here as well as you can. Work, you know. The great anodyne." He paused as they climbed the broad stone stairs and purposefully lowered his voice. "By the way, Hen, there's some sort of rumor around that this thing has gotten to the students. They even say that there's a petition circulating. Do you know anything about it?"

Henry held himself taut. Experience had taught him that surprise of all reactions was the most difficult to imitate, for one was always an instant too late. He therefore remained immobile, as though frozen to stone by what he had heard, while considering what to say. *"I don't believe it,"* he finally said, in measured tones, biting off the words, one by one. John scratched his ear, which had a rather pendulous lobe from being pulled, thoughtfully, in many a long discussion. "So they say," he repeated. The moment prolonged itself, awkwardly. "I heard it," he added, as though apologizing, "from Bill Fraenkel, who had it from a student. There's a girl, Lilia Something, a freshman, who's supposed to be passing a petition." Mulcahy laughed. "Why, I don't even know her," he cried with exuberance; for a reckless moment, he had been on the verge of an admission, which the slightest real encouragement from Bentkoop might have succeeded in wringing out of him. "It just goes to show how the smallest thing gets distorted and magnified. I never heard of the girl. Probably some student grievance petition that has nothing to do with me, and Bill Fraenkel gets wind of it and tries to make me responsible." He stopped and gnawed his

lip. "As a matter of fact, John," he suggested, "Fraenkel
was in the store yesterday when I was talking to Domna—"
Bentkoop put an end to this speculation. "Let's hope you're
right," he cut in, on a note of weariness. "I'd hate to see
the students get their teeth in this one. Bad business, Hen.
Bodes no good for anybody, including you, you know.
I'd like to see this thing settled quietly. Maynard's amenable to reason if you don't force him out on a limb. If you
do, there'll be a fight, I'm afraid, and somebody's likely
to get hurt." He scratched his ear again. "Technically, I
assume you know, Hen, Maynard's well within his rights.
Since you don't have tenure, he's not obliged to show
cause." He broke off and held open the storm door for
Mulcahy, who preceded him into the vestibule. Despite
this deference, natural and proper from a younger man
to an older, Mulcahy felt suddenly uneasy, as though
binoculars were trained on his back.

This religious young man, he suspected, had been giving him a series of tips, like one of God's strong men
or gangsters; there was an aura of pleasant-spoken omnis-
cience about him that reeked of spiritual blackmail. Could
he be seeking to convert him to Protestantism by establishing a ghostly commerce with his conscience? Bentkoop
held open the inner door, and again Mulcahy passed
through ahead of him but pulled up and waited while
Bentkoop stamped nonexistent snow from his overshoes.
How he dallied, observed Mulcahy; as though expecting a
keyword to be passed, like a priest who sits secure in the
confessional, confident from long experience of the sins
that will come tumbling out! Nothing further, however,
was said, beyond a short good-bye, as they discerned their

tutees waiting outside their separate doors. The interview, thought Mulcahy, as he unlocked his office, had a
curiously raw, unfinished, and provocative quality, as if,
to state it flatly, Bentkoop knew something. He felt a sudden interest in discovering Bentkoop's real motive for
supporting him, for Domna's explanation—that Bentkoop
wished to see at least one theist in the Literature department—seemed to Mulcahy all at once terribly thin and
unconvincing: if this was one's motive, one would certainly not avow it at Jocelyn. Impatiently, he wrote off the
human element: Bentkoop was too intelligent to be taken
in as the others were. There was something else, he was
certain, some inscrutable purpose, of which he himself was
either the tool or the beneficiary.

Ushering the student in, he took stock of the boy, wondering whether this weedy sophomore could be trusted
to carry a message to Sheila McKay without letting the
whole campus in on it, yet scrupling as to whether to call
off the petition—if indeed there was one in existence—
merely on Bentkoop's say-so. There were certain interests,
he abruptly perceived, notably Mr. Maynard Hoar's, that
might be very well served by having a student movement
nipped in the bud; and what could be cleverer than to
persuade him, through the mediation of Mr. Bentkoop,
their agent, to do the job himself. It went without saying
that the Administration cabal would have a spy planted, yet
who would have thought they could have acted so promptly
and with such amazing foresight? And what a master-
stroke, he breathed, to have their spy actually appointed
to serve on the proposed deputation, with only Domna to
ride herd on him, a shy, high-minded girl with no experi-

ence of academic politics. Yet still, in the back of his mind, Mulcahy seesawed, accepting a paper from the student and running his eyes absently over it, while his pencil jotted corrections of spelling and punctuation: was he not being too astute, he rebuked himself, and ascribing to them a cleverness which was an attribute of his own intelligence and quite out of keeping with their own clumsy maneuvers?

It was always possible that Bentkoop had spoken to him in all good faith and sincerity, to warn him of what might be a costly mistake in timing, in which case he would do well to heed the admonition and curb his impatient disciples before they could do him harm. And yet how had Bentkoop known to come directly to him? There were a thousand ways, he assured himself, in which the students could have got hold of the story without *his* intervention. Why behave as if *he* had set the damned petition afoot? A spasm of irritation shook him. He could not determine where *their* machinations ended and his own, over-active intelligence began the work of conjecture—it was the old philosophical stickler: how to distinguish the mind's knowledge of its objects from its experience of its own processes? In short, *can we know anything,* he muttered under his breath and raised his eyes from the paper. "Before we get on to this, Jerry," he commenced, "could you take a message for me to one of your fellow-tutees? Don't give it to just anybody in the dormitory. See that you tell her personally. Sheila McKay. Tell her to come to see me directly after lunch; she forgot to take her assignment and I want to explain it to her." The boy nodded. "Glad to, Dr. Mulcahy. Do you want me to go now?" The

teacher smiled at this alacrity. "No," he said, lightly, seeing with relief and a certain pale regret that the name,
Sheila McKay, had no special meaning for Jerry, and
that the petition, therefore, could not be making great head-
way, "afterwards will do very nicely."

CHAPTER VIII

The Deputation

DOMNA AND JOHN BENTKOOP sat side by side on a small horsehair-covered sofa in the anteroom of Maynard Hoar's office. They both looked extremely nervous, like a young couple being detained in the waiting-room of a doctor's suite or an employment or adoption agency. The role they were about to play in the history of academic causes was in the foreground of their thoughts, so that they glimpsed themselves from the outside and strove for a correct demeanor that would combine assurance with naturalness. But merely by keeping them waiting, Maynard Hoar had turned the tables on them, so that they came, they began to fear, not as advisers, *amici curiae*, but as petitioners, facing an interrogation. Conscious of Miss Crewes, the secretary, typing in the next room, they spoke in slightly raised voices of indifferent matters, meanwhile exchanging certain eye-signals commenting on the furniture, which reflected a recent visit to Wanamaker's on the part of Mrs. Hoar. The room had been redone, to cite the *Alumni Bulletin,* "in the spirit of the old College," with white walls, white straight linen curtains, and black Shaker reproduction chairs. On the walls were dark paintings of the first presidents, clergymen and theologians, a primitive engraving showing William Penn and the Indians, and a pastel portrait of the Founder done by a woman friend. On a table, beside the catalogue and a brown glass ash-tray, was a framed snapshot of Maynard, fishing in a local stream. Domna indicated this, and John gave a short laugh, which came out over-loud, like a bray. To cover himself, he got up and pretended to examine the picture. Domna became immersed in the catalogue.

Each in his own mind was sorting out the arguments at his disposal and setting them aside, provisionally, in hopes that the other would take the initiative. They did not know each other well, but the constraint of their detention was beginning to draw them together, like pupils called before the Principal, and to invoke in each a silent trust that the other was the bolder and stronger of the two. John's wife had just had a baby, so that he did not go out much, and he met Domna now, as if for the first time, in the intricacies of the Mulcahy case, like a man meeting a girl in a grand right and left and finding that their steps agreed. Though an ocean and a gulf of class had separated their childhoods, their upbringing had much in common in strictness and isolation; both held the advanced ideas that had been current in the eighteen-sixties and that remained advanced in the present era, though with a certain pathos, like an old hat that has never been worn.

Ten days had passed since they had written to Maynard, asking for a date for an interview; he had answered, begging them to postpone it until the beginning of the field-period, when all concerned would be freer. This morning the college was deserted, save for the Administration Building, the Library, and one wing of a dormitory kept open for the five or six students who remained. Thanks to this postponement, Mulcahy's supporters were already scattered: Ivy Legendre had taken a train to Florida; Aristide, with a group of French majors, was en route to Quebec with his ice-skates; Alma had gone to New York. This left no one for the deputation to report to but Van Tour and Kantorowitz and, of course, Mulcahy himself, who justifiably felt that he had been let down, despite the fact that before leaving, Ivy and Aristide had penned hasty notes to the President, questioning the termination of the appointment. Mulcahy prophesied to Domna, whom he came to see every night, that the whole movement would evaporate during the four weeks' hiatus; he was in a baleful mood, privately ruing the day when he had let himself be tricked into squelching the student petition, and vowing vengeance on Bentkoop, whom he only spared temporarily, till the conclusion of this morning's interview. Domna, though she did not say so, feared that he might be right, in the main—she was ignorant of his sentiments toward Bentkoop and did not know how to interpret certain darkenings of the visage when the young man's name was spoken. She too felt that those others, if they were serious, might have sacrificed a day or two of pleasure to stand by in the crisis. Even the writing of those notes, as she murmured to Bentkoop, had become suddenly a concession bestowed on her like a papal indulgence. Like most people intent on selfish ends—she swiftly continued, looking sidewise at him, through lowered eyelashes—they had an air of strained concentration, as though on a higher duty, as though the obligation to catch a train were a species of

martyrdom, exacted from them by the schedule, by name-
less people who were waiting for them, i.e., hotel-keepers
and the like. John nodded.

" 'You and John will handle it; everything will be all
right; don't worry,' " she quoted the guilty ones, broodily.
"And such an outing suit, I assure you! Such veils and
toques!" John's noiseless laugh was tolerant; he perceived
that she needed to work herself up by gloomy prognosti-
cation, and this inspired in him a protective feeling both
toward her and the others. "It's not going to be so easy!"
she threw out with a foreboding look at the closed oak door
into Maynard's sanctum. The truth was, she felt abandoned
by her colleagues and had begun to have doubts, not only
of the outcome but of the justice of the cause, which she
turned into blame of the deserters. What she longed to
confide in John and dared not was that Mulcahy had been
acting most strangely, coming to her house late at night,
letting his satirical laugh ring out over the snowy fields
till the neighbors wondered, talking excitedly over the
phone in a crazy code-language, which must surely be
audible to Cathy, making friends with Mr. Mahmoud
Ali Jones and demanding that he be added to the deputation, confabbing with Herbert Ellison, whom he named his
"new disciple." Like most Russian women of her class,
she had a horror of the bizarre that could only be tamed
by mirth and she feared to laugh at Henry. She had the
feeling that he was slipping away from under her influence
and wondered even whether she really knew him as well
as she asserted to herself. The idea that she was in too
deep to get out was becoming her sole reassurance, em-
bodying all her fatalism. At the same time, of course, she

reproached herself for disloyalty: these doubts, she crisply declared, were marshaled in her by selfishness and a social dread of identification with another person's conduct.

As she sat there, on the sofa, brushing her hair back, smoothing her skirt, she kept trying to restore the image of Henry, as he had seemed to her before he became, so to speak, her dependent, but only an image of a rather colorless man whom she had first seen at a department meeting came at her behest. When she first met Henry, she desperately admitted, she had not liked him at all. "Now it is too late," she said to herself, relievedly, as the oak door began slowly to open, and John, gripping her arm, whispered, *"Now,"* and pushed her gently ahead of him. As she rose, she observed for the first time that he was wearing what must be his best suit, also a white shirt and staunch, dark, conservative tie.

"Now," said Maynard, seating them in two chairs on either side of his desk, "I infer that you two children have come to give me a scolding." John stole a glance at Domna, who looked woefully pale and tense. "Right," he said coolly, folding his arms and settling himself into a more comfortable position, as though he did not intend to be budged. As a Jocelyn alumnus, he had memories of this room, with its high dark oak wainscoting, white plastered walls, and heavy oak window embrasures, that well anteceded the President's. This was the only Victorian building on the campus, and the room remained what it had always been, a Protestant minister's study, with brown leather-covered chairs, a bay window looking out over the main drive, glassed-in bookcases of golden oak. It was an atmosphere into which John fitted rather more easily than

Maynard, who this morning was wearing a tan jersey with a little collar, open at the throat, and a pair of khaki trousers. He was one of those rugged men who looked exactly like their photographs—dark, resilient, keen-eyed, buoyant, yet thoughtful. Like all such official types, he specialized in being his own antithesis: strong but understanding, boisterous but grave, pragmatic but speculative when need be. The necessity of encompassing such opposites had left him with a little wobble of uncertainty in the center of his personality, which made other people, including his present auditors, feel embarrassed by him. He was much preoccupied with youth, with America as a young country; he tried to have up-to-date opinions which were as sound as grandpa's digestion. He had a strong true voice and liked to sing folk songs, especially work songs and prison chants.

At Jocelyn, he was somewhat of an anomaly and half knew it, being the first of Jocelyn's presidents who was a political progressive and neither an intellectual, strictly speaking, nor an esthete. This made him placatory to his faculty and dependent on them to "sell" him to the student-body, whose subversive streak he did not at all understand and who, in turn, regarded him rather warily, like a group of native coolies confronted with the new type of promotion-conscious colonial administrator. John Bentkoop more than once had counseled him through an incipient student rebellion.

"I'm not going to be stuffy," he announced, having taken out a folder, put on his glasses, and glanced through it. He looked up at them over his glasses and pushed it aside. "I recognize the right of this faculty to oppose

what I do and if they can to amend it." The echo of the
Declaration brought a faint, curving smile to Domna's
lips; she breathed easier. "I want you and Domna to know,
John, that I'm grateful to you for coming to me man to
man about this. What Alma has done"—he tapped the
folder—"seems to me unforgivable." His handsome face
slightly reddened and his voice rose. "It speaks to me of a
basic disloyalty to the college and the ideas of free exchange it stands for." Domna opened her mouth to put
in a word of objection but closed it as the President flashed
his dark eyes on her in a histrionic blaze. One does not
argue with theatricals, she told herself; one submits and
deafens one's ears. He knocked out his pipe and slowly
filled it. "Now in the case of Henry Mulcahy, which I presume you're here to plead"—he lit the pipe, as they
eagerly nodded, and puffed a few puffs—"I don't want
to be hasty. I want to hear everything you have to tell me
about him. From where I sit"—he gazed ruefully out down
the drive—"one is apt to get a narrow view. I was surprised, to tell you the truth, when these letters came to
me. And now you two, whom I respect and admire. I had
supposed that everyone would agree that poor Hen, whatever his merits, had neither the desire nor the aptitude to
fit in here at Jocelyn."

John interrupted. "For your information, Maynard," he
declared in his deep cool voice. "Domna and myself are
here officially as delegates. We've been empowered to speak
for Ivy, Kantorowitz, Van Tour, Aristide, and now, I hear,
Mr. Ali Jones." The President smiled. "Ah," he said,
good-humored, "the humanist faction. I ought to have
known there was ideology behind this. *That's* the nigger in

the woodpile." "The Negro in the woodpile," murmured Domna and was instantly ashamed of the joke. The President threw back his head and roared. *"Touché!"* he cried and grew thoughtful. "It's an ugly thing how our language is defaced with expressions of prejudice. 'Catch a nigger by the toe'—did you use to chant that as a boy, John? Sometimes I think we ought to make a clean sweep and invent a new world-language. I guess our friend Hen would have something to contribute there." This "courtesy" reference to the Book was not understood by Bentkoop. "Joyce," telegraphed Domna, across the desk, silently moving her lips. She was not able to make out what this after-dinner tone of the President's portended; nevertheless, she felt encouraged. "So," inquired Maynard, "the wicked scientists, headed by myself, a renegade philosopher, have set out to 'get' one of your persuasion?" John nodded, imperturbable; this was precisely what he felt.

But Domna grew hot. "No," she said, "Dr. Hoar, that is not our contention at all. I do not defend Henry as a humanist but as a human being." Bentkoop tried to deter her with a slight shake of his head. "And a distinguished mind," she threw in. "The outstanding *homme de lettres* on your faculty." Maynard puffed on his pipe. " 'A human being?' " he mused. "What do you mean, Domna? We're all human beings, I think; at least until proved otherwise." He sighed, and Domna was startled by the heavy fatigue in his voice; this interview, she suddenly suspected, was an ordeal for him, which he had apparently undertaken on principle. "I mean Cathy's situation," she murmured, lowering her eyes. "Dr. Hoar, how can you defend what you are doing?" He stared at her, rather

warily. "What do you refer to, my dear girl?" John cleared
his throat. "Cathy is in bad shape," he declared, on a grave
note of admonishment. "The doctor has told Hen that any
shock may kill her."

Maynard clasped his chair-arms and sat dynamically
forward, his dark eyes turning from one set, shut face to
the other. "So," he said, in a flattened tone, having probed
them. "There was naturally bound to be something like
that. What is it, do you know?" John repeated what he
had been told. "And a secondary anemia," capped Domna.
The idea that the President was acting seemed scarcely
tenable to her, and yet, as she knew, Henry had told
Esther Hoar all this himself. "We have been assured
that you knew this," she prompted. Maynard shook his
head with decision. "I? Not a word," he affirmed. "Henry
told your wife some time ago?" "No," he repeated. "At
the time, surely you remember," she insisted, "when he
was asked to bring her on here from Louisville?" Maynard
slowly knocked out his pipe. "I remember the occasion
very clearly, Domna," he assured her. "There had been,
so we were told, some little trouble of the kind you mention, after the birth of the baby. Esther urged Hen not to
try to bring Cathy here till she was perfectly well. Hen
promised us that she was."

Domna had turned very pale. "But it was my understanding," she cried, "that you insisted on his bringing
her. No?" Maynard laughed richly and easily at her
alarmed, disoriented expression; he had regained his control of the talk. "Far from it," he proclaimed. "Esther and
I both begged him not to bring her unless and until I
could promise him something permanent in the way of an

appointment." He edged himself forward in his chair and raised a forefinger. "Let's get this straight between the three of us. There was nothing permanent for Hen, then or now. I offered him the job as a stop-gap, at the instance of certain friends of his who happen to be friends of mine. Hen knows that perfectly well, knew it all along; I took care to see that he should. I believe I can even show you letters, explaining our position. Our budget for Literature-Languages doesn't allow for another salary at the professorial level, which is what Hen needs at his time of life, with his family to consider. I could carry him as an instructor, pro tem, but I couldn't promise him promotion and tenure; there were no vacancies higher up. I had my three full salaries: Aristide, Alma, Furness. Hen, for all his reading knowledge, isn't equipped to teach languages as you are, Domna, for instance, and Alma was, when she used to give Goethe in German. Even at the instructorial level, Hen has been nothing but a luxury for us. He gives a course that Howard Furness can give, and always has given, in Proust-Joyce-Mann, and Furness, to oblige him, teaches the freshman Introduction, which Hen ought to be giving and hasn't the patience for. He gives another course in Critical Theory, for which at present two students are registered, one having dropped out at midterm. And of course, he has the usual tutees. For one term last year he gave a course in Contemporary Literature, which turned out to be a replica of Proust-Joyce-Mann and brought us a lot of complaints: the kids say Hen wouldn't teach the authors they were interested in, Hemingway, Farrell, Steinbeck, Mailer, you know what I mean, the red-blooded American authors, no offense, Domna, that kids

today want to hear about. Right now—I could show you
the books—Hen isn't being paid out of department funds;
he's on a special stipend, borrowed from the emergency
reserve. That sort of thing can't go on; I've warned him
of it from the beginning, and he's pretended to be perfectly
reconciled to a short-term appointment, to get him on his
feet again. Naturally, I resisted the notion of his bringing
Cathy here; I did everything short of forbidding it. I foresaw, as it turns out, exactly what would happen. With the
wife and kids installed here, he'd fight like an old-time
squatter," he concluded, smiling, "for his title in the job."

"Then how," said Domna, breathing quickly, "did you
come to dismiss him now, so suddenly, without consulting
the department?" She stared meaningfully at John and
waited.

Maynard took off his glasses and rubbed the indentation
left by them carefully between thumb and forefinger. To
her surprise, he did not appear to take offense at the point-
edness of her query. "Why, Domna," he mildly countered,
"how would you have managed it in my place? Hen was
slated to go; the bursar and I talked it over some time
ago; the enrollment has been dropping—I've been told to
cut down to the bone. The normal procedure would have
been to let him out in May or June, when the new contracts were made up. Instead, I tried to make it easier on
him by giving him a little notice. It seemed to me that
during our field-period he would have time to look around,
in New York and elsewhere, get a head-start on his com-
petitors. I assumed that he would prefer to keep the department out of it. No point in broadcasting that a teacher
is being let out; he stands a better chance if he tells poten-

tial employers that he is thinking of making a change.
You know the formula, and Hen's whole career here would
support it. God knows," he laughed, "he's made no secret
of his disapproval of us and our teaching methods."

He sat back with an air of having said the conclusive
word. The two young teachers stared at each other; John's
Adam's apple moved under his collar, and he shifted his
long jaw. "I believe you," he said, earnestly. "How about
you, Domna?" Domna nodded, with a stricken face. "I
should like, please, to see the letters, though," she ventured. Maynard picked up the telephone. "The Mulcahy
correspondence, Miss Crewes—may we have it here in
my office?" The idea that these two stony youngsters were
sitting in judgment on him appeared to amuse the President. "What did Hen tell you?" he asked, with a quizzical
look, while they waited. "That I'd promised him a permanent place here if he stuck it out as an instructor?"
They remained silent, not wishing to betray their colleague. "Worse?" he pressed them, gaily, and when they
did not yield he sobered. "You couldn't shock me, I promise you. During my day in teaching, I've heard many a
tall tale and told many a whopper myself. There's never
been a poor devil yet that doesn't get it into his head some
way that the President has made him promises. The wish is
father to the thought. Hen, with his Irish imagination, is
just a more striking example of the common teacher char-
acter-type. We're essentially public servants spiced with a
dash of the rebel. Hence the common fixation on tenure;
we feel that we serve for life like civil-service employees;
we accept low wages and poor housing conditions in exchange for the benefits of a security that we consider im-

plicit in the bargain. And for some of us, like Hen and
myself, this security usually covers the right, from time
to time, to be agin the government." While he twinkled, a
rapid look passed between John and Domna. Miss Crewes
hurried in with the correspondence, which he glanced over
and distributed between the two teachers. "I've fought all
my life," he went on, idly watching them as they scanned
the carbons and passed them back and forth across the big
desk to each other, "for better teaching conditions, more
benefits, recognition of seniority along trade-union lines,
and yet sometimes I wonder whether we're on the right
track, whether as creative persons we shouldn't live with
more daring. Can you have creative teaching side by side
with this preoccupation with security, with the principle of
regular promotion and recognition of seniority? God
knows, in the big universities, this system has fostered a
great many academic barnacles. What do you think, you
two? Give me your fresh young views. Suppose we allowed
Hen tenure, would it furnish him with the freedom he needs
to let that tense personality of his expand and grow or
would he settle down to the grind and become another old
fossil? *I* don't know the answer. I've observed in the course
of my career that a teacher grows stale after a maximum
of three years with his subject, and nowhere, by golly, is it
truer than in an experimental college like our own, where
a teacher's excitement is the spark-plug behind the whole
system. In two years, John, I'll warrant you, your Kierke-
gaard-Barth-Tillich course won't be worth listening to,
and yet we'll continue to offer it because of the require-
ments of the curriculum." John had long since replaced the
papers in the folder and laid it on the desk, but Maynard

paid him no heed; like most administrators, he was a man who felt himself to be misunderstood and welcomed any opportunity, like the present one, of displaying his broad humanity to a relatively captive audience; John, who had had a good deal of experience with his ability to slip into free-wheeling, hastily applied the brakes. He coughed and tapped lightly on the folder.

"Ah," exclaimed Maynard, "you've read them. What do you think? Are you satisfied?" He smiled on them with disconcerting friendliness as they confessed that the evidence did indeed bear out what he said. In fact, to their dismay he seemed disposed to treat of the whole affair as past and forgotten, a mere slip of judgment on their part which he gladly extenuated. "Don't think," he said, "that I bear Hen any grudge for this. I don't, in all honesty, and I don't want to see you two blame him. He needs every friend he has. What's passed between us this morning will stay right in this office. I'll do anything I can to help him find another place." The two looked awkwardly at each other; the President's manifest sincerity and even kindliness made the next step difficult.

"Maynard," brought out John, after a short silence, "has it occurred to you that the termination of Hen's appointment will be a sort of vindication for the critics of your stand on the rights of the dissident to teach?" A flicker of uneasiness appeared in the President's eyes; he shifted in his seat and said nothing. "When you hired him," John continued, "it wasn't from motives of utility, as you say yourself in these letters. You hired him to make a profession of faith, not in Hen as a teacher of English, but in the principle of freedom of conscience. You asserted that

neither the state nor a mere concert of opinion professing
to uphold the state had the right of search and entry into
the privileged domain of the soul." Maynard made a sign
of assent that carried with it a certain impatience. "What
you proclaimed to the world was not your perspicacity as
a judge of English teachers, which you compared favorably
to the perspicacity of a group of ignorant politicians, but
your duty not to inquire into the private beliefs of a
teacher, whatever they might be. If you let him out now,
for motives of utility, you'll supply a sorry footnote to a
courageous action. You won't persuade anybody that he
was let go for budgetary reasons. It will be assumed, as a
matter of course, that you had your eyes opened, got your
fingers burned, learned a thing or two, tasted your own
medicine—all the ugly phrases coined by the demon in us
to describe the deceit and disappointment of the spiritual
by the material factor."

"Deceit and disappointment," echoed Maynard. "I'm a
tired man, John. The material factor is a mite bulkier
than I supposed when I was your age. I'm afraid I must
heed the bursar's realities here, as I did on the Jewish
quota. Fifty per cent." He ruminated. "It's a high quota,
I console myself. The usual half a loaf. I sometimes pretend to myself that what we have is a Gentile quota." He
smiled a fleeting smile of self-disparagement. "In Hen's
case, I've done what I could, within the limits of necessity;
more than most would do." He looked at his watch. "Let
my critics crow. I won't deny that as a man I've found
Hen a bit of a disappointment; like all martyrs, when you
get to know them, he turns out to have quite a chip on his
shoulder. But I accept that. I make allowances for it. After

all, we all know that old Hen is no Communist; nobody in his right mind would think so but some fool state senator —when I watch him, I say to myself, 'Was ever man more unjustly treated?' " He laughed and a strange look passed between John and Domna, which Maynard appeared to sense, like a shadow or a draught of cold air. "At any rate," he continued, "we can give him a clean bill of health here as to political activity; why, I don't even believe he's signed up for Blue Cross."

"Dr. Hoar—" said Domna quickly, and hesitated. If he genuinely did not know, as it almost seemed, her revelation might harm Henry. But how was it possible that he did not know, if not from the F.B.I., then from Furness, the incorrigible gossip? "You're thinking of the loyalty oaths?" he half-asserted. She nodded. "Ah, don't tell me," sighed Maynard. "I've considered that angle myself. I've said to myself that Hen, as we all know, is just the fellow to refuse to sign a loyalty oath out of sheer principled cussedness; I respect him for it. And yet, as we all know too, Hen really belongs in one of the traditional colleges, where they're asking more and more for an oath or some sort of signed statement to the effect that the applicant is not a member of any subversive organizations. You know where I stand on that. I've asked myself whether I had the right to send him out of here to face that decision. But I've established to my own satisfaction that in Hen's case we have an unusual situation, where he's been smeared in the past, and so would be justified in signing such a thing to clear himself, and for family reasons; nobody would blame him for it—in fact, I'd say, go to it. I don't ordinarily agree with the position which says that if you're not a

Communist, why not say so and show some consideration
for your family; but in this special case I think it has
relevance." As he dealt with this curious scruple, his manner became more tranquil, as though, contemptuously
thought Domna, the capacity to entertain such a small
scruple testified to his largeness of mind. "Hen," he continued, "has the training and ability to make good in one
of our big universities: let him do it then; *I* won't condemn
him if he makes his peace with society." The two young
people, by common consent, avoided looking at each other.
Maynard suddenly coughed. There was a silence.

"So, Dr. Hoar, you scruple about the loyalty oath?"
asked Domna, in a suffocated tone, her nostrils quivering.
"But you will turn him out without a qualm despite what
we tell you about Cathy?" Whatever she had promised
Alma, she knew that in another moment she was going to
resign; the interview had reached its crisis. She half-rose
from her chair, but the President waved her back. All at
once, he temporized, looking into the two taut faces. "Why
not wait and see?" he suggested. "Let him try and find
another post and if nothing turns up for him by June, say,
or mid-summer, we will try what we can do with the bursar.
In the long run, I don't suppose, Domna, that we'll literally turn him out into the streets. But let him make an
effort, I say, and show me that he means business."

"Impossible," she retorted. "How do you imagine that
a man of Henry's temperament will stand such a strain?
He can keep a secret from his wife for a week, ten days,
two weeks; but how will she not learn of it if he is looking
for other work?" The scorn she felt for his callousness
made her fearless of offending him; in her own mind, she

had already resigned and spoke to him brusquely as an
equal. "Whoa," cried the President, genially. "Let me get
this straight. You mean to tell me that Hen hasn't told her
yet? That defies all the laws of matrimony." "Naturally,
he has not told her," replied Domna. "If he had, she might
be dead at this moment." The President's face wore a look
that vacillated between amusement and curiosity. "You
take this very hard, Domna," he said, wonderingly. "I
scarcely think Cathy's heart condition can warrant such
drastic attitudes. I myself have a slight heart condition," he
warned her with mock severity. "Shall I complain that at
this moment you're endangering my life?"

"You mean you don't believe it," she asserted. "Oh, I
believe it," conceded the President. "Hen would scarcely
make such a statement without some medical backing. I
doubt whether it's as serious as he thinks. What you can't
understand, Domna, is that most of us, after a certain age,
are living on borrowed time. The doctor has told Hen, in
all probability, to spare Cathy any unnecessary shocks.
My doctor has told *me* to avoid worry." Domna coquetted.
"If you say yes to us, Dr. Hoar, you will have no more
worry." She gave him a dazzling smile.

"*That's* an idea," he said, jesting. "Let me think it
over." He turned to John. "You back Domna up, do you?"
John nodded. "Why?" asked the President, as confronted
with a real mystery. "You have a level head on your
shoulders. What I'd like to hear from you is one positive
concrete reason for keeping Hen—what Jocelyn would gain
by it; never mind what Hen would gain by it, or humanity,
or the liberal tradition. I don't hear anything from either
of you about Hen's qualities as a teacher—what do the

students think of him?" "They admire him," put in Domna, passionately, knowing, as she spoke, that she had no evidence for this statement, which however she believed to be true. The President, as she saw it, was yielding, and it was not a moment for exactitude. "You think so?" asked the President, turning to her with a look of thoughtful regard, as if she had made a weighty statement which could tip the balance of his opinion. "Oh, yes," prevaricated Domna. "I have several tutees who talk to me of his Joyce course. And I hear them discuss it in the store. And he is wonderful in the Sophomore Orals, very kind, very thorough." The President bit on his pipe. "And you, John?" "Same here," said John. "I have one student who is doing Critical Theory with him—a first-rate girl he's taken great pains with. Otherwise, our fields don't coincide but I have the same rough impression as Domna. Or, rather, to be exact, I would say that there was a division of opinion about him, with his partisans very vociferous."

"Hmn," said the President, looking up. "It may be that he has settled down this year and gotten the bit between his teeth. Your information is probably more recent than mine. What impresses me most, however"—he studied them —"is the fact that you and Domna are here to represent him. That speaks to me very well for Hen. You're intelligent and quick and straight as a die, both of you, two of my finest young teachers and one of you a writer as well." He gazed appreciatively at Domna, who had just published some poems in a little magazine. She stared at the carpet, in embarrassment, since she had just told him a lie. His eyes once again canvassed them. They looked at each other and hesitated. They had not yet directly mentioned the main point—the issue of political freedom—and now that the interview appeared to be ending, they could see no suitable avenue of approach to it. It seemed, in fact, irrelevant to the friendly understanding which had finally been established among the three of them. As upright young people, moreover, brought up in an old-fashioned tradition, they had a trained distaste for outright lying that extended to the outright act of catching another in it; to come on the President in a lie, to see him flush up and betray himself, would be to come on Noah in his nakedness and commit the sin of Ham; they felt a pudent loyalty to the President's façade. John's wiry dark eyebrows knitted, and he gave a slight warning shake of the head.

"You'll hear from me within the next few days," said Maynard, rising, "and many thanks for your information. You can tell Hen from me that he has two pretty potent advocates." Domna seized his hand and nearly kissed it. "Oh, thank you," she cried, beaming. John gave him a steady grip. "Thanks, Maynard," he said earnestly. The President watched them go and turned back to his desk with a sigh. From his window, he could see them bound down the outside steps and perform a sort of caper of victory, like a pair of students he had favored against his ruing judgment.

CHAPTER IX

Discovered

MULCAHY WAS not much impressed. "You let him pull the wool over your eyes," was the verdict he returned to Domna that same evening in his car, when he came to fetch her for the chicken supper that Cathy, despite his remonstrances, had spent the bulk of the day preparing. "You aren't supposed to know," he pointed out to Cathy, as he gloomily observed the festive preparations: the silver-polish brought out, books dusted, pictures straightened; even the photograph of Joyce's death-mask received a sweep of the dust-rag. "What will she think of all this?" he demanded, running the vacuum-cleaner, borrowed from the next-door neighbor, over the tan living-room rug with its dark-brown border. "The house stinks of fatted calf." But Cathy, self-contented, had simply gone on humming a love-ballad. "You old fuddydud," she finally teased him, dropping a kiss on his tiny bald spot, as he sat slumped on the davenport, staring into space, "do I have to have a special reason for keeping a nice house?" And she smacked the green cushions on either side of him, singing the trashy ballad, a suspiciously recent favorite with her, that she had got out of one of the children's songbooks: " 'Oh, what care

I for my house and my land? What care I for my-y-y treas-ure-oh? What care I *for* my new-wedded lord?' " Patting her back hair, she glided out to the kitchen, leaving him with a bottle of Windex and instructions to polish the glass tray on top of the coffee-table. In the back of the house, the children were being read to by a sitter at fifty cents an hour.

It was not so much, he assured himself, that he feared Domna's guessing. He had been crediting her with normal intelligence and assuming that, of course, she knew by this time and was simply going through the forms as he was: did she suppose Cathy was deaf to what was said on the telephone? What got under his skin was the *unseasonableness* of this celebration: the way the two women, separately, but in perfect unison, had leapt to the conclusion that it was all settled and done with, when Maynard, as far as he could see, had yielded nothing but a vague promise to think it over. Every jangled nerve in his body warned him against accepting this formula; as he drove off to return the sitter and get Domna, he was fully conscious of the dangers attending a premature *détente*. So much so, that he was half tempted to disobey orders and not stop at the liquor-store for the bottle of whiskey decreed by Cathy, since Cathy, though she would not admit it, had a poor head for liquor and had begun to take all too readily to these little nips with Domna that now seemed to be the order of the day. But, thanks to his fear of displeasing her and setting off some sort of scene, the bottle was in the seat beside him when he called for Domna and learned from her reluctant lips the tell-tale fact that she had been suppressing: Maynard, it turned out, had led the conceited

pair through the interview without once permitting a mention of the only issue that counted!

He caught his breath when he heard it, and only his
feelings as a host prevented him from letting her have it,
straight out, in the car. He drew on his reserves of mag-
nanimity and spoke to her with patience, as he had learned
to do with the children, analyzing a process step by step,
taking into account their slower rate of learning; the drive
home seemed to him endless and at the same time too
short. "It's a dead give-away, Domna," he expatiated.
"Analyze it out for yourself. Assume Maynard was ignorant, when he fired me, of my Party record—something
I don't concede for a moment but which seems to appeal
to your generous heart. Is it likely that his pal, Furness,
whom you insisted on taking into your confidence, wouldn't
have rushed around to inform him the minute he heard the
news? Not 'arf likely, is it?" he gloated, unable to keep a
thrust of plebeian malice from his tone. "Henry, I've
thought of that," said Domna, in her low, restive, *bien
élevé* voice. "It's strange. I can't explain it." "*I* can explain it very well," he asserted. "Having got his briefing
from your friend, Howard, he met the two of you with a
well-prepared story. Don't imagine that a single word of
that interview was extemporized; every gesture, every
pause, I'll wager, was rehearsed before a mirror, and all
very carefully calculated to steer you away from the main
point. Why, he took you through that session like a regular
Intourist guide with a party of dumb fellow-travelers. One
direct question from either of you, and Maynard's goose
would have been cooked. You had him on the ropes and
you didn't know it. The bloody fool's scared to death,

Domna; he can't afford to have a charge of bias made; his whole career of straddling is at stake. He's a corpse, a well-preserved corpse, rotten with inner corruption, *pourri,* my girl, *pourri*—one breath of fresh air, and he'd stink, like the estimable Father Zossima. Don't think he doesn't know it." He turned up the hill into his driveway and lowered his voice as he did so; the elucidation of his topic was banishing his first irritation; he began to feel content, as though everything were back in its place. "As a matter of fact," he descanted, "Maynard proved to you by his silence that he had something to hide. Put yourself in his place. If he were innocent, and Howard came running to him with the charges, what would be his natural reaction? He wouldn't wait ten days to blarney you. He'd have you and me too on the carpet inside of sixty minutes to demand a retraction pronto. Right? *Of course he would.*" He headed the car into the garage and jerked on the brake with emphasis. "Why say with such offhandedness," he prodded her, " 'we all know Hen is no Communist,' when nobody has mentioned the possibility, if not to put a denial into the record?" He switched off the lights and the motor but made no move to get out. From the other end of the breezeway, through the open door of the dark garage, they heard Cathy's voice thinly calling, "Hen, is it you? Have you got Domna with you?" He tooted the horn, their signal, and listened for the door to close. "You see," he said swiftly, "it's the same thing with Cathy and her heart. Do you suppose Furness didn't tell him all about it and yet, according to you, Maynard put on a bland face and pretended great shock and surprise. *He couldn't let you know that Furness had been talking.*" To his annoyance,

the garage-lights came on; Cathy, in the kitchen, he supposed, was manifesting impatience. "Hadn't we better go
in?" urged Domna. "Cathy must be wondering. . . ."

Obediently, he got out and hurried round the car to help
her, but his lips, in their solicitous smile, stiffened with
mistrust and umbrage. What, he would like to be told, had
transpired from the interview that made her so anxious
now to be rid of him, to hurry off into the house and avert
further questions and discussion? He had guessed, straight
off, as soon as he saw her, that she had learned something
that discredited him slightly in her judgment, but not too
much, apparently—else she would not be here. Obviously
—he felt satisfied on this point—it had nothing to do with
his "confession," for how could she have discovered anything to impugn that, when the topic had never been
broached? Yet there was something, he thought, tightening his guiding fingers on her elbow, and congratulating
himself on his acute sensibility, that made her draw away
from him a little, even while she smiled and deferred to
him—some little thing, perhaps, that failed to jibe with
Maynard's account of things and on which, naturally, without hesitation, like a true friend, she had taken Maynard's
word. Why all this sudden concern lest Cathy "wonder"?
Was it simply a feint to get away from him or was there a
rebuke to his carelessness behind it?

Watching the two women kiss in the kitchen doorway,
he frowned and shook his head, as a warning, over Domna's
shoulder. Cathy, in his critical view, was going much too
far in trying mutely to convey to Domna her gratitude
and happiness over this morning's interview. Woman-like,
in fact, she had been picking at him all day, ever since

Domna's telephone call, for not treating his supporters properly, not showing sufficient gratitude, and so on; she had even been at him to "tell" Domna, with the usual wifely implication that she understood the girl better than he did. The love of taking needless risks was something in the feminine temperament that he did not pretend to explicate.

He helped Domna off with her rubbers and hurried her into the living room, leaving Cathy in the kitchen to put the dumplings into the pot. On the table by the davenport was a doily and a plate of involuted pink-and-white sandwiches in the shape of pinwheels that Cathy had got out of some fancy cookbook or other. He eyed them with disfavor and sampled one. In the back bedroom, baby Stephen was crying, which told the whole story of the day. Red-haired Eileen, wearing her best dress, with her dirty underpants hanging down, approached, made a curtsey to Domna, and snatched a sandwich from the plate; Mary Margaret, the eldest, in middy and skirt, followed and, without taking any notice of Domna, marched up and gave her sister a slap. The children, he supposed, had been fed while he was absent on scraps of bread and colored cheese; they were accustomed to eating with their parents and wore looks of sullen suspicion as they watched their father and Miss Rejnev raise their old-fashioned glasses to each other. When Miss Rejnev set her glass down, Eileen's fingers darted into it and came up with the cherry. In the girls' bedroom, Nora, the three-year-old, who had been put to bed by her sisters, set up a howl to go to the bathroom; he flew down the corridor and whisked her out of bed too late. The ammonia-smell of urine in the back rooms, owing to the pads drying out on the radiators, was pungently noticeable to him, for the first time in many weeks—no vacuum-cleaner or furniture wax had penetrated this area. He twitched his nose and searched in the bureau for a clean pad; finding none, he settled for a dry one, which he arranged under the child, who put her soft face up to him for a kiss. "Daddy's girl," he murmured, stroking the silky head. Pity for himself and his children became, as he stood there in the darkness, hearing the women's voices, a sort of pride and militancy. He felt gravely offended with Cathy for her betrayal of their anti-bourgeois ethic—had all their years together at the kitchen-table with the tea-pot between them on the oilcloth been a sham and a sacrifice to her that she could so readily turn her back on them and follow the Pied Piper down the road of least resistance?

He knew the signs all too well, having catalogued them, together with Cathy, in a dozen faculty-wives of their acquaintance: first, cocktails, cocktail napkins, inedible fancy sandwiches, the children shoved into the background, the dinner hour receding farther and farther into the night, then pressure-cookers, dish-washers, deep-freezers, an unending procession of sitters groping their way into the upstairs region as into some segregated ghetto, and downstairs, answering the door, a neighboring farm-girl in cap and uniform with tin buckles on her shoes—"May I take your wraps?"—fraternization with the local gentry, the Episcopal lawn fete, the deadly round of entertaining, domestic hatred, hangovers, name-spending, literary revivals, fawning on imported celebrities, the publisher's contract at last for an anthology of the literature of the Crisis, the invitation to lecture to a book group, traveling expenses,

padded, the bottle in the suitcase, the professor's wife from
Pennsy, "Jesus, what a head!" He closed the door softly
and went in to see Stephen, who had lost his pacifier, an
old teething-ring that had served the little girls before him.
Finding it where it had fallen on the rag rug, he wiped it
off with his handkerchief and tucked it in the fat clenched
fist. Stephen's cries halted; he gurgled—a series of luscious
primal sounds. He was waiting for the Irish air that his
mother was wont to croon to him, and Mulcahy, whose
voice was tuneless, struck up instead with "Mulligan's
Ball." There was sorrow in the jig for Mulcahy; he was
minded of Joyce's household and the gloomy fate of the
children—did Nora Joyce, like Cathy, look back in her
splendid years of exile to the lost Sodom of infantile satis-
factions, the "toy fair" of material civilization that her
husband had wrenched her away from? The child, however, laughed contentedly. Mulcahy went out.

In the kitchen, he found Cathy, red-faced, drinking her
second cocktail; wisps of hair protruded from the brown
bun at the nape of her neck; there was a rich smell of
burning from the oven, where the chocolate bread-pudding
had bubbled over. In the living room, Domna was reading
to the two children; the plate of sandwiches was nearly
empty. He sent them off to bed rather sharply and refilled
Domna's glass. The single drink, he discovered, had
loosened his tongue a little and removed the inhibitions he
put on his curiosity. "You know, Domna," he said to her,
pulling up a chair to her and taking the picture-book from
her lap, "I've the feeling you're keeping something back
from me. What did Maynard tell you this morning that
you're afraid to tell me?" Domna's brilliant eyes slid

away from him; she reached into her pocketbook for her
cigarettes and her lighter. "Do you know," he said, as if
idly, "whenever you're uncomfortable you reach for a cigarette?" She smiled uncertainly, "Do I?" and then added,
swiftly, with an air of taking a plunge, "It's you, Henry,
who make me uncomfortable. You demand so many par-
ticulars. I've given you the gist, I promise you." A queer
hesitant light flickered in her eyes. "Since you wish to
know, I'll admit to you: certain things in the past, Maynard
recalls differently. He doesn't remember that you told him
of the state of Cathy's health." Henry shrugged. "Naturally not," he remarked. "You've got it balled up yourself.
I didn't tell him; I told Esther." "So I said," blurted
Domna, with an after-look of guilty consternation. "He
says he doesn't recall this. He says he received the impression that Cathy had been ill but was better." She raised her
eyes and confronted him and then looked quickly away.
Was she "giving him his chance" to contradict this or bring
his own story into line? He was not such a fool, he could
assure her, as to rake up all that old business which lay too
far in the past for anybody to swear positively to what had
been said and what hadn't. "A convenient memory," he
said lightly. "It's possible that Maynard persuaded himself, even then, to hear what he wished to hear. I don't
hold it against him; we all tell lies to ourselves." "*Sans
doute*," agreed Domna, with a sly face. "But now that
he's been told, Henry, he'll do the right thing, I'm sure of
it." Henry made an irritable grimace; he flexed a muscle
in his cheek. "*Please*," he begged. "I'm older than you.
I've seen more of the world and its administrators. The
leopard doesn't change its spots."

"Domna may be right." The loud words came out a little furrily. Cathy, without their hearing it, had slipped out of the kitchen behind them and was standing in the doorway arch with an eggbeater in her hand. They wheeled around to look at her; Henry winged a prayer to God. "You weren't there, Hen," insisted Cathy. "How can you be so sure?" There was a fearful pause; the eggbeater dripped cream onto the carpet. As she digested Domna's expression of horror, Cathy began to laugh. "I don't know what I'm talking about," she said gaily. "I must be a little tiddly. Didn't I hear you say something about Maynard? I thought Domna went to see him this morning about a salary raise." "She did, darling," said Henry. "You're quite right. We were discussing it. I told Cathy all about it, Domna; you don't mind, do you, if I let out our little secret?" His wife's eyes grew drunken again. "I think you've been wonderful, Domna, just wonderful," she said with feeling. "We all need that raise so badly." "I've done nothing," said Domna, rather shortly. Henry bit his lip. "Dinner's in just a minute," said Cathy. She turned and slowly exited toward the kitchen. Henry followed her. "Why did you do it?" he whispered in a fury. He took her cocktail glass from the kitchen table and threw the contents into the sink. "She knows," he despairingly exulted and struck the table a blow. "She doesn't know," replied Cathy, airily. "I carried it off very well, I thought." Henry came closer to her. "She has good manners," he said in her ear, vindictively. "She won't call you a liar to your face. She'll ignore it till she gets out of here and then, excuse her dust! I watched her. She was vibrating all over like a plucked string." His eyes swept over the table set in the dinette off the kitchen with Cathy's wedding silver and an old lace table-cloth. "Why did you do it?" he repeated. "I've warned you again and again to be careful. How many drinks did you have?" "Two," retorted Cathy, determined to brazen it out. "I'm not drunk. I was just playing drunk to cover myself. Listening to you laying down the law. I simply lost my head and forgot that I wasn't supposed to know. It could happen to anybody. It's all your fault anyway, Hen," she continued, with a sharpening and sobering of her features, as she spooned the dumplings out, one by one, efficiently, and set them out on the big platter. "I *told* you you ought to tell her. You're too conspiratorial in your methods." "Do you still think so?" he said with breathless sarcasm. "*I*'ll tell you why you did it. You hate to be left out of anything. You couldn't stand the idea that these discussions were going on every day and you were supposed to be kept in the dark. You resented the implication that you were stupid and didn't have the mother-wit to guess your husband's troubles. And you're jealous of my relation with Domna. You want to have her all cosy to yourself with your lace tablecloths and your confidences. You're dying for an aristocratic friendship. Everything has changed here since you met her; the children are neglected; you have to be driven into York to the hairdresser; you're dieting and yet you want to have wine with your meals. You lie in the bathtub and feel your breasts in the mirror; you use French expressions. You're a beautiful natural woman and all of a sudden you want to be a *femme du monde,* a vulgar *femme de trente ans* in the style of Maupassant."

Cathy's eyes sparkled; she tilted her angular chin complacently—these sudden and secret quarrels between them she took for a manifestation of worship. She picked up the loaded platter, strewed it with parsley, balanced it on a pile of plates and proceeded grandly with it into the dinette. A vapor of steam followed her, tantalizing him, like one of the veils of Salome. "Dinner is served," she announced, sliding the plates onto the table. "Go and get her, you fool." She readjusted a hairpin and sat coolly down at her place; next to her, stood her old tea-wagon, recently exhumed from the basement, stacked with dessert-plates and a coffee-service. Henry hurried back into the living room. "Cathy's not quite herself," he apologized. "I was afraid for the moment she'd heard something disturbing. But it's all right; I've been talking to her. She has no conception of what she seemed to be saying. It's a lucky thing I gave her that salary-raise story as a blind. Whew!" He made a half-laughing motion of wiping the sweat from his brow, and when she did not smile back, he grew serious. "Alcohol isn't good for her. That's why we seldom serve it. There's a little history of that kind in her family—the curse of the Irish." He held out his hands. "Come! She'll be better when she's had something to eat." Domna put down the quarterly she had been gripping. "Would you rather I didn't stay?" she said abruptly. She appeared exceedingly tense and disturbed. Henry shook his head with decision. "What a scare you must have had," he said warmly. "I could see it. You turned a sort of yellow —your Tartar blood, I'll warrant. You still look a little queer. Can I get you something more to drink?" Domna gave a quick, strained smile. She rose. "No. I'm all right." He led her into the dinette. "What a wonderful dinner,

Cathy," she murmured, looking at the table, but the tribute
escaped her mechanically; she seemed to fix her eyes on
the flatware and napery with the same hypnotized effort
that dragged her fork to her lips and back again. She ate,
observed Henry, like a stupefied goose of Périgord subjected to forced feeding; indeed, her whole demeanor
was that of a creature in a vise.

Cathy, however, had recovered her poise; she led the
conversation and they discussed theories of love. "What
you love in a person, Domna," she explained to her, "is
his essence, not the dross of appearance. Love is the discovery of essence." Domna looked up from her bread-
pudding. "I think you are too dualistic," she said,
brusquely. "Even in Plato, essence is perceived through
existence. There is no gross contradiction, no belying.
Shadow is a partial aspect of substance. Appearances inti-
mate to us; they do not flatly deceive." She put down her
spoon. Henry affably nodded. "You're a handsome girl,
Domna," he reminded. "All handsome people are monists.
For the rest of us, there is always the temptation to gnosti-
cism. What we are is not what we see in the mirror, and we
know therefore that appearances are fickle. We look to
somebody else to discover our imperishable essence." He
smiled uxoriously at Cathy and wiped his lips with his
damask napkin. "She," he signified, "has been good enough
to do me this service. Could you love a leper, Domna?" he
continued, musingly. "I wonder whether you could. I
think, if you did, you would love the leper in him, from
defiance, and not seek to discover what there is in him that
the loathsome disease hides. That is, you would love in
defiance what the world sees and hates, and your love

would be simply an affirmation of repugnance overcome."
That he repelled Domna physically he had known for some
time, without rancor and even with a kind of objective,
scientific interest, and he observed once again, with detachment, seeing her drop her eyes in embarrassment, that this
repugnance he now calmly alluded to was still the strongest
hold he had on her: was it feasible, he asked himself, to
try to exercise the same attraction-repulsion in the moral
sphere? He saw that she understood very well the drift of
the conversation, which, he had to concede, had been splen-
didly maneuvered by Cathy to come athwart the subject
at hand. Domna's fine nostrils indented; she raised her
brows in distaste. "Why are you R.C.'s so fascinated by
leprosy, like children? It is all simply a bogey of legend
and crude mass superstition. But in answer to your question: if you mean a moral leper, no. Fair without and foul
within has no charm for me. Nor the reverse, for that matter. One must love in depth. I cannot be interested in people
whose inside contradicts their outside. Such people have
neither essence nor existence." She folded her napkin. "I
must work tonight," she declared.

Cathy warmly protested. "It's a holiday," she reproached her. "We can have a good long gab. No students,
no classes, no convocation. You don't really have to work."
"I have papers to do," said Domna, with a sidelong glance
at Henry, "and achievement sheets to get in." Yet she
stayed, when pressed, and helped wash up the dishes as
usual. Henry saw plainly that she was ashamed for them
but that this very shame, also, was preventing her from
making a difference in their relation. Certain acutely telling little things, however, betrayed her reluctance to be

any longer "at home" here; she made a show, for example, of not knowing where to put the china and glassware, though she had helped wash up a dozen times before and knew the cupboards like the palm of her hand. In the past, too, she had busied herself wiping the tables and counters; she would get out the broom and sweep the floor and sometimes even set the table for breakfast, putting a silly glass ornament in the middle and pleating the children's napkins. But tonight she was irking to get away; she dried the dishes at top speed, like a kitchen worker in a hash house, and was off to get her coat on before the sink was emptied. Henry drove her home, with a sick, empty feeling, as at the end of something, knowing that she knew and that she knew that he knew that she knew. If she turned on him, the others would follow her; they had all been looking for an excuse to lose faith in him, and one apostasy would be ample to show the others the way. And at the moment, he blamed himself completely for what had happened; he felt humbled for his lack of trust in her and let himself grovel in the feeling with penitent abandon—all of which he tried to convey to her at the ultimate moment on her doorstep, in a fervid, miscreant's handclasp and a quick, blind turning away. To admit culpability was to open the way to amendment, he repeated to himself on the way home, and he was tempted suddenly to appear at her door and make a full confession; yet he knew at the same moment that it was too late— his confession should have preceded Cathy's slip if it were to have any air of *bona fides*. What more, he asked himself, could he tell her in words than he had already indicated wordlessly? Words and explanations had no place

in true friendship, which was a connexion of souls. Had
he need to beg her in words not to give him away, when
eye and lip and hand beseeched her higher understanding?
Moreover, he thought, with a sudden dry cackle, she *dared*
not tell on them—anybody she confided in would think
her an utter fool and a turncoat.

John Bentkoop and his wife, Virginia, were in their
night-clothes when Domna cranked the old bell. He came
downstairs, blinking and pulling on his bathrobe, followed
by Virginia in a pink woolen dressing-gown. She would
not let him open the door until he turned on the flashlight
and they saw through the side-panes the Russian girl
standing on the porch. Virginia, who was a sensible girl,
instantly drew her into the dark house, put an arm around
her and guided her into the living room. She had met her
only once, at a college lecture, but she divined correctly
that her feet were wet. John hastily made a fire. Domna
sat crouched on a hassock by the fireplace; she would not
take off her shoes or her polo coat at the beginning, apologizing that she had been pacing outside the house for hours,
trying to make up her mind whether to intrude on them,
and would go at once when she had said what she had to
say. After the first few words, Virginia absented herself;
she came back with a pot of coffee and big, white, cheap
cups on a tray, served them, and sat down by the oil lamp
in a rocker—there was no electricity in the house. "You
must stay," she proffered. "I've made up a bed upstairs.
I've always wanted to know you. Next year, I'm going to
take your course." Without further parlance, she took up
her knitting, a pale green baby sweater; the motion of her

needles kept pace with the conversation. She had pale, almost greenish fair hair, pale sea-like green eyes, a pink and white complexion, fair brows, delicate hands; everything about her was pastel and tranquilly decided—in short, she was the complement of Domna, whom she scanned with earnest attention, as though the other girl were something—a flower, a chemical process—she had read about in a book and she was now satisfying herself as to her reality. This child-like faculty of attention was her notable characteristic; nothing appeared to strike her as aberrant in a world that was myriad with difference; she looked at her husband carefully whenever he made a point, as though studying afresh the whorls of his personality. Before the discussion was over, she had finished the sweater, laid it aside in a basket and begun casting a new set of stitches on the yellow needles. Toward the end, when it was nearly morning, she added her voice to the symposium. This voice, surprisingly, was rather clear and loud, like a boy's voice that has not changed yet.

John threw another log on the fire and paced up and down before it. "I think, Domna," he said judiciously, "you're doing him a minor injustice. It doesn't seem to me likely that they cooked it up between them, as you say. More likely she half guessed and he told her. I'm willing to buy that for what it's worth." Domna's shadowed face showed a faint stirring of relief; as she listened, she slipped her coat from her shoulders and Virginia silently came and took it. "I've never put much credence," continued John, easily, like a wound-up bobbin unreeling, "in Hen's power to keep a secret. To the best of my knowledge, he told one of his tutees the very first thing, probably before he told you. If he hadn't told Cathy finally, she would have been one of the few people in the community he didn't favor with his confidence. The town's buzzing with it; I heard it from the garage-man and the grocer and the druggist, all very concerned about Mrs. Mulcahy and about Mr. Mulcahy's prospects for paying their precious bills. Why, I think Hen could get up a real rank-and-file movement among the tradespeople here to petition for his continuance." He laughed but Domna sighed restlessly. "I would pay them myself to be rid of him," she declared in a passionate tone. John studied her concernedly, with a pursing of the large lips. "You're really suffering," he discovered. "Drink some more coffee. It's mainly shock, you know. You're one of the few people on this campus that really had faith in Hen. It's a shame it had to be you to discover this. Those of us who've known him a little longer would have been better prepared." "Oh, that dinner!" she suddenly moaned, as it came back to her. "They talked about *love*, Virginia. 'Could I love a leper?'" "Could you?" asked Virginia, setting the cup in her hand. "I don't think so," said Domna. "Neither could I," said Virginia. "At least, I never have." "But what I was supposed to understand by this," said Domna, raising her eyes to John, "was that Henry was a moral leper and that I didn't love him sufficiently. Of course, it's perfectly true. I don't. Not sufficiently for this." Her face stiffened. There was a silence. "Did you really suspect it?" she demanded, in a different, half-hopeful tone. "Honor bright," said John. "Ask Virginia." Virginia paused in her knitting. "Yes, he did. You aren't married or you'd see how hard it is to keep something from your wife." "And you really

think," insisted Domna, "that it wasn't cooked up, deliberately, beforehand, as a bid for sympathy?" John shook his
long head. "That's not how these things work, Domna;
one begins by persuading *oneself*, and this germ of persuasion is infectious. Hen has a remarkable gift, a gift for
being his own sympathizer. It's a rare asset; it could be
useful to him in politics or religion." He spoke with perfect seriousness. "He's capable of commanding great loyalty, because he's unswervingly loyal to himself. I'm not
being sarcastic. Very few of us have that. It's a species of
self-alienation. He's loyal to himself, objectively, as if he
were another person, with that feeling of sacrifice and
blind obedience that we give to a leader or a cause. In the
world today, there's a great deal of free-floating, circum-
ambient loyalty that fixes itself on such people, who seem
to offer, by their own example, the possibility of a separation from the self that will lead to a higher union with the
self objectified in an idea. It's Hen's fortune or his fate
to have achieved this union within his own personality;
he's foregone his subjectivity and hypostatized himself
as an object."

He settled himself on the hearth-rug and wound his
arms round his long, bony legs in their white pajama bottoms. Virginia laid down her knitting and joined him; she
rested her head on his shoulder. The fire threw a ruddy
light on the three absorbed faces, as in a painting by La
Tour. Around them, outside the circle of the lamp, the
room was nearly dark: they might have been sitting by a
campfire on a chill beach after a night picnic, or in a
forest-clearing, keeping watch. The even heat of the fire
in their faces, the lateness of the hour, the shadows, the

rattling of the small-paned windows, the eeriness of the
man they spoke of, produced a sensuous content and numb-
ness; they felt close to the primeval mysteries, the chiaro-
scuro of good and evil. John hugged his knees. His olive
student-face assumed a didactic mien. "The criteria of
truth and falsity, as we know them, don't exist for Hen.
He doesn't examine his statements from the point of view
of the speaker but from the point of view of the listener.
He listens to himself as you or I might listen to him and
asks himself, 'Is it credible?' Even in private soliloquy,
credibility is the standard he applies; that is, he looks at
truth with the eyes of a literary critic and measures a statement by its persuasiveness. If he himself can be persuaded
he accepts the moot statement as established. This is real
alienation. In the critical part of his mind, he's extraordinarily cold with himself, cold and dedicated. Hence his in-
cessant anxiety, like the anxiety of a military commander
or an author or a stage-director; he's busy with problems
of reception, stage effects, cues, orchestration; his inner
life is a busy rehearsal and testing for activity on the larger
stage of tomorrow, where the audience, as usual, will miss
the finer points. Immersed in all these difficulties, hung up
on the little snags of production, he's impatient, understandably, with outside interrogation. 'Is it true?' you
want to know, but the question's irrelevant and footless.
Do you ask an amber spot whether it's true? Or an aria?
At bottom, he doesn't give a damn, Domna, what you or
I think, any more than a general cares about democratic
opinion. We're not his critics or even, primarily, his audience; we're amateurs whom, unfortunately, he must use
in his production, green troops whom he has to put up

with since the great Commander we all act under saw fit
to send him no better."

Domna cupped her pointed chin in her hand; she stared
reflectively into the blaze. "So," she pondered finally,
"when Cathy guessed or he told her, he had no hesitation
in going through with the imposture? He felt justified
in doing it since she *might* have found out and *might* have
been dead by this time for all Maynard cared?" John
laughed. "Such might-have-beens are for neophytes," he
said, stretching. "When Cathy found out, Hen as an intelligent man saw that it was simpler that she knew. The
worry of protecting her was removed and he was supplied
with a consultant he could trust." He sat up cross-legged
on the hearth-rug and conned the two girls' faces. "Be
honest with me, both of you," he demanded. "What would
you have done in his place? Would you actually have interrupted the proceedings to announce that Cathy knew
and there was no further worry on her score? Think what
it meant to him. What were his chances of being rehired
if the college didn't have Cathy on its conscience? Most
people, I'm afraid, would do pretty much as Hen did.
What about you, Virginia?" "I really don't know," said
Virginia, "I like to think I would come out with the truth,
but probably I would try to play possum until the matter
was settled. I would stay away from my supporters and
hope that nobody would ask me." Domna leaned forward.
"Is it conceited of me? I think I would tell the truth." The
taut declaration made a silence. Virginia's look consulted
her husband. She spoke. "You don't really know, Domna,"
she argued. "You've never been in the position he is. In
your situation, it wouldn't cost much to tell the truth." A

look of pride glittered in Domna's face; her nostrils
flared. "It costs nothing to tell the truth when one has
the habit. One becomes entangled in self-pity and lies."
She drew out the last word with a strong diphthong and
sibilant hissing of the *s*. "He threw himself on our pity.
This was not an honest act. He lied to Maynard about
Cathy and lied to us about the lie. Or is he lying to us
now and she is healthy and it is all a fantasy that we believed?" Heated and gleaming in the firelight, her pure
features were almost ugly. "And now we are all in it;
we are all lying for him. I lied this morning to the President: my students do not praise Henry—it is I who praise
him to the students, who sit with their faces *so*." She made
an idiot face with sunken jaw and goggling eyes. "I lied
tonight at his house, two, three times. I lie to myself
about him." She jumped up and lit a cigarette and stood
by the mantelpiece, puffing. "And now what am I to do?
I am to lie some more, I presume. You know that I cannot
carry this nasty story to the President. I cannot. I tell
myself that it's my duty but I cannot. If Henry had not
been my friend, still I could not do it. Do you blame me?
And I cannot tell Henry, either, that I know and am not
deceived by him. I think this is a weakness. I'm ashamed
for him; I cannot face him; I am afraid of him and
that terrible white freckled face." "Undoubtedly, he knows
that you know, Domna," put in John, by way of comfort.
Domna flared up. "So what will he do, murder me? Let
him do it," she cried recklessly, striking the mantelpiece
a blow. John smiled at these heroics and then grew
thoughtful. "He's more likely to accuse you of something," he said gravely, after due reflection.

He appeared to consult again with himself. "Look here, Domna," he finally suggested, "there's a good deal to be said for Hen on the plus side. You felt it once yourself or you wouldn't be suffering disillusion. Your friendship wasn't a deception; Hen is extremely likable in the early stages of an acquaintance. He has a taste for abstract conversation that makes him peculiarly accessible, like some of the old philosophers. He's interested in ontological questions, which are the great binders of diverse humanity. On some of the better students, he has an extraordinarily tonic effect. To my mind, he's worth keeping here aside from the question of Cathy and the four children and the bills and all the rest. He has an agile mind and excellent training. What I said at our first meeting is a true statement of what I believe. I think it valuable for the Literature department to have a theist teaching in it. Hen's brand of theism and mine differ; in his personal life, he may belong to the devil's party, but the devil is a theist too. What's needed at Jocelyn or any college is a mind concerned with universals and first principles; the students take to them like catnip if they're given half a chance. Your department's monstrously one-sided—you're concerned with formal questions exclusively: Tolstoy's method, the method of Virginia Woolf, the elucidation of Mann's symbols, the patterns of Katherine Anne Porter. All appropriate enough for criticism, but it isn't what the student reads for. A student reads an author for his ideas, for his personal metaphysic, what he calls, till you people teach him not to say it, his 'philosophy of life.' He wants to detach from an author a portable philosophy, like the young Joyce in *A Portrait of the Artist*—a laudable aim which you discourage by your insistence on the inseparability of form and content."

"But that is true," protested Domna, dropping to her knees on the hassock. John shook his head in reprimand. "True, but also not true. And not relevant to the student's purpose. Content *can* be paraphrased. What we're doing here at Jocelyn is a sinister thing for our students; we're turning out classes of sophisticated literary hollow men, without general ideas, without the philosophy or theology that's formed in adolescence, without the habit or the discipline of systematic thought. Our students have literally no idea what they think or believe except in questions of taste, and they've been taught to fear formulation as a lapse in literary manners. Hen is the one force here that runs counter to this tendency. His Jesuit training formed him in an older mold and his Joyce studies confirmed him in the habit of universalization. *Finnegans Wake:* one book which shall be all books, the Book of Life."

Domna interrupted. "John," she said tensely, "I have to tell you something." Her pale, severe face was sharp with trepidation, as if she feared being overheard; they moved a little closer. "This is *my* confession. I think Henry is mad. He comes to see me at night and talks, talks, talks. He has a delusional system centering on Joyce. He speaks of Joyce's life as a Ministry. He speaks of the Book, the Revelation, the Passion." John raised his eyebrows. "Most of the Joyce brotherhood are a little batty," he cautioned. Domna shook her head firmly. "This is different; it's not an ordinary obsession. He believes that he's been subject to persecution for propagating the

Word. This, he insists, is at the bottom of his troubles; all the rest is pseudepigraphal—that was his own word. He is hated, he says, by Joyce's enemies, who comprise the whole academic world, with the exception of rival Joyce experts who hate him also, since they are really Joyce's enemies in disguise." Virginia laughed delightedly. "How wonderful!" she cried in sincere enjoyment and admiration. Domna laughed also, but more grudgingly. "Yes, it's funny," she admitted, "but terrifying, too. You know that stick he carries; he's put it aside, he says, for the duration of this emergency in token of symbolic burial. His Communist period, he says, was a ritual conversion symbolizing Joyce's baptism in the religion of naturalism—the precursor. And the Communists hate him because he transcended naturalism, just as they hate Joyce. Behind Joyce, you see, is the identification with Christ. Bloom was Christ; Earwicker was Christ—Henry Mulcahy is Christ in the disguise of Bloom and Earwicker, the family men, the fathers eternal consubstantial with the Son." The laughter died out of her voice. "I've tried to assure myself," she declared, "that all this is merely an allegory, the pastime of an ingenious mind, that he uses to give form to his experience, to console himself in a rather bitter way by the sense of repetition, but, John, I'm afraid he believes it literally, just as you believe in the Incarnation."

John's dark eyebrows knitted; like an upright young judge he seemed to search his experience for precedents and normative explanations. At the same time, with his short black hair standing up, there was something alert and lively about him, like a hare after its quarry: understanding. "Christ's experience," he announced finally, with an odd eager smile, "is the great paradigm for the persecution psychosis. It displays the whole classical syndrome: belief in divine origin, special calling, chosenness, the cult of exclusive disciples, betrayal, justification—one might even add, following Freud's analysis of paranoia, homosexuality, for it's noteworthy that He not only eschewed women, but that His betrayer was a man. The betrayer for the paranoid is always of his own sex, the loved and feared sex. One could say," he continued breathlessly, with a sort of awkward ardency, "that by becoming man precisely God underwent what could be described as madness: the experience of unrecognition fusing with the knowledge of godhead, the sense of the Message, the Word, the Seed falling on barren ground, the sense of betrayal and promised resurrection. And like the mad, who use symbolic language, He spoke in parables." Domna huskily laughed. "*Jésus-Christ, c'était un fou qui se croyait Jésus-Christ.*" John nodded. "Yes; in so far as He was human, this was his predicament. But is it any wonder that man who seeks in his highest moments to identify himself with God, should do so also in his time of tribulation, in the dark night of the soul. And if Hen is mad, Domna, to choose to imitate Christ, in the pattern of his sufferings, where are all the Thomas à Kempises?"

"You're playing on words," she protested. "Though to me, John, to speak frankly, all religious people seem a little mad." "That's because you don't believe in godhead," he retorted. "You don't believe in the black reality of the night of separation our friend Hen is undergoing." The three moved closer to the fire. Domna

met John's eyes. "No," she said, squarely, "I don't.
Except as a metaphor. But I am willing to pity him if
you want." John firmly shook his head. "You don't pity
him, Domna; you're ashamed for him; you've just told
us so yourself." Domna considered. "I think I feel pity
mixed with horror. I should like to avert my eyes. This
is not the proper Aristotelian compound, as Henry himself would be the first to say. What is requisite for the
tragic spectacle is pity and terror compounded—pity for
the tragic victim, terror for oneself, in so far as the victim *is* oneself, universalized, by extension. But I cannot
feel that Henry is myself and I can only feel horror of
him. *Noli me tangere.*" She shuddered. "I had the mis-
fortune to be born into the upper classes and I cannot
respond to suffering when the sufferer is base. And it
seems to me now—forgive me for saying it—that this
arrogant Henry has the soul of a slave. No doubt this
cringing soul reflects social conditions; one has only to
look at Henry to imagine the matrix that formed him—
a poor heredity, hagiolatrous parents, a nasty and narrow
environment, sweets, eyestrain, dental caries. I detest the
social order which sprouts these mildewed souls—all that
should be changed, for everybody; nobody should be
permitted to grow up in such a bodily tenement. But
there is also in each individual the faculty of transcend-
ence; there is in each of us a limited freedom. I myself have
been poor and I am not sentimental about poverty—poor
people must be judged, like the rest of us. Poverty has
certain favorable aspects: the poor are free of money-
guilt and the sophisms and insincerities that go with it.
Poverty and bad heredity are not a blanket pardon; need

palliates Henry's behavior but it is not a justification."
"Very true," agreed John. "But who is to do the judging, Domna? You? I?" She hesitated and then grew reckless. "Yes, I. Why not? I, you, everybody. Everybody who will judge himself has the right to judge others and to be judged also. This abrogation of judgment you practice is an insult to man's dignity. Everybody has the right to be judged and to judge in his turn. This 'understanding' you accord Henry is dangerous, both to him and to you. God is our judge, you will tell me. But there is no God. God is man." The blasphemous words rang out; the windows rattled; but John seemed unaffected. "God is man, Domna, if you wish," he said gravely. "But He is not men."

Domna suddenly looked tired. "No," she admitted. "I suppose in a certain way I am on *your* side. If I presume to judge Henry, I don't presume to punish him. That is not my affair." She sighed. "And yet I can't help but feel that I'm implicated in a frightful swindle. When I think of how soundly I rated Dr. Hoar this morning!" She gave an unwilling laugh. "After all, you were in good faith," said Virginia. "I wonder," replied Domna. "I think really, in my heart, I knew all along too. I think I hid from myself what I did not want to see. I didn't dare ask myself what Cathy must be thinking; to ask would have implied an answer I didn't wish to get. My pride, I imagine, undid me; I could not stand to be wrong."

John gave the fire a final poke; the last red ember dissolved in a shower of sparks. "Let me console you," he said abruptly, as though he had been withholding this last piece of information till Domna had spent herself.

"I don't think Cathy's health had much to do with Maynard's decision—assuming he made it this morning. What impressed him most was the faculty support for Hen: he hadn't quite expected it and was relieved, in a way, to find it was there. I think between ourselves, as Maynard would say, that Maynard had a good many qualms about letting Hen go. Quite aside from Cathy, Maynard has a pretty fair idea of the employment picture and he knows as well as the rest of us that Hen's prospects aren't too bright. Nobody likes to have the feeling that he may be sending a man with five dependents out onto the relief rolls, and whatever Hen may say of him, Maynard, in his way, is a very decent fellow. The letter he sent Hen may have been something in the nature of a trial balloon, to test faculty reaction. He wasn't anxious to let Hen go, but on the other hand, he couldn't keep him in the face of the bursar and the trustees, without some faculty backing. Now he can go to the money-bags and announce that a valued group in the faculty considers that Hen's departure would be an intellectual loss to the college. That was what he wanted to hear; so long as he had the impression that Hen was an intellectual liability, he couldn't in fairness to the students argue for retaining him as a teacher. Maynard himself is quite at sea in these cultural matters; he honestly wants to be told who is who and what is what. He meant it when he told us he was grateful to us for our visit—we forced him to take a line he'd been half wanting to take. In a word, we accepted responsibility."

He got to his feet rather stiffly and solemnly. The fire had died out; it was nearly dawn; a few roosters were crow-ing; a high-pitched dog barked. "Milking-time," he said, going to the window. "Time to go to bed." Virginia lit a candle and let the wax drip into a saucer to fix it; she handed it to Domna, who reluctantly pulled herself up. The word, responsibility, seemed to lie on her shoulders like a burden. John's practical and reassuring exordium, it appeared, had sunk her into new perplexities. With Virginia in the lead, carrying the oil lamp, they went single file up the stairs, on tiptoe, so as not to wake the baby, whose six o'clock feeding was less than an hour off. In the upstairs hall Domna suddenly detained John. "Responsibility," she whispered, "what does it mean, we accept responsibility for Henry? Does it mean we underwrite him for one year, or are we stuck for life?" Her candle trembled as she laughed, rather nervously. "For one year, I should think," said John. "And Communism," she murmured, "do you still think that had nothing to do with it?" In the darkness, he looked at her rather oddly, with a wry twist of the long jaw, but she could not see this; the flame of her candle lit up only her own face. "No," he said, stolidly, in his ordinary speaking voice. He gripped her arm and drew her toward him till he could kiss her, dryly, on the forehead. "Sleep well," he adjured, with a curious creak in his voice. "The sleep of the just."

CHAPTER X

Mulcahy Finds a Disciple

HENRY MULCAHY's contract was renewed late in February. He at once let it be known that he signed under pressure; the new contract contained no provision for the rise in salary to which length of service now entitled him. But faculty opinion, as he probed it, was neutral for once on a salary question. Nobody denied the facts, but nobody seemed anxious to act on them. There seemed to be a movement to flee from the subject, as from an embarrassing connection, even while it was being admitted that, yes, there was a certain "hardship," as if the admission wholly relieved the speaker of the need of doing anything about it. Of all those who assured him, with an air of expert knowledge, that he had better settle down and forget it, nobody volunteered to tell him how he was going to support six people on thirty-two hundred a year. The common prescription was that he should try "creative" writing— with four children in the house!—even his wife, Cathy, subscribed to this vulgar success-dream and kept urging him to enter a contest sponsored by an influential quarterly for the best long short story by a person in academic life. To be told to write for money was the final insult to his talent and to a lifetime of sacrifice to an anti-commercial ideal. The very suggestion informed him that there was a new and subtle influence at work against him on the campus. He knew where it came from—Miss Domna Rejnev, who went about murmurously confessing that she had just sold some of her wretched mannerist verse to that same influential quarterly and advising everybody else to seek publication, like a woman in an advertisement who has found satisfaction in the use of Pond's cold cream.

And it was *this* modest young lady who was daring to gibe at him to her classes under the pretense of deploring what she called the "scholasticism" of contemporary criticism, the egoism of the modern artist-figure; he recognized her characteristic touch in the phrase that he began to hear parroted by the students: "the theophany of modern literature," ecod! She flushed whenever she saw him, and with good reason, for she could not face the plain fact that he and Cathy had dropped her; to hide this from her following, she always pretended to be concerned and friendly, asking about the children and threatening to "look in" on Cathy, "when she had a moment to spare." She held her head very high these days, as though her pretty ears were burning; she ought to have known that to break with him and join the herd of success-mongers and philistines was going to be a risky play.

He watched her strolling about the campus with Bentkoop and Milton Kantorowitz, the painter, holding an arm of each and looking up earnestly into their faces, the square Dutch head and narrow, long-nosed Jewish one making, as the students said, an interesting pictorial composition, and he smiled to think that Domna regarded the two melancholy men as bucklers of invincibility, a very foolish illusion, since Bentkoop, according to his wife, was thinking of leaving Jocelyn to study for holy orders, and Kantorowitz was a learned simpleton like all painters and had no understanding whatever of the verbal disciplines and their problems and was more likely to embarrass Domna than to help her in a literary crisis.

And that, Mulcahy assured himself, was what was on the cards. Domna had made a cardinal error in using an attack on modern literature to strike at him through the students. True, the immediate trend on the campus might seem to justify her conduct. There was a moment in the spring when the whole Jocelyn sideshow seemed to be boarding the gravy train, on to fatter triumphs of platitude and mediocrity. Dr. Hoar won an award in the field of human relations and was presented with a scroll by a United Nations luminary at a little ceremony in the chapel. Warren Austin, through an emissary, consented to speak at Commencement, and the creator of Li'l Abner was to be made a Doctor of Letters. Aristide (the Just) Poncy copped a Fulbright to lecture on Amiel in Lebanon and promptly rented his house to a grateful Mr. Mahmoud Ali Jones, whose contract, as if by jinn-magic, found itself renewed. Considine Van Tour, at the age of forty, announced his engagement to a widow with a fortune of twenty thousand a year, whom he had met at a writer's conference in Iowa during the previous summer. Grünthal, of Psychology, got a grant from the Rockefeller Foundation for a study of the learning process, and his students were posted in every class, like Pinkerton men in a museum, observing and making assayments of the retention of auditory material. One of Furness' long-tressed Ritas was promised a movie-test, and her father was reciprocating Furness' introduction to an agent by a gift of a thousand dollars to finance a poetry conference, to be held in the chapel in April, with a panel of ten poets; already, of course, there was great rivalry over where they were to stay, who was to give the dinner for them, who cocktails, and so on. Yet this very poetry conference, at which Domna was expecting to scintillate, was going to teach her a little lesson in the workings of retribution— as her friend, Bentkoop, might have told her, you cannot serve God and Mammon, and she had had her first inklings of this truth at a recent departmental meeting when the committee for the conference was selected and her name was wonderfully not included.

Mulcahy himself took no credit for this stroke; he owed it to his protégé, young Ellison, an extraordinary poet in his own right, with a firm sense of true values, and no sentimental hesitations in making them operative. The boy's doll-like exterior, pink cheeks, Episcopal-school manner and pale, hoarse voice were belying; he had a center of iron and absolute professional integrity. Domna, who contemptuously described him as a neo-traditionalist ultra, showed her own incapacity for assessing the true direction of the modern movement as well as a pitiable lack of judgment in selecting one's adversary. The real enemies of the future of poetry, as Mulcahy could have told her, were the sentimental progressives, like Consy Van Tour, with his flaccid, prosy devotions to K.A.P., Hemingway, Lardner, Saroyan, and the bristling methodistical moralists, like Alma Fortune, who, following

Leavis and the Cambridge school, pretended to see in a man's style glaring revelations of his personal faults and evasions, the public health inspectors placarding *Finnegans Wake* and the late James as diseased—these were the trough-wallowers and the trimmers, whom Domna chose to rally with in today's crisis in contemporary art. The rediscovery of George Eliot, indeed! As he laughingly remarked to Ellison, who's traditionalist now?

It was Ellison, all honor to him, who had foreseen from the start the importance of keeping her off the committee and the ease with which this could be maneuvered, merely by conciliating Furness, who held the purse-strings and cared for nothing but that he should be allowed to put up two or three of the more *réclamés* poets and give the official party for the conference in his handsome, dark-beamed, long living room. A few walks with Ellison, in his bohemian sweat-shirt and sneakers, and Furness was reluctantly able to see that to put Domna on the committee would make the wrong impression on the poets, who were surfeited with Radcliffe misses and faded libertarian poses. There was no fear in the boy and no truckling to convention. "Her verse isn't taken seriously," Mulcahy heard him explain to Furness, within Domna's hearing, as if he were calmly citing some incontrovertible natural fact, and when Mulcahy poked him, he let his eyes rest square on her, coolly and neutrally, while continuing his exposition. All this, admittedly, excited Mulcahy very much; he felt something remarkable in this friendship, which reminded him, in some of its reversals, of the friendship of Verlaine and Rimbaud. Though he knew himself to be the boy's intellectual superior, both in age and attainments, he often

felt like his pupil in the ordinary affairs of life. Ellison
seemed to have achieved, through youth and singleminded-
ness, a dizzying simplification; he did not recognize the
existence of obstacles felt to be palpable by timid and
second-rate people. The fact that he was not liked in the
department neither grieved nor interested him; he saw
that the voting strength was divided three to two against
himself and Mulcahy, with Furness as the pivotal figure,
and he treated Furness frankly for what he was—a pivot
—making no attempt at friendship and merely assuming,
at certain critical junctures, that Furness would want to
be told how to vote. And simply by virtue of this assumption, his sway over Furness was near-absolute. He did
not forget, either, that Domna had only half a vote, which
seemed to him, in fact, her primary characteristic; he did
not, like Mulcahy, worry over what she might think or do
if she "caught on" to what was being planned against her.
"She has only half a vote," he replied tranquilly, whenever such conjectures were broached.

This foresight and lucidity made a great impression on
Mulcahy, who watched with respect while the department
voted, unanimously, on Ellison's suggestion, for a committee of two. Ellison was then elected, without a single
dissent, and immediately nominated Mulcahy to serve
with him. This was the ticklish moment; Van Tour, with
an aggrieved expression, nominated Domna; Furness, looking uneasy, proposed a secret ballot. When the votes were
counted, Mulcahy had won easily—there were only two
counters against him, Van Tour's and Alma's, as he as-
certained from the wastebasket; it had been an unnecessary precaution to vote for himself. Irrationally—for it

had all gone according to schedule—he felt a little ashamed and supinely gave in to Furness, who also appeared to have qualms and truculently insisted that Domna should be invited to chair the important afternoon session—a quite unnecessary concession, as Ellison remarked later to Cathy, who was in full agreement.

What fascinated Mulcahy about Ellison's attitude toward Domna was the fact that it was completely literary and devoid of personal ill-feeling. He simply paid her no heed in extra-poetic connections, as if she were a superfluous quantity. So he treated all people who bored him and most general ideas. To people and ideas his adaptation was functional, as to food, drink, and clothing. He used only what was necessary to his immediate purpose, and his life, in Mulcahy's eyes, in comparison to his own, had a wonderful spare, stripped beauty, like that of a Mondrian painting. When he came to the house in the evening, he brought his own bottle with him, which he placed on the floor beside him; he accepted a glass from Cathy and refilled it till the bottle was gone. He was fond of charades and singing. He made Cathy take up her music again, so that she could sing to him in the evenings. He liked to have Henry read Joyce to him, for the rhythms and vocabulary, he explained, though Joyce did not interest him as an author: his work was too naturalistic. He ate very little and often drank himself stiff— the legend put about by the students, that he wore nothing under his outer clothing, was correct, Mulcahy found, when he put him to bed on the sofa.

For his friends, he was full of energy and a multiplicity of plans. He discouraged Cathy from cutting her hair, in imitation of Domna, but counseled instead a permanent and large, regular old-fashioned waves, like those shown in the old Nestlé advertisements or in Morris Hirschfield's women. One evening, he brought a shawl with him, which he said he had stolen off a piano; she put it on and danced while he blew on a mouth-organ which he produced from his dungarees' pocket. It was he who got her to write poetry again and advised her not to show it to Henry, lest she be thought to be influenced by him. He promised to send it to *Furioso*, which had published some of his own verse, as soon as she accumulated enough and urged her meanwhile to write constantly, at every hour of the day, to develop that first verbal facility; he had her read Pope and Dante and listen to Caruso's records. Encouraged, Cathy wrote steadily, on the backs of the children's drawings, of laundry lists and achievement sheets; it was her fancy to stylize herself as a naïve or housewife poet, in the style of Grandma Moses—a shrewd idea, commended Ellison, and suggested she try *Partisan Review*, with an eye to being picked up by *Life*.

Mulcahy was not offended by these managerial gestures toward his wife. He recognized in them the creative impulse, the longing of every poet-Pygmalion to make his own Galatea; in Cathy's milk-white skin he too could feel a temptation that was not of Eros but of Apollo. It pleased him, moreover, that his wife had decided to challenge Domna on her own ground. He himself, thus far at any rate, had been unable to muster Ellison's objectivity; he was hurt by Domna's covert attacks and mistrustful of the spread of her influence. Hearing of parties she had given, which he ought to have been asked to for

form's sake, he was heartened by Cathy's successes with
a growing circle of admirers. Thanks to Ellison, the news
of Cathy's poetry was spreading, and many people who
had never been privileged to hear a line of it described
it to each other in detail; the little house on the hill was
rapidly becoming a center of literary and artistic pro-
nouncements, for Cathy had the Irishwoman's gift for
pithy and prophetic utterance; her decrees began to be
quoted, like the manifestoes in the latest little magazines in
the library. Her admirers included Furness, who made a
point of dropping in, offhandedly, to settle his little score
with Domna, and to whom Cathy, in her whimsical fem-
ininity, had suddenly taken a fancy. The turn of fate
which had brought him into the Mulcahys' orbit while
Domna plummeted into ignominy appealed, obviously, to
his Proustian sense of pattern; Furness adored, as he
frankly confessed, reversals and sudden shifts of fashion—
the life of a small college charmed him as a microcosm
of high society.

He laid his cards lightly on the table, with a disarm-
ing emptying of the sleeve; Mulcahy, nevertheless, could
not be persuaded quite to trust him, and Cathy's cry,
"But of course one can't trust him, that's the whole beauty
of him," was too Jamesian an accolade for his taste. It
struck on his ears rather falsely, with a timbre of luxury
and idleness, suggestive of a leisure-class life which could
afford to collect people as objects—a far cry from the
realities of Jocelyn. "He doesn't matter," said Ellison,
expressing a truer view. To Ellison, it was of no importance that Furness still seemed to have a soft spot
for Domna, despite everything Cathy had told him of

how the girl used to malign him behind his back. Beyond
a certain point, Furness did not care to hear her decried,
and it amused him even to try to play the peacemaker between her and the Mulcahys. "We must all make friends
before the poetry conference," he announced sentiment-
ally, throwing his arms around the Mulcahys, and he was
threatening to give a pre-conference party at which everybody should pair off with his worst enemy. "That would
be rather difficult," observed Cathy, "since Domna has
so many. For once, she would get her wish and have all
the men to herself." Furness laughed pacifically. "I will
cede my place to Henry," he said. What was behind this,
Mulcahy suspected, aside from general perversity, was
Howard's indefatigable curiosity. He could not find out
the reason for the coolness between the Mulcahys and
Domna and naturally itched to know, since it would surely
be discreditable to somebody. Mulcahy himself had stood
firm; he did not propose to tell a story that would damn
Domna forever with people of feeling—after all, she had
once been his friend and he did not wish to provoke her
into denials that would only make her uglier. That she
had doubted him, unwarrantedly and without a second's
hesitation, was shameful, apparently, in retrospect, even
to herself, for she had not said boo to anybody, so far as
he knew, about that revealing evening and chose, rather,
to hide her guilt in sallies against the modern movement
and its "unholy alliance" with tradition, which meant, of
course, in plain English the friendship between Ellison
and himself. Everything he heard of her from the students
inclined him to think that she had gone a little mad, as
people will, on occasion, when they find that they have

been seen in their true colors—one curious sign of this was the fact that she still refused to have anything to do with Furness, as though in her own occluded mind she inflexibly declined to admit a changed situation. She was adhering, that is, to the past, to a time prior to that fatal dinner, and this in its turn cast an interesting sidelight on her violent thrusts against the modern: what she hated about the modern was her own refusal to face the present.

All this, of course, gave grounds for pity, and he would have pitied her wholly, if she had not been dangerous. It was unfortunate that he himself, in an unpardonable fit of rashness, had given her weapons with which she could do harm. He had not yet heard of any direct charges linking himself with the Communist party, but he lived in quiet expectation of the inevitable anonymous letter posted to the local authorities. It was distasteful to him to have to ascribe such potentialities to her, even in self-protection, but history, alas, had shown to what lengths an hysterical anti-Communism, combining with a personal grudge, could carry an unbalanced woman who had a score to settle with herself. She had no corroborative evidence, naturally, which our legal system still weakly asked to see, and her own unsupported statement that he had "confessed" membership to her would not carry much weight with impartial minds, but who in these days was impartial or even wished to be? Luckily, whatever currency the tale had gained on the campus could be shown to be traceable to Domna, and to her alone—it had been his good angel, he now saw, that had guided his reluctant hand when he had agreed to let her assume full charge of his destiny. He could not be made responsible for her fabrications on his behalf, however well meant they were —so any sane person would admit—and the fact that she had no backing from him, in this matter of the "confession," ought to have warned sensible people against giving her too much credence. He was too honest, of course, to deny to himself that the inspiration for the story had come from him, but who would have thought that the crazy girl would make so much of so little? She had apparently had a real wish to believe him a Communist, to take him *au pied de la lettre* when he had spoken metaphorically—a foreshadowing, had he but guessed it, of her later attitude toward him, which was one of cold-hearted crimination.

How weirdly irresponsible this was could be judged by a comparison with Furness. Furness, for all his malice, was a man of the world who used reasonable prudence in his estimates of other human beings. If he was no knight errant, on the one hand, he was no credulous clown on the other. It was plain that he had taken Domna's wild stories of Party membership with the requisite grain of salt, which was the thing that perhaps, even now, she could not bring herself to forgive him. Indeed, even to Mulcahy's mind, he rather overstepped the bounds of what was permissible in jocular allusions to the "thirteenth floor," "Gospodin Mulcahy," and so on. What Mulcahy found tiresome about this was the assumption, so characteristic of Furness, that we are all a parcel of rogues and confidence-men; he seemed to regard Mulcahy as Domna's confederate in a hoax on the college's credulity. His wised-up air was as irritating, though not of course

so dangerous, as Domna's exaggerations. His little store
of worldly knowledge had made him overweening and
captious: he knew just enough to know that Mulcahy was
not Party timber and not enough to see that Domna was
but the latest of a long series of persons who, for good or
bad reasons, had chosen to think otherwise. Since the
idea of Mulcahy as a Communist was fantastically comic
to his mind, it diverted him, evidently, to regard it as
Mulcahy's own fantastic invention, but for Mulcahy, who
had suffered because of this mistaken idea, the joke was
not funny and did not gain by repetition. It stung him to
see that Furness had so little appreciation of his life—
the supposition that he might have been a Communist was
not so far-fetched as all that. To be told that we would
be ludicrous in any life-role, even an uncongenial one,
is an insult to our sense of human possibility.

The first premonitory signs of Furness' treachery came
to light late in March, along with the skunk-cabbages in
the damp places and the first bouquet of spring beauties
brought by Alma Fortune to the department office. The
whole campus was, as usual, unsettled by the vernal influence and the prospect of Easter vacation: hitherto well-
satisfied students came before the department wanting
to change their major or their tutor and were dissuaded
with the greatest difficulty; roommates broke up; love-
affairs were blighted; girls wept in the washroom; Miss
Rejnev's Russian literature class sent her a petition that
they had had enough of Dostoievsky. But it was the coming poetry conference that provided a focus for the general restlessness and disaffection. From nowhere and
everywhere, all at once, came the cry that this affair—

the first of its kind ever to be held at Jocelyn—be run on democratic principles. The campus, suddenly, was seething with rumors of a "loaded" panel; it was said that Mulcahy and Ellison were planning to use the symposium for an attack on contemporary verse, on formlessness, on "pure" poetry, on "impure," i.e., paraphrasable, poetry, on the idea of progress, on progressive education. Conflicting stories circulated, but every story run down by Mulcahy agreed on two prime assumptions: (a) that the conference would not be representative and (b) that it would be the scene of an attack.

At first blush, these rumors and spiteful charges seemed merely amusing, as illustrating the perennial tendency of philistia to suspect what it does not understand, but as they grew in volume to a regular chorus of detraction, Mulcahy felt his smile becoming thinner and anxious. He was tired of denying the weary old lies that were carried to him by his students from every corner of the campus. It was all very well for Ellison and Cathy to advise him to pay them no attention; his nature, unfortunately, thanks to long ill-usage, had become a gallèd jade that chafed at the needless and quivered to the goad of baseness. The number and variety of these stories made him fear, moreover, that there was more than one force at work against him in the college. As with all symposia and anthologies, criticism fastened on omissions. It was claimed that certain allegedly leading figures had not been invited: Dr. Williams, W. H. Auden, Cummings, Yvor Winters. Humbugs like Mr. Mahmoud Ali Jones were expressing the gravest diplomatic concern over the affront to Mr. Robert Hillyer, as though the slight to his poetic gift were an international incident capable of world-wide repercussions.

But more disturbing than these manifestations from the extreme right was a notice posted one night on the bulletin-board by somebody unknown—WHERE ARE THE POETS OF THE MASSES?—lettered in crude red ink. Mulcahy, hurrying into the store to find Ellison, discovered the room buzzing with it. It was a student prank, perhaps, as some of the old guard tried to assure him, but he could not help but suspect something uglier and more personal behind it. And he was not alone in thinking that there was a faculty hand involved. Fraenkel of Social Sciences was explaining, in his usual dry-as-dust way, that the student body this year conformed to a national trend observed in a New York *Times* survey in being conspicuously a-political; hence he did not think, and so on, meticulously, *ad infinitum*, while Consy Van Tour, giggling, pointed out that the word, *where*, was spelled correctly, which *proved* faculty assistance. Mulcahy, not finding Ellison and spotting Domna and Kantorowitz and Bentkoop in one corner with their heads together, as usual, turning in concert to survey him, was on the verge of leaving in some alarm and dubitation when Furness appeared, a large frown writ on his forehead, and called a department meeting.

"I don't like this, Hen," he announced, when the flock was gathered in his office. He had just been seeing Maynard and had carried away with him, apparently, something of Maynard's fussy severity. "Maynard tells me the whole campus is in turmoil over this poetry conference. We can't seem to find out who posted that notice,

but the wildest stories are going around about some coup
you boys are supposed to be planning. What's up, anyway?" A note of pugnacious cajolery edged into his voice.
"Let Uncle Howard in on the plot." To Mulcahy's surprise, everybody was looking at him, tensely, almost
accusingly, except Ellie Ellison, who was leafing through
a volume of Apollinaire that he had selected from Furness'
bookshelves. "Yes," reinforced Van Tour, full of breathless righteousness. "Where *are* the poets of the masses?
That strikes me as a *very* good question."

Faced with all those eyes, gleaming on him expectantly,
Mulcahy reacted with laughter. "Am I on trial?" he demanded. "What are you accusing me of?" Furness scraped
his clean jaw and glanced, as if for succor, at Alma, who
at once took charge of what was apparently to be an in-
quisition. "We've been told," she declared forthrightly,
"that the conference is going to be rigged. A certain
elderly poet is going to be asked here, to be attacked by
his juniors and by certain members of our faculty. The
same treatment, we hear, is to be accorded a well-known
foreign poet who is a guest of this country. The panel is
being organized to exclude all contemporary tendencies
except those of the attackers and of those under attack.
A manifesto for a new kind of verse, calling itself the
Mythic, is supposed to be drawn up, if all goes according
to plan. One of our own members is also to be under fire
and to be censured, poetically, from the podium. We've
all heard this and don't wish to believe it, but there it is.
The students who tell us these things are resentful also,
evidently, of a conference that isn't fairly representative
of the leading tendencies in verse and of a symposium

that will reach conclusions already prearranged. That, I presume, is the meaning of the placard we all saw this morning, if it is not simply a joke at the expense of Jocelyn and of the department."

Her leathery face flushed; her jaw clamped shut suddenly. All eyes turned again to Mulcahy, who in his just shock and fury thought for a moment that he would not deign to answer such trumpery charges, but Furness' blue eye gave him a look like a nudge, which he interpreted as an encouragement to turn the tables on his accusers. "You hear these things from the students, Alma?" he said gently. "It surprises me that you believe them unless there's a prior wish in you to take me at a very low valuation. I understand all too well the mechanism that makes this possible. You defended me once in a crisis and now you fear that I may not have been worth defending, so that you take at their face value the first ugly stories you hear that seem to corroborate this little fear. In a word, you now feel responsible for me, all of you good people, and there's no richer soil for mistrust than an awareness of responsibility." He smiled. "Didn't it occur to you to doubt the veracity, I won't say of the students, but of those who fed them this rubbish to regurgitate back to you?"

Domna suddenly spoke out. "Henry," she said boldly, "the one who fed them this rubbish is you. We have it from students who heard the plan for the conference from your own lips, in confidence. We did not seek this information. It was brought to us by students who felt that what you were planning was not fair to the poets and a bad thing for the college. They felt someone should be warned." Henry moistened his lips. "How many students?" he demanded, quickly, to catch her off her balance. Domna's eyes calculated. "Three," she replied, obviously lying—he set it down at two. He himself made a rapid calculation. "I would like to be confronted with the students who so valiantly abused my confidence." He sat back in his chair, smiling, arms folded; a disobedient muscle twitching in his soft cheek.

Furness shook his head. "No," he remonstrated. "Nix on that stuff, Hen. Come off it. There's no accusation. The department's merely asking you to take it into your confidence. A report from the conference committee. What has it got up its sleeve?" The pleading note had come into his voice again, a strange raucous sound, like that of an itinerant hand-organ. Ellie Ellison looked up. "If you wish to know who posted the placard—if that is what this meeting is about—I can tell you. I did." Everybody swung around to stare at him, Mulcahy along with the others. At the boy's self-possessed words, he felt tears of relief and admiration well into his eyes. "Why?" demanded Alma, shrilly. "I think it's outrageous," said Considine. There was a babel of curiosity and reproach. But Furness' white teeth flashed in a smile of complaisant understanding; his love of mystifications was fired. "It seemed an appropriate device," explained Ellison, "for stirring up interest in the conference. There can be no proper debate if the passions are not roused. You mistake what Hen and I have been doing, sowing fear and anticipation among the students. They're being taught to take poetry seriously, like a baseball game." His look lightly dropped on Domna. "Choosing up sides. It's the

only way to run these things, to give them the quality of
a mythic contest. We intend, by all means, to have a
poet of the masses, if only for our private scapegoat. But
first it seemed advisable to create a demand for him. I
should not wish to be held responsible for inviting one
for poetic reasons; they all write so badly that they can
be interesting only as specimens, embodiments of a class
myth." His tone was matter-of-fact and serious; he looked
startled when Furness laughed. He drew a paper from his
hip-pocket and handed it to Furness. "Here's the invitation list," he said and looked on, detachedly, while the
department gathered round and peered over Furness'
shoulder. There were four or five well-known names followed by five or six others, belonging, for the most part,
to friends of his, whom Van Tour and Alma had never
heard of. "That is the most important poet writing today,"
he remarked, casually, pointing to one of them. "This is
the greatest poetic talent, which may or may not realize
itself." His forefinger tapped a third name. "That's the
poet of the masses. Like so many of his inspiration, he
lives out West, in Carmel, but I think we shall be able
to get him if we simply pay his bus fare." He folded the
list and put it back in his pocket.

    Mulcahy eyed him with trepidation. He was conscious
of being out of touch himself with contemporary poetry,
owing to the perplexing fact which often troubled him in
his friendly relations with Ellison: most "new" poets
were hostile to Joyce's work. Even in Eliot's recognition,
duly paid out like a tithe, he sensed something official
and perfunctory, cautiously charitable and concessive. The
true attitude of Eliot, he suspected, was manifest in his

disciples, who in all their voluminous New Criticism had
given Joyce scarcely a word of exegesis. Auden could shed
a tear on the grave of James at Mount Auburn; a whole
band of singers could hymn the dead Fitzgerald; but where
was the *Lycidas* for the blind minstrel who was the greatest voice of all of them? The pipes of Ransom were silent
and the reed of Tate was hollow. The envious neglect of
the "new" poets had embittered him against their verses,
perhaps unjustly so, for he could see in Ellison's new
poem, for example—an experiment with a modern epic
form, based on the heroic couplet, but relying on assonance
and a syllabic line—unmistakable evidence of the influence of *Ulysses*, whatever Ellison himself might choose
to say about it. The poem dealt with the life of Jocelyn
in a mythic semblance, using the plot of the Epigones,
that is, of the Seven who came after the Seven, and the
structure of the whole was that of a series of Epicycloids
arranged around a fixed circle. Mulcahy, who was going
to figure as Adrastus, was enchanted with the conception
of the poem and with the few lines he had heard of it—
a thing which had made him trust more willingly to Ellison's judgments of his contemporaries in drawing up the
list for the conference. Between them, they had elected to
give an interesting version of the pocket-veto to certain
stuffy figures whom the department had insisted on inviting: Ellison had disposed of them with his usual economy
by deciding not to write to them at all, but Mulcahy had
had a safer idea—he had written without mentioning
any honorarium, which had achieved the desired effect
in all but one instance, where the poet had accepted with
joy, not even inquiring about the railroad fare, and had

sent on several of his records as a gift to the college
library.

Yet now, in the presence of the department, Mulcahy
experienced misgivings. Would the department swallow
these poets, whom, to tell the truth, he himself had boggled
at somewhat until Ellison had reassured him? He cast a
curious look at Domna and at Furness, who appeared
to be struggling with what he could not help but recognize as a desire to laugh. "Herbert," said Furness, in a
muffled voice, "the purpose of this conference is not to
emulate Columbus. We need a few of the old landmarks
—*you* know, Stevens, Dr. Williams, Miss Moore—to give
the students their bearings." Domna gave a delighted
laugh. It was plain to Mulcahy that he and Ellison had
erred, since she did not seem at all offended but truly
and spontaneously amused. "The list," she cried, "is perfect to be buried in a time-capsule. In twenty years, we
will dig it up and find whether the promise has been ful-
filled." Ellison regarded her calmly. "You find bliss in
your ignorance," he stated, like one making a scientific
discovery. Domna opened her mouth sharply to answer,
but on a sudden placatory impulse Mulcahy intervened.
"Who would you like to ask, Domna?" he queried, with
an anxious, appealing smile. "Have we overlooked somebody whom *you* think important?" Furness' smooth jaw
dropped; he stared; everybody's gaze followed his to
Domna, who looked nonplussed and yet touched.

"My private opinion," she said finally, "has no special
right to be considered. There is always injustice when a
conference claims to be representative—any tendency that
exists, if only in one person, can demand a right to be

heard. My real criticism of this list—please excuse me— is that it seems to be based on an expectation of cruelty in its confrontations. You have listed several pale, respectable old men, with a long history of publication, one man in middle life whose poetic reputation is in eclipse, and four or five fledglings who have published very little and are noted principally for a critical intransigency. What do you expect to happen? Those young men will tear their elders to pieces, to the joy of the student-body, and the older men will not retaliate because they are disarmed by their success and will not stoop to in-fighting with puny adversaries, who have no body of work to put at stake. You're planning a Roman holiday, for what motives I can't imagine, unless you expect publicity. And how is it you ask no women? Do you think that a sentiment of chivalry might be a deterrent to blood-thirst?"

"But it's those pale respectable old men who have everything their own way in poetry," protested Mulcahy, aggrieved. "Nonsense," said Domna. "Every one of those old men lives in terror of some youthful thug who plays bodyguard to him and dictates whom and what he shall endorse. What you're doing is asking them to come here without their customary protection—the poor things, it's pathetic—to face a gang of hoodlums. You *must* show a certain piety by inviting the usual flappers and buffers: the poets of the middle ground."

"*What* an appraisal of the poetic situation," murmured Ellison. Domna flared up. "The trouble with the poetic situation," she said, "is that it has become organized, like the Skull and Bones society, on the lines of mutual assistance, not to let the fellow-member down.

With the advent of the new criticism to America, we've learned to become 'readers' of poetry and lost our critical standards. During the past fifteen years, criticism within the fold has been reduced to a minimum. On the other hand, no poet of any real merit has been excluded from the fold, so that complaints appear unjustified. You and your friends"—she turned to Ellison—"are too impatient. You want to make a *putsch* for the sake of tighter control, more daring methods of promotion, but violence is unnecessary. Time will bring you power."

"Is she accusing me of being a fascist?" said Ellison, speaking to the room at large. There was no answer. Furness coughed. "Why don't you make a practical suggestion, Domna?" But Domna suddenly turned obstinate. "The omissions are obvious," she declared. "You have a wide choice—Tate, Ransom, Miss Moore, Empson, Jarrell, Shapiro, Auden, Winters, Roethke, Lowell, Miss Bishop. Who am I to say?" At the mention of these names, Ellison shuddered and directed his gaze out the window. With the defection of the two poets, Furness stepped into the breach and made two or three recommendations. The meeting adjourned.

Henry caught up with Domna as she was passing through the swinging doors into the other part of the building. He touched her on the sleeve. "Domna," he said, "I don't want you to misunderstand Herbert. He meant nothing personal, I promise you. You and he are not really far apart; the very things you said this afternoon I've had him tell me a dozen times. It's the old business of the ins and the outs. He's a natural out like you and me and deeply fears any compromise. This makes him standoffish

and touchy, just like you." Domna shook her head. "No,"
she insisted. "Not like me. I'm not a natural out." He swung
into step beside her as she started across the campus.
"Domna," he said, suddenly, "who was behind that meeting?" Domna's face froze; the faint, musing smile died
on her lips. He felt her stiffen as he took her arm. "Was
it Furness?" he asked. Domna shook her head. "Or Alma?"
he prompted, more softly. "No," she cried. "It was all of
us, the whole department."

Henry smiled. "Dear Domna, I was not born yesterday.
There is always an initiator. Who spoke first? I think I
have a right to know." "We all did," she reiterated. Henry
laughed aloud. "I can find out very easily, you know,
but let's try guessing and you will tell me if I hit it
right the first time." He held up his bare hand and began
to count on the plump, shortish fingers, as though playing
with a child. Domna continued to shake her head, but he
could see that she was curious to know whether he guessed
right. "We'll eliminate poor old Consy," he said. "He
bears no grudges and knows nothing about poetry. If it
had been a short story conference, we might have expected him to fight. You?" He scrutinized her carefully,
down to her narrow fine-leather shoes. "No. I think not.
If it had been you, you would have said so, out of sheer
incontinence. It is Furness, then, or Alma. Which one?
On the whole, I think Alma. A little bird has been telling
me that Alma is angry with me. Somebody has put it
into her head that I am 'angling' for her job and trying
to push her into leaving Jocelyn." Domna flushed, uncon-
trollably. "Just ask her," he went on, "whether she re-
members the morning when I pleaded with her not to go

through with her resignation. Now, naturally, it's too late and she has only herself to blame if she can't find another position. I've done all I could, God knows, written stacks of letters for her, but nobody seems to want her. Let's say, then, I guess Alma. Do you deny it?" "No," said Domna, stopping in her tracks and whirling on him. "I don't deny it or assert it. You have no right to ask such things." She hesitated. "But if you're going to suspect Alma, I'll tell you. You're wrong. It was me." Henry gave a pitying laugh. "Dear Domna, don't you think I know that you and I have no students in common? If a student betrayed my confidence to a teacher, it could not have been to you. You gave yourselves away when you told me you had student sources. The others were too canny to do that. It was you who made the slip."

Domna drew a long breath. "As it happens," she announced, "you're wrong. We do have a student in common, but it was not that student who told me. I beg you, leave this thing alone. Nobody meant you any harm; we were merely thinking of the college and of the unfortunate effect on the students of a débâcle at the poetry conference. If Ellison was planning some outrage, we owe you a debt of gratitude for telling your students about it. There was no intent to injure you, only a public solicitude which was possibly exaggerated. You *must* not harbor vindictive feelings against anyone, including your students, who acted also for what they thought was the best."

Henry squeezed her arm. "I don't harbor them against you, Domna," he said cheerily. "I congratulate you for a valiant attempt to shield your friend, Alma." He doffed his old gray hat to her and turned quickly back on his steps. In the Administration Building, in the registrar's office, he found the class-file he was looking for. "Miss Rejnev, Oral French, Sheila McKay (transfer)," he noted and hurriedly slipped the card back.

CHAPTER XI

What Would Tolstoy Say?

DOMNA, WHEN Henry had left her, turned on a guilty impulse sharply to her right and made for Linden Hall, where Alma had her apartment. She was going to confess to Alma the thing she had just done and purge her soul of the falsity in which Mulcahy had left her. It seemed to her that she had committed a very unfriendly act: the embarrassing truth was that it *had* been she, just as she had said, who had first alarmed the department with the prattle of Mulcahy's student, the pale, anxious, little McKay girl, who had recently attached herself to her, hanging about after French class, waiting to walk with her to the post-office and confiding to her all the worries and scruples of an over-conscientious nature.

The burden of this conventional child's avowal was that she was afraid of Dr. Mulcahy, who was making her read *Ulysses*, which shocked her, pumping her about her other teachers, filling her up with all sorts of menacing theories about the artist as arch-conspirator, demanding that she and her friends baby-sit free of charge and do all sorts of menial work for Mrs. Mulcahy, who spent a great deal of time at the hairdresser's or in her bedroom, lying down, writing poetry. According to this wide-eyed Sheila, some of the boys in her circle were "slaves" to Dr. Mulcahy: he was coaching them to play a disruptive part at the poetry conference and running them ragged in his household so that they had no time to study and were finding themselves conditioned in all their courses but his. This gush of confidence imparted twice a week had in it something of awe and pristine wonder that had tempted Miss Rejnev to listen to it, at first, from a sense of intellectual duty—to Sheila, Dr. Mulcahy was a phenomenon, like thunder, for which she sought an adult explanation that would restore tranquillity to her cosmos. And the child herself, in her timid way—as Domna, torn between amusement and solicitude, related to Alma and Considine—had been groping toward understanding while holding tight to the rail of analogy: the boys revolving around Mulcahy in charmed servitude, she breathlessly discovered, reminded her of the followers of Ulysses turned into swine by Circe's spell. Hence, in a certain fashion, it was conceded, the experience of Mulcahy had been valuable to her, as the beginning of her mental life.

One scene, however, described by Sheila, had made Domna and her colleagues very uncomfortable: an account of how Mulcahy, coming home one afternoon, had endeavored to make a boy confess to breaking a serving-dish which in fact he had not broken, sending him out of the room to "think it over," and agreeing grandly to accept his apology when the boy remained uncommunicative. Such a scene, nevertheless, they all acknowledged, belonged, all too horribly, to the purlieus of private life; it was not the department's business to regulate Mulcahy's personal relations with his students nor to pry into the details of his hold on them. "They *love* him, Miss Rejnev," Sheila explained simply, when asked why they stood for such treatment. "He flatters them, you mean," sharply corrected Mrs. Fortune, who had been detailed to be present at this interview. And yet the two teachers, once the frightened girl was gone, had exchanged looks of bafflement—they believed in love and its inviolable sanctities. It was the same with Consy Van Tour's excited report that he had seen Mulcahy borrow money from a student to pay for a huge bag of groceries in the village store, so heavy, affirmed Consy, that the student staggered as he carried it out to the car. This was not the department's affair either—there was no college rule forbidding loans from students to faculty—and, for all anyone knew, this might have been an isolated instance. Such insights into Mulcahy's personal life fell under the heading of gossip, and not only Domna, but her two friends and Aristide, to whom these stories were confided (eliciting an "*Inouï!*" and a bulging of the big, flat eyes), felt somewhat guilty for dwelling on them. Yet it seemed as if everything conspired, in this particular period, to bring to their attention damaging facts about Mulcahy, which rained on them like reproaches; and this concurred, very awkwardly, with a sudden coolness and haughtiness shown by Mulcahy to all of them, a coolness to which Domna held the clue, which she felt that, in all honor, she ought not to divulge. And the fact that she had not, despite greater and greater provocations—including a most damnable attempt to woo her favorite girl-student away from her—said a word to anybody but the Bentkoops of her unpleasant little discovery gave her, she was persuaded, a certain leeway in listening, not only to Sheila's tales, but to the tales brought to her ears by every little bird on the campus.

It would seem, she inwardly protested, that she had been singled out by fatality to learn the worst about Mulcahy, as though in punishment for her credulity. Hardly a day passed, she swore, but that some student tapped on her door, to complain that Dr. Mulcahy was not in his office for his tutorial and did she know where he was, or, if it were not a student, it was the librarian, asking if she would speak to Hen about sending in his reserve list on time. There was, as she knew, a natural explanation for these recurrences: it was supposed by the ignorant that she and Mulcahy were still friendly, and those who needed to complain of him had found, by experience, that it was pleasanter to do so through an intermediary. Hence, it had fallen to her lot to be, where Mulcahy was concerned, the bearer of bad tidings, which soured their relations still further. She had no doubt that he presumed that she was spying on him—a warrantable conclusion from the evidence. Therefore, as March had worn on, with its flurry of spring colds, leading to unavoidable absences, latenesses and so on, she had delegated the task of mediation to Alma, who at once fell under Henry's displeasure, and at length to Aristide, who sped back and forth on his errands of conciliation, with the invisibility and discretion of Hermes, winging between mortals and Olympus. All these reprimands and reminders ought, of course, to have fallen to Furness to deliver, but a conspiracy of delicacy spared him, so that he alone of the original group was unaware of the real state of affairs and even supposed, as the three guiltily recognized from remarks of his casually thrown out, that Hen had finally buckled down to the job.

And Domna and her two colleagues were unable to determine, reluctantly listening to Furness, what color their own affrighted imagination was lending to the picture of Hen's delinquency. *Was* he worse, as it certainly seemed to them, or were they merely conscious, awkwardly, of certain features of his behavior which they had firmly overlooked in the past? And if he *was* better, if he was now "behaving himself," as Furness lightly noted, then what must he have been in the past, when they had all so staunchly underwritten him? The very thought made their reason quake. And the fact that he had drawn away from them, that he sometimes indeed seemed positively *unfriendly*, as Consy declared, aghast, gave their investigations a certain posthumous character, as though, like Proust's Marcel, they were tracking down infidelities of a lover dead and beyond the grasp of their reproaches.

The stories they had inevitably begun to hear of the goings-on in the little house on the hill, of Cathy's extravagances, of the close friendship with Ellison, made them, in fact, wonder whether this was the same Henry. "It doesn't sound like the Henry I knew," Alma kept repeating, as though her own Henry had strayed from her, like a household cat. And the two women, in particular, sometimes fell victims to the temptation of tracing the faults they now saw in Henry directly to Ellison's influence and of dating Henry's deterioration from the day he threw off their soft yoke. Hence, it was only natural

that they should fasten on Sheila's report of the deep-
laid plans for the poetry conference as a pretext for
bringing Henry to book, censuring the insufferable Ellison,
and restoring order to the department under their benevo-
lent tyranny; and they found no difficulty in enlisting the
indignation of the gentle, public-spirited Consy, whose
Writers' Workshop students had told him enough already,
he asserted, to freeze his balls blue.

From this moment, they all three ceased to feel guilty
and became animated by a spirit of public interest. Up
to then, though greatly disturbed by the stories brought to
them by Domna from Sheila, which were corroborated
by their own canvassing among Mulcahy's students, they
had felt that reluctance to intervene that characterized
them as true liberals. They were conscious of owing a duty
to the students to protect them from the eccentricities of
a teacher whom they themselves had sponsored, but they
could not be sure how far this duty extended and where
it conflicted with their duty to Mulcahy as a fellow-being
with certain gifts and certain handicaps, for which due
allowance must be made. There was also, they could not
help but feel, a duty to themselves, a duty not to spy, not
to be underhanded, not to encourage informers or welcome irresponsible gossip, but this duty, likewise, was in
conflict with both the other two, for how were they to determine the limits of their responsibilities if they did not
inform themselves precisely as to what was going on?

But the poetry conference, they had all agreed, was an
entirely different matter. They owed it to the college as a
whole, to the poets, to the national cultural scene, not to
permit Henry, led on by Ellison, to abuse a trust that had

been voted to him by the Literature department. Only Domna, with her anarchistic sympathies, showed, at the last moment, a tendency to balk at the idea of a departmental confrontation or showdown, but the others had quickly overridden her. It would be better to seek safety in numbers, they argued; to send Aristide as their deputy with such a commission as this one would not be fair to Aristide. And when Domna, almost inaudibly, volunteered to go herself to Henry, she was grateful when the others cried her down. "You mustn't *think* of it," they exclaimed tenderly, gazing at the fragile girl. "Think what happened to Bentkoop." For Bentkoop, it seemed, had ventured to remonstrate with Henry on some matter touching a student; and just the week before the amazing story began to circulate that John had tried to run down Mulcahy on the streets of Lancaster, a story that nobody believed but that everybody, Mulcahy's enemies in particular, repeated for a few days for the fun of it—it was said to be attested by a student and there were a number of variants in currency: that it was not Mulcahy but Mrs. Mulcahy, that it was one of the children, that it was the other way around, that Mulcahy had tried to run down Bentkoop.

Domna had given in, with a rueful backward glance at what Tolstoy would have thought of this performance; she was teaching *Anna Karenina* that week and had little doubt of his opinion. But she made no objection when it was decided to call in Furness, like the family doctor, of whom Tolstoy also disapproved. Yet when Furness was summoned and made privy to all their fears regarding the poetry conference, everybody, including Domna, experienced great relief. She had been wondering in secret whether they had not been making a mountain out of a molehill; but Furness listened to what they told him with a look of the gravest concern. To him, scandals were amusing only when they had become unavoidable, that is, after the fact; he anticipated them, so to speak, in retrospect.

And the fact that he had had no knowledge of these rumors that were spreading of boding indignities to elderly poets seemed to convince him of the existence of an emergency. He left Alma's apartment in a state of spruce discomposure and telephoned back, almost at once, to say that his own researches among the students confirmed what the three had told him. The campus was seething with gossip; it had even reached the village. Mulcahy, to judge by the evidence, had been colossally indiscreet, talking not only to his students, but telling every local tradesman and repairman, in confidence, of the strategies of the poetry conference, which figured now in the local mind as an event like Armageddon, to be followed by Judgment and the final separation of the sheep from the goats. "They're counting on seeing it in television," he observed with a despairing laugh. This, in itself, had a certain professorial charm, to which Furness' wit automatically responded, as to anything apocryphal or fabulous; but as head of the department, he admitted, he could not indulge his own taste. He was obliged to call a halt and play the old fogey. A private summons to a department meeting was already in Domna's possession when Ellison played into the hands of the enemy by posting that absurd notice.

As Domna legged it up the worn stairs to Alma's apartment, she was suddenly conscious, not only of a weakening of purpose, but of a wild, truant feeling of amusement and sympathy for the dreadful Mulcahy. "You know what Tolstoy would have said?" she demanded, bursting into the apartment. "He would have said we are all fools." Alma came out of the kitchen in an apron, with her short, wiry hair tied up in a scarf. With her usual efficiency, she had already started cooking her supper. Seeing the single chop in the pan on the hot-plate, the frozen peas garishly bubbling in the copper saucepan beside it, the tray set with a woven straw mat, earthenware plate, large blue-green Mexican glass already filled with milk, Domna felt a light compunction toward the regularity of this woman's life, so different from her own, which was ill-organized and haphazard like her moods. She herself, for example, could never have planned a series of hot menus around her solitude; she ate the same meal every night—an apple, some cheese, a roll, some salami—with the rare variation, after one of her aunt's visits, of a can of cold borscht with sour cream and some pâté made by a Russian lady in New York. Even so, she had to force herself to do the dishes by deciding every night not to do them, which, as she pointed out to one of her tutees, was a homely illustration of Kierkegaardian freedom; by deciding not to do the dishes, she recovered her freedom to choose to do them. Her whole existence at Jocelyn had a transient and picnicky character, like that of a train trip on hard boards, in the European third class. The sizzling chop in Alma's pan appalled her, as though it were a foretaste of eternity. It was Domna's frailty, as a young and egoistic person, to experience in a heightened way a common subjective il-

lusion, which was that her own life was free, determined
only by voluntary choices, while the lives of other people
around her were subject to harsh necessity. She was now
under the impression that she pitied Alma very much,
while in reality, on a sudden impulse, she somewhat
scorned her.

"Why would he say that, Domna?" said Alma, indul-
gently, taking out a bottle of wine and two old-fashioned
glasses and pouring them both a drink. She clicked down
the heat under the chop and gently pushed the girl into
the sitting-room. "Oh," said Domna, impatiently, tossing
the wine in her glass, "we are all so concerned with trivialities—this ridiculous poetry conference; why are we
excited about it?" Alma looked grave. "You know," continued Domna, lightly, "I have a new obsession. All the
time, these days, I say to myself, 'What would Tolstoy
think?' And you know, one always knows. One does not
have to call him up on the telephone." She laughed. "It's
not at all the same with Dostoievsky. I don't give a damn
what he thinks." Alma leaned forward. "Perhaps that's
because Dostoievsky is the greater artist," she said seriously. "It's all *there*, in the novels; there's no injunction
to action, no trailing moral imperatives, no direct preach-
ing, as they used to say; the morality's inseparable from
the form." Domna shook her head. "You are wrong.
Tolstoy is the greater artist, even in style, which is not
important. But Dostoievsky wrote badly. He was slip-
shod, like a journalist or a popular crime-novelist. 'Pyotr
Stepanovitch flew into the room.' Not that it matters."
Alma flung up her hands. "Ah," she laughingly cried,
"I hear the terrible things you tell your students. That

Dostoievsky is good only for comedy. You're very reckless, Domna. You ought to be very sure you're right."
Domna felt a temptation to get into a literary argument;
but she checked herself, watching Alma as she arranged
her dinner on the tray. "No, thank you," she said. "Nothing
for me." She hesitated. "I came here to make you a confession," she said, smiling. "But I don't seem to be able
to do it."

"A confession?" Alma's face was troubled. "Yes," said
Domna, as if carelessly. "I'm afraid I've just done something rather awful." "No!" exclaimed Alma, politely,
but with a shade of uneasiness. "I don't believe you could."
"Wait until you hear. Henry followed me just now, out
of the meeting. He wanted me to tell him who was behind
our *démarche*. I'm afraid I may have left him with the
impression that it was you." Alma gave a shrill cry of
horror. "Domna!" she exclaimed. "I don't believe you!
How could you have done such a thing?" Domna dropped
her eyes. "Purely from motives of self-protection, I'm
afraid. The thing is that I don't know whether I really
did it or I didn't." Alma made a gesture of impatience;
she dropped her fork on her plate with a loud clatter.
"You see," added Domna in a low voice. "I *said* it was I,
after *he* said it was you. Taken together, this, I *think*,
may have given the impression that I was lying in order
to shield you." She considered this formulation and quickly
nodded. "Yes, I think that is right. I believe I may even
have wanted to leave that impression. But, as I say, I am
not sure. I find it quite impossible, I discover, to describe
to you exactly what happened. My words become disobedient, like the vocal cords of a person who habitually

sings off key. I thought I heard the truth for an instant; somewhere I think I can still hear it, very faintly, but it eludes me, like perfect pitch." Her whole manner was peculiarly *dégagé*; she set her wine-glass down on the lowboy and began to button her coat. "Domna!" ordered Alma, pointing to the chair opposite her. "Sit down there this instant and tell me what happened, straightforwardly. No more hints, if you please, and leave the interpretation to me."

Domna obeyed, with a slight shrug, observing, as she listened to her own words, as to a performance, that this "straightforward" account was extremely misleading—it left her in a better position than she knew herself to be in. But Alma appeared relieved. "You talked too much," she conceded. "How *could* you have been so wobbly, Domna, as to let that man stand there and pump you? Couldn't you at least have been silent, if you knew your own weakness? You ought to have turned on your heel the minute he accosted you with his questions." Domna laughed. "You look on him as a seducer," she suggested. "To me, he is more like Hamlet, with his soul-searching questions to Ophelia, 'Are you honest?' " "Well, for that matter," said Alma, "I think you were honest enough. Too much so. Has it occurred to you that you may have put your little friend, Sheila, in a pickle?" "Naturally," agreed Domna. "But what am I to do? Must I go and confess to her also?" Alma failed to see that this question was intended ironically. "Of course not," she said nervously. "You mustn't think of such a thing. I already shudder to imagine what tales she must be bringing home to her parents." She carried her tray out to the kitchen and put water on for her coffee. "And yet," she pondered, returning, "I wonder whether we shouldn't take measures to protect her, if Henry should be mad enough to try to trace her down through the files. Could we have her come to the department and petition for a change of tutor? You could take her on and she could shift to Aristide's French section—no, that would be too crude. Oh, I rue the day, Domna, when you called us together to back that man." The tea-kettle whistled and she hurried out to the kitchen. "And how we treated poor Howie!" Her voice rose above the whistle. "I blush for us in my bed of nights."

"Howard was wrong," said Domna, abruptly. "He was motivated by cynicism and hardness. And you know, Alma, *I* think that we are wrong now. That is what Tolstoy would tell us." Alma laughed. "What would he advise us to do, Domna?" "Leave it alone," called Domna. "It is all nonsense, you know, like worrying about balldresses and fans." "Hardly that," said Alma, coming into the room and handing Domna a cup of coffee rather coldly. "Yes, nonsense, Alma," repeated Domna intensely. "What could Henry do to that wretched well-meaning little Sheila? He is not dangerous, you know." "He could fail her," said Alma, succinctly. "And so?" queried Domna, with a laugh. "To fail a course, is that so serious? She could make it up in the summer. None of our students would be damaged by a course of summer reading." "You young monster," said Alma, quizzically, shaking her head. "But the emotional experience, Domna," she added on a rising note. "Think of the emotional experience for that soft, unformed little child." Domna shrugged. "There are worse emotional experiences. Henry is an interesting man."

Alma pounced. "Look into your own soul, Domna. You're simply minimizing the effects on Sheila to extenuate your own behavior." Her dark eyes glowed; she leaned forward, with something in her aspect, thought Domna, of a fishing stork. "Examine your behavior, Domna," she said coolly, folding her arms. "You come here to confess a mistake and you fall to condoning Henry, which is only an indirect way of condoning yourself for being weak with him." Domna colored. "And yet what I say may be right," she murmured. "I may have been led to truth through error." Alma tapped impatiently on the table but Domna went on. "This poetry conference, think of it, are we not being nonsensical? Who can be hurt by it if it turns into a fracas? And there will be no fracas. It is all some mad vain delusion in the minds of Ellison and Mulcahy, which we pretend to be frightened by for mad vain reasons of our own. And if we do not pull back and examine we will find ourselves, precisely, doing what Henry fears of us—leading a crusade to force Maynard to fire him." She stood up and rebuttoned her coat. Alma looked thoughtful. "It's something we must be on guard against," she admitted, rising. "Heaven knows," she interjected, alarmedly, "I should not like to hurt poor Cathy and those children. Thank you," she exclaimed, after a moment's reflection, and leaned over and gave Domna a quick, warm hug. Domna responded. "You know," she murmured, "I sometimes think Henry knows us better than we know ourselves. He forces us to choose whenever we see him. He asks only one question, 'Are you with me or against me?'" She lifted her eyes and smiled. Alma walked her to the door; they stood for a moment, arms interlinked and swinging. "That, I suppose," mused Alma, "that imperative, I mean, must be the heritage of that unfortunate political past of his. I often wonder how he came to it. I was very close once myself, Domna, and yet never, never!" Domna felt a vibrant shudder run through Alma's frame. "It was a question of my freedom, I suppose," Alma continued, with a faraway, firm look in her eyes. Domna's lips parted and closed again, with reluctance. She had been about to make a suggestion but Alma's dreamy, romantic expression restrained her, just as John Bentkoop, on a previous occasion, had been restrained, though Domna did not know it, by the belief in her own eyes.

CHAPTER XII

The Poets Convene

JOCELYN'S MOOT poetry conference opened on a fine Friday afternoon in April with the usual difficulties of transportation. Like so many small colleges, Jocelyn had preserved its historic atmosphere at the price of having been passed over by the railroads, the nearest main station being in Harrisburg, twenty-eight miles away. This fact having been made known to the poets, an afternoon train was named, which could be conveniently met by the official welcomers after the last class hour and before the appointed baptism of cocktails at the President's house —this arrangement, as was pointed out in an official purple hectographed schedule issuing from the President's office, would give the men poets plenty of time to "get acquainted" with the department and the lady poets time to "wash up."

Yet the poets, as usual at such affairs, elected to display their individualism and their freedom from the trammels of the academic by ignoring the train suggested and arriving by diverse routes and at different hours of the day. Some came by car too late for the cocktail party, and also for dinner in commons, having stopped, so they said,

to explore the cloisters at Ephrata, so that some faculty-
wives in their dinner dresses were obliged to turn to and
make sandwiches and coffee. One deaf old poet appeared
in the morning and spent the whole day wandering about
the campus, lonely as a cloud. One, taking unfair advantage of the provision for expenses, arrived by plane
in Pittsburgh, whence he telephoned collect for somebody
to come and get him; one came on Saturday morning;
one did not come at all. The poet of the masses hitchhiked
and was picked up on the highway by some students, who
carried him off to Gus's. The English poet arrived in
York, unannounced, having discovered a local train that
no one else knew existed. One old freedom-loving poet
descended from a parlor-car with his wife, who had not
been specified in the invoice; this produced a momentary
upheaval in the sleeping arrangements, for it had been
planned to create a men's dormitory in Howard Furness'
upstairs and a women's dormitory at Miss Rejnev's. The
problem was solved at the last moment by Mrs. Fortune's
offer to vacate her apartment—after a number of beds
had already been hauled about by members of the baseball team. In short, of the eleven poets who accepted (rep-
resenting, in many cases, a second choice on the part of
the committee, since a number of the original invitees
had to decline, citing prior commitments to attend several
other poetry conferences being held the same week on The
Contemporary Neglect of Poetry), only one, a woman lyri-
cist, arrived at the proper time and place, and this, as it
turned out, proved most inconvenient, requiring two special trips on the part of Considine Van Tour in his new
red convertible, which could not travel more than twenty

miles an hour, for he had failed to recognize, at first
blush, in the large woman with the grip, whom he took
for one of the church-workers so prevalent in the neighborhood, the subject of the Cecil Beaton photograph
that appeared on the back jacket of her books.

Yet in this large, comfortable woman, with tight-drawn
bands of black hair and a Sunday-meeting hat, who
alighted at long last soughing on Miss Rejnev's doorstep,
he had found much sharp discrimination and a worldly
understanding of life. They had had a most rewarding
conversation on the trip back, concerning the various
factional struggles within the department, which he felt
it his duty to apprise her of, lest she be made the victim
of a deception; she listened with great acuteness to what
he himself feared was a rather confused account of the
outrageous behavior of Henry Mulcahy and Herbert Ellison, whom he did not hesitate to warn her against by
name; and it pleased him to be able to turn her over to
Domna with the assurance, "I leave you *in good hands*,"
and see her nod in return, a great, calm, capable nod,
like a wink of the universe, that accepted the reliability
of her landlady in supra-mundane matters. Meanwhile,
other poets, riding perilously in Mulcahy's swaying old
Plymouth, were also "getting to know" the department,
an experience they took quite calmly, since it happened
to them at every college.

Led upstairs by Domna, to the larger bedroom, the
lady poet tried the bed, approved it, asked for a medicine
glass, a saucer, an extra pillow and a shoelace; she loosened her corset, looked out the window, inquired the age
of the house, the local agricultural product, remarked that

she had been born on a farm, and that she would like to press out a skirt—if it were not too much trouble—before the evening session. She then took off the skirt she was wearing, revealing a pair of long pink bloomers, and allowed Domna to persuade her to take a nap while her evening apparel was being ironed. Domna being a slow ironer, and the evening skirt being long and wide, they arrived at the President's house at seven-fifteen, just as the last poet was leaving; Esther Hoar hastily telephoned commons to save some hot food and a table for four, and to Switchboard to post a notice that the lecture would be fifteen minutes late. The President in his dinner-jacket appeared somewhat distrait, but the guest politely ignored this; she was accustomed to find small colleges on her arrival in a state of tension and disorder, like some small mountainous country on the verge of a revolution. Over the remains of the Christian Brothers', they leisuredly discussed train schedules, botany, Mennonite customs, agricultural patterns, the Pullman Company, a conversation which tortured the President with the idea that he was being patronized, as though by some stately fellow-passenger in a parlor-car, as they glided into the alien West. It was a peculiarity of this woman poet that she turned her whole body slowly from the waist when addressed by a new interlocutor, as though she were an obliging ear-trumpet maneuvering into position to take account of some strange new noise reaching her from afar; and her discourse also had something of this measured adjustment or focusing. As one of her old friends took pains to assure a group of students later, this was not really a sign of condescension on Harriette's part, but only a trick of her corseting.

Nevertheless, the President, early in the conference, had developed feelings of inferiority; as he sat there, glancing at his wrist-watch, the terrible sensation that he was something infinitely small, at the other end of a telescope, or a very faint, pre-verbal noise assailed him.

What troubled him even more, however, was the fact that the poets, as he observed them gathered together this first night in commons, showed no inclination to discuss poetry. He had imagined something very different—a two-day Platonic banquet of the mind, from which the students might garner the crumbs at the public sessions—but all he could pick up, when he and his party finally took their places in the dining room, was a clamor of personal allusions that made him fear for his eardrums, a good deal of profanity from the younger members, and several unflattering references to members of his own faculty. The only similarity he could detect to Plato's banquet was that some of the poets seemed to be tipsy, or "high," as he preferred to call it, genially, and this, despite the fact that acting on Furness' advice he had decided to serve only sherry, which had elicited, according to Esther, several very rude comments from the corduroy-clad youth element. It occurred to him that some of the poets must have a bottle in their rooms.

Yet, in spite of his apprehensions, which he tried to mute even to himself, believing, as he did, in every man's right to regulate his own behavior, once he reached the age of discretion, that is, when he graduated from college —so long, he silently stipulated, as the other fellow was not injured—the first or Friday night session went off on the whole pretty well. Alma Fortune was mistress of ceremonies; she wore a low-necked black beaded dress and black jet earrings that served to bring out more worldly gleams in her twinkling personality than the college generally saw. Under her sharp eye, a contingent of youths from Ellison's Verse-writing who were lounging against one wall slowly took seats toward the rear, where their comments, at any rate, were inaudible, thanks to the overhang of the gallery. In Alma's introduction, she showed to great advantage, thought the President, that gift for the local allusion that was her strong point as a teacher. A light reference to the mishaps of the afternoon, to the saga of missed connections, led her back to the early history of the college, to the frontier, and thence to the Epic, the topic around which the poets had been asked to frame their remarks. She hoped—with a side-twinkle for the students, to whom this was a twice-told tale—that the hex signs on the neighboring barns would serve to ward off all evil influences from the vicinity and not, as the ignorant sometimes thought, to attract them or indicate their presence. With a glancing hint at the dual function of poetry—as black and white magic—, at the role of the daemonic in art (the Mann students pricked up their ears), and at the witchery of Miss Harriette Mansell's verse, she gaily sat down, tucked her skirt under her and turned her bright, wizened face, dancing with a thousand expectations, up to Miss Mansell, who strode toward the podium. Miss Mansell was wearing a very high-necked black heavy crêpe blouse encrusted with sequins and a long black crêpe skirt. There was a patter of applause from the poets, who were seated on benches that gave the effect of choir-stalls on the right-hand side of what had

once been an altar and now served as a stage. Several of
the poets leaned over to tap a shoulder or whisper in an
ear and receive a quick nod in reply, as though in con-
firmation—it was apparent that Mrs. Fortune's speech had
given satisfaction. The poets, in fact, indicated that they
were agreeably surprised by it, a thing which they made
no attempt to hide from the audience: they would not,
they rudely pantomimed, have expected to find such tact-
ful literacy here. Having thus consulted with each other,
like birds on a telephone wire, they unanimously folded
their arms and settled down to listen to Miss Mansell's
talk, which proved to be on Virgil.

A faint sigh rustled through the faculty. From the point
of view of the student-body, the choice was not a happy
one. The majority of the students present had never heard
of the person being alluded to as the Mantuan; they
supposed he was a modern poet whom their faculty had
not yet caught up with—a supposition correct in a sense,
as Howard Furness, maliciously grinning, remarked in
his slippery voice afterwards. A few scowling scholarship
students who had not had the good fortune to be educated
progressively moved restlessly in their seats, as though
fighting being awakened from a dream to the realities of
their old Latin teacher and the abhorrent learning-by-rote.
There were stifled cries of "Let me out of here," "This
is where I came in," and boisterous pummelings and
punchings, quieted by a glare from a bright Austrian girl
named Lise, who was doing her major project on Hermann
Broch and *The Death of Virgil*. Lise's major project, as
the news of it spread around the room, evoked instant respect and attention; heads turned to nod at her approv-

ingly, as though some member of her family had just
been mentioned from the dais, and Lise sat blushing
joyfully, like a bride. Unfortunately, this dark pretty girl
did not understand Latin, which was Miss Mansell's forte;
nevertheless, she strained forward, not wishing to miss a
word.

Miss Mansell did indeed read beautifully; she made
a majestic Dido, and from her flashing orb and classic
bust something of passion and tragic nobility did communicate itself even to those who were unable to appreciate her control of the hexameter. At a whispered re-
quest from Mulcahy, who darted up to the podium, she
read aloud her own recent translation of the Prince-of-
peace eclogue and followed this with a free sight translation of Dido's speech, a real virtuoso performance, which
she finished with streaming locks, moistened eye, and
flushed cheek, to a salvo of applause from the poets,
which informed even the soundest sleeper in the audience
that something stirring had taken place. Even to students
who had never seen her published photograph, it was suddenly manifest that she had once been very handsome and
had loved in the heroic style, just as they felt something
of the Augustan amplitude in the tidal swell of the dactyl
breaking on the shoal of the caesura. To Maynard and
his wife, the reading had been "a rare treat," as they
exclaimed, coming up to Miss Mansell afterwards; they
knew, however, that they would have to pay for it later,
at the bench of progressive judgment, for they could see,
two rows in front of them, the head of the Social Sciences
division vigorously conferring with the head of Natural
Sciences—to these two Robespierres there could be no

question of the President's connivance in this reactionary coup of the Literature department; and it was a mark of Maynard's moral courage, therefore, that he went up, publicly, to shake the hand of the victorious Calliope.

Fortunately for the President, there was an irregularity in the solid front of the Social and Natural Sciences. Dr. Muller, the historian, one of the pillars of the college, had listened to the lecture with the greatest approval. "Fine stuff," he called out to the President, patently holding him responsible also. Dr. Muller, like many historians, had certain regressive tendencies arising from the nature of his subject, which called forth a tolerance for the past, in the same way that some occupations, like sandhogging, give rise to their own occupational diseases. He had just been reading an article in a learned journal which strove to show, by quotation, that Virgil, far from upholding the centralized tyranny of Augustus, had been secretly a republican oppositionist, giving his poetic sympathy, not to Aeneas, but to the conquered and unfortunate, exemplified by Dido. Hence, he had been in the throes of scholarly anticipation from the very first moment of the lecture, so much so that he had paid little heed to the stated theme—the problems of a heightened language raised by the epic form—and had concentrated all his powers of attention on the moment when, after the lecture, he would sequester the handsome Miss Mansell and put to her the question that was throbbing through his brain: Could the Prince-of-peace eclogue, in the light of these discoveries, be now considered spurious or was it to be read, rather, as a powerful example of irony? When in due course, after the lecture, he did have the opportunity of laying the problem before her, he met with a set-back. Perhaps he had spoken too fast, being, like a boy, so full of his spermy question that he crammed it all into one sentence, without consideration for the lady's slower pace. But either Miss Mansell did not hear him correctly, as she leaned slowly sideward, like a tronometer, to apprehend his presence, or she did not perceive the cogency of his question for the understanding of the phenomenon of imperialism in our own times. Arrested, no doubt, in an historical phase of the development of language, like a magnificent fly in amber, she took him to be offering some new and purely verbal definition of irony and directed him to somebody named Empson—if he caught the name rightly—and his treatment of the pastoral mode. And her answer was so richly complete in itself, so rounded and duly meditated, that he did not have the heart or the temerity to put the question again. He forgave her, very shortly, from the brisk egoism of his nature, as he had learned to forgive other provocative lecturers and fine students who failed to live up to their promise. Indeed, at the next week's meeting of the Social Science division, he administered a rebuke to his colleagues; granting, as he said, a certain bias in the handling of the poetry conference, an exception had to be made in the case of Miss Mansell, who had shown, he thought, a fine understanding of the vital relation between democratic principles and sanity in art.

The second and final speaker of the evening was a very old poet, clean and fresh as a rose, a bank president in private life, very mild and courteous, with a gentle quavering voice and a tight set of the long soft lips, like a

Presbyterian pew-holder. He had a style of old-fashioned, elaborate compliment, in which there could be detected the flourishes of an antique penmanship and the scratching of a bookkeeper's quill. He began his address with a series of tributes, to Mrs. Fortune, "our gracious Janeite," to the President, the student-body, the college as a whole, and to each of the poets on the platform, individually, with a special gallantry toward the two ladies; as his keen powder-blue eye passed over the audience, he did not omit favorable mention of "our audacious friend, Dr. Mulcahy," or of "our young friend, Mr. Herbert Ellison," or of Miss Domna Rejnev, "whose verses we have been reading with astonishment." These compliments, under which some of the recipients could be seen to bridle, amazed the student-body, which was given the illusion of having been inducted, personally, into some venerable temple of commerce, treading, like new depositors, reverently behind the soft, padding footfalls of the manager of this very old and reliable firm, which kept nevertheless a spry pace with the times and for which, as the slogan had it, no account was too small. The President, however, shifting uncomfortably on his haunches on the cushionless bench and smiling an appreciative smile, felt a country boy's wariness of this old party, who reminded him of the original John D. Rockefeller dipped in attar of roses; he made a jovial note to watch his mental pocketbook in the transactions to follow.

The lecturer, pinkly smiling, announced that he would speak on Lucretius, which caused a flurry of interest among the poets on the platform: was this the long-awaited beginning of a new phase? They leaned forward tensely, alit with professional excitement. In the audience, the President frowned; the faculty was uneasy. Had the poets conspired among themselves to make game of the students? Feeling the President's eye on him, Furness turned and flung out his hands in a gesture that pleaded his innocence. He, like many of his colleagues, was recalling, with some disquiet, the old poet's bland question at the sherry party—"Is this the fabled college where everything is run backward?"—and the air of gentle disappointment with which he bore the news that no, indeed, it was not, that the courses ran normally from the immediate past to the present, Mrs. Fortune interjecting, proudly, that *her* modern novel course, as distinguished from Mr. Van Tour's and Mr. Furness', began with Jane Austen and stopped with Henry James. Yet the idea that Jocelyn was being "had" subsided in all minds but the President's as the lecturer proceeded to block out his subject with the greatest care for the students' understanding. He read his speech from a prepared manuscript, looking up from time to time to insert a date or an historical footnote, and making no sorties into the original text. Indeed, he admitted to an "otiose" preference for reading the philosophers in translation, a side-remark that made the President long to tell him to take his tongue out of his cheek and put it where it belonged, into his utterance. For the truth was that, contrary to all expectations, which were based on the notorious "difficulty" of his verse, the poet's essay had an innocuous and guileless character, like a schoolboy's précis or a junior-encyclopedia article on its subject—there was nothing new in it, as the Literature department began to murmur among itself, with puzzlement.

His talk was, in fact, so clear that the best disposal the
Literature faculty could make of it was to assume that
they had not understood it, that of the proverbial four
levels of meaning that they so stringently enforced on
their classes they themselves had seized only on the
literal and had failed of the moral, the allegorical, and
the anagogical. Or had Consy Van Tour seen something
of the second in the allusion to Democritus and the atom?
Was the poet, as Consy divined, suggesting that the atomic
bomb represented today's most promising theme for a
philosophical epic? Like Dr. Muller with Miss Mansell,
Consy could hardly wait for the speech to end in order
to tell the speaker of the interesting work being done in
his radio verse drama seminar on the hydrogen bomb,
bacillic warfare, interplanetary rockets; he turned full
around in his seat and nodded triumphantly at his friend,
Ivy Legendre, of the Theatre, who had been trying to persuade him that science fantasy was hick.

To the Natural Science Division the talk was not, per se,
objectionable. Lucretius, Democritus, Pliny—these were
names of honor with them; and they sat back contentedly,
once they had made sure that the speaker was not going
to use Lucretius to attack modern science, something always to be feared when the names of the ancients were
invoked. They were glad, moreover, to be able to give
their tolerance to at least one part of the conference, for
they found themselves in a peculiar position *vis-à-vis* their
best students, who were enthusiastic about literature and
rated very high in it on the achievement sheets. This
strange morganatic alliance between the Literature faculty
and the top science majors, most of whom were boy

prodigies, was always upsetting to the professional scientists, and at no time more than now when to their discomposure, as they applauded, they heard their young
physicists and chemists pronouncing the talk elementary.
But this was a minority judgment. The majority, hearing
the poets' applause, more prolonged and respectful than
what had been given Miss Mansell, concluded, like their
teachers, that something must have been lacking in their
own understanding.

This led to an unfortunate incident during the question period. A very literal-minded girl, the terror of her
instructors, with pink snub nose and flaxen braids, dressed
in a laced bodice like a peasant in an operetta, got up
and boldly asked the poet whether he was a primitive.
"A primitive, my dear young lady?" pondered that Mr.
Turveydrop. "What *can* you mean?" He looked quizzically
around him, as though for assistance. "Do you wish to
know whether I am an aboriginal or a savage?" The
poets laughed. "Or do you mean to imply that I am
primordial, that is, ancient?" The President ground his
teeth, but the girl, blushing in great red disks, stood her
ground, as she had stood it in a whole series of Sophomore
Orals. "No," she said firmly. "I meant that your lecture
was very simplified, like a primitive painting. And I
thought you might like to tell us whether this was deliberate." In the front row, Furness groaned. *"Touché!"*
exulted Domna Rejnev, beside him. Mulcahy caught her
eye and winked. Across the whole short front row that
was the department passed a sudden smile of pride: one
of their worst students had just voiced the question that
no critic, for twenty years, had dared voice even to

himself. A red-faced, white-haired poet on the platform
unexpectedly slapped his knee, but the majority looked
frostily disapproving. "Deliberate?" repeated the poet,
rather angrily. "I'm afraid I cannot tell you. But there
is nothing in art which is not studied." The girl opened
her mouth again and struck a rather "cute" pose, putting
one finger to her open mouth and scuffing her ballet-slipper
along the floor, a pose which the department sadly recognized as the sign that she had outlived her moment.
Alma Fortune rose from her chair on the platform. "Sit
down, Gertrude," she ordered, but kindly. "We mustn't
tire our speaker."

Howard Furness, smiling, got up to propose that the
poet might read some of his famous poems, which were
already known to the students through the college record
library. But the old man was disinclined; on his stiff, thin
legs he moved out of the limelight and sank into a chair
at the back of the stage, where he sat, chafing his hands.
The audience began to clap in unison for his return; it
was felt that he had been offended, and there was a general friendly desire to pay him homage for poems that
had given pleasure in the past and that remained, even
now, in the modernist canon, preserved, like his fresh complexion. When the old man continued to refuse, the poet
who had been dubbed by Ellison the poet of the masses,
a middle-aged, heavy-set man with a scarred prominent
jaw, wearing a red flannel shirt and heavy boots, stood
up suddenly in his place, at the very end of the bench,
and declared that he would read them. There was a movement of incredulity among the poets; it was not supposed, obviously, that this person, smelling of beer and

doubtless of sweat—for he boasted of having been seven
days on the hoof—was familiar with the old man's frail,
difficult poems, which had emerged from the Imagist movement, convoluted and pale, like sea-shells. Throughout
the whole audience, in fact, there was a feeling of alarm
as the red-shirted poet, without waiting for an answer,
made straight for the lectern, like a worker resolutely
moving to seize the power-switch in a factory. It was feared
that he would read his own poems or somehow do the old
man outrage. But to everyone's surprise, when the old
man's books were not forthcoming and a student was sent
out to look in Furness' office, the proletarian poet began
to recite from memory those forty-year-old verses written in the counting-house, on the backs of checks and
deposit-slips, celebrating merchant princes and their ladies
and the life of the summer hotel. To these crabbed and
yet fastidious verses, the proletarian poet's delivery added
something uproarious and revivalistic, hell-and-damnation
thunder lit up with a certain social savagery and wide-
open bohemianism, which suggested a good deal of the
atmosphere of *The Outcasts of Poker Flat.* "Preserve us
from our admirers," whispered a young poet, sardonically,
to his ally. Yet an obscurity in the old man's poems, or
rather the uncertainty as to how he had meant them hit
upon by the student, Gertrude, made this dramatic interpretation possible, and though the old man sat picking
at his buttons throughout the recitation, it was a manifest
success with the students, the boys in particular, who
stamped on the floor and called out for more, until Mulcahy, at a cue from Ellison, whispered to Alma to put

a stop to the reading. The poets, it seemed, were displeased.

This did not arise, as might have been thought, from
professional jealousy, but from a deeper feeling, the
natural antagonism between the poet and his audience
that now began to be exhibited at the Jocelyn poetry conference. It was a profound, suspicious, almost animal
antagonism, without necessary basis in outward circum-
stance but arising, as it were, from the skin, from a
bristling of the hair on the nape of the neck, and the
proof that the proletarian poet was not really a poet was
the fact that he did not appear to feel it. The true poet,
unlike the prose-writer, explained Howard Furness in
lowered tones to the President, does not care to be ad-
mired or even to be read, except by a few chosen fellow-
poets; a taste for public admiration in a poet is already,
as he himself knows, the fatal sign of his deterioration;
he has ceased to be proud, protective, and fiercely pos-
sessive of his work. Hence—he airily continued, while
the President listened, aghast—all attempts, on the part
of well-meaning academics, to persuade the poet that he is
loved are futile and self-defeating, for the poet does not
wish to be loved and flocks to symposia on the Contemporary Neglect of Poetry to be reassured that he is not.
And the spontaneous applause, just now, accorded the
proletarian poet's rousing reading of the old man's work,
was, from the point of view of the poets on the platform,
an unmitigated disgrace and catastrophe. Even Domna
Rejnev—he pointed out, guiding the President's attention
to where she stood in the front of the hall, nervously talking to the proletarian poet, whom everybody else was

shunning—was finding her libertarian principles sorely
put to the test; and, in fact, as they watched, she slipped
away from the poet and took neutral refuge with Alma
Fortune, who was chatting with Miss Mansell. The President was shocked. "Why, it's like the old Greek ostracism,"
he commented, reaching into his pocket for his pipe.

An impulse of hospitality led him to start through the
emptying hall to where the proletarian poet was standing,
alone and conspicuously abandoned, scratching his jaw.
Senior girl-students were passing punch and cookies; the
poet took a cookie from the tray and made some remark
to the girl, who blushed and hurried on with her duties;
this particular student, as the President recalled from her
advisers, was unfortunately very shy. Before the President
could get to him, however, the poet, with his mouth full
of cookie, suddenly reached out and seized the arm of
Henry Mulcahy, which was hovering over the refresh-
ment tray. Mulcahy, observed the President, was in very
good form this evening; the continuation of his appointment seemed to have put a little weight on him; the fixed,
precise smile had lost its baneful character, and he dif-
fused an air of good fellowship. Up on the platform,
Cathy, accompanied by Ellison, was the center of a little
group; her rich laugh rang out. The poet grasped her
husband's hand and shook it. "Hello, old friend, don't
you know me?" Mulcahy paled under his freckles; he
peered at the poet mistrustfully and endeavored to withdraw his hand. "I don't believe so," he said coldly. "I
know your work, of course." He started to veer away and
caught the President's eye, in full rebuke, resting on him.
"At Brooklyn College in the old days," reminded the poet.

"In the old John Reed Club. I was using my Party name, then." Furness, who had caught up with Maynard, threw the President a quick look of interrogation and wonder. Both men, by common consent, moved closer. A pair of curious physics students, noticing this, nudged each other and edged up; Alma Fortune's attention was caught; Miss Mansell's body slowly turned. "And what *was* your Party name?" inquired Henry, with a faint smile of derision. "John Marshall," chuckled the poet. "*Now* do you remember?" Henry bit his white underlip. "Indistinctly," he admitted. "I've changed," conceded the poet, with a sudden note of bitterness and significance. "In more ways than one." He touched his chin. "I got that in a San Francisco dock-strike. With the Sailors' Union of the Pacific. That was after I broke with the Party." He laid a finger on his broad, thick-flanged nose. "When I broke with the Party, they broke that for me. Twice. When I was laid up in the hospital, my new life began. New name. New ideas. I began to do some reading. I went into the hospital a Trotskyite and came out an anarchist, thanks to an old Wobbly working-stiff who used to bring me books."

By this time, half the room was listening. The tall young girls put down their trays on the empty benches and came nearer. Several attenuated young poets and the red-faced, white-haired poet who had slapped his knee and was noted for his dynamic Americanism and metrical intransigency now pushed purposefully forward. The old poet had left, accompanied by two of his cohorts, and, with his departure, a desire to make some gesture of solidarity with the proletarian poet had overtaken the poets remaining, who felt a certain human compunction and also curiosity. The

proletarian poet, moreover, was unobjectionable to them
as a man of action; indeed, they found him picturesque,
as did the students crowding around him, with talkative
wonder, as though he were an historical remain, a chipped
statue in a square. Everybody, it seemed, had expected
him to be much younger; and the explanation, which he
himself cheerfully volunteered, lay in his rebirth. His
poetry, he explained, with citations, was youthful, direct,
and sensuous, celebrating free relations with women, red-
wine parties, bull sessions, hitchhiking; as a poet, in
short, he was the same age as the Jocelyn literary set,
while as a man he was forty-five years old. But it was as
a man, sad to say, that he interested the students, who in
their turn quickly explained to him that their own literary
age was about fifty, thanks to the Jocelyn system of individual instruction, which had made them old before
their time. Much later that night, in one of the social
rooms, a girl Philosophy major showed him that he had
paid the price of a robust and time-conscious nature, that
is, that he was dated, that he embodied a militant yesterday, which seemed farther from today than the pyramids;
and it was precisely this fact that drew the students to
him and permitted Dr. Mulcahy to hurry out of the room,
unnoticed, while the poet continued to talk of frays with
the Bridges union, mutiny on a banana boat off New
Orleans, the strike at Ohrbach's, the old John Reed Club.
When the poet finally looked for him, he was gone, like a
spectral vapor.

In the moonlight, on the chapel steps, the President and
Furness turned to face each other. "Who would have
guessed it?" exclaimed the President. Furness shook his

smooth head. "Not I," he disclaimed. "I still wouldn't
credit it if I hadn't seen Hen turn tail and run." They
took a few steps into the reviving mountain air, on the
gravel of the circular driveway. "It puts him in a better
light, you know," remarked Furness, finally, in a tone
of apologetics. Their feet crunched as they walked. "For
us, Howard," distinguished Maynard. "But we must look
at the whole picture. How many students, would you say,
got in on the beginning of it? *Oh, my God!*" he cried,
suddenly, as the whole picture smote him afresh. Furness
regarded him with a certain amused tenderness. "Two
or three," he hazarded. "But there's a fifty-fifty chance,
Maynard, that they didn't take in the meaning of it. The
kids here aren't very political these days; you can't
seem to get that through your noodle." The President
shook his curly head. "There's no such animal, Howard.
If the kids aren't political, as you call it, it means that
they've given in to the forces of conformity and reaction." His handsome face tightened. "If this thing gets
out, I'll have the trustees on my back again." They
rounded the drive again. "Poor devil, poor hunted devil,"
he mused, "he *was* perjured, apparently, before the legislature." He lit his pipe and spoke through clamped teeth,
indistinctly; a terrible new thought had occurred to him.
"Howard, you don't think . . . ?" Furness looked at
him sharply; his strong, active face was ravaged in the
moonlight. "That he's still in it?" supplied Furness. The
President sorrowfully nodded; he looked eagerly into
Furness' face, with a consciousness of his own pathos—was
he once, twice, or thrice deceived? Furness shrugged. "I
should doubt it," he replied. "But am I a competent

judge?" He grinned. "I would have *sworn*, I would have *sworn*," he insisted, "before a legislature, that it was all a blague." They walked for a time in silence. "Who knows most about all this?" said the President, suddenly. "Domna," replied Furness. "She's the only one he told directly." "We'd better get her," resolved Maynard. "Right away. Tonight." "What about the poetesses?" objected Furness. "She's supposed to be driving them home, to my house." "You do it," said the President. "Take them to Domna's. And then come back. I want you to be there." Furness made a deprecatory gesture. "I was planning to serve a little whiskey," he said. The President blew up. "For God's sake, Howard!" he said bluntly. "My whole career is at stake. We've got to cover this thing up, as soon as we can find out what to cover. This is no moment for a drinking-party. Is there any way, do you think, that we could call off this damned conference and send them about their business?" Furness laughed. "We could abduct the poet of the masses. That's what his former comrades would do." "Stop using that silly name," exclaimed the President. "What is the fellow's name, for that matter? I rather liked him," he added, to soften the effect of his outburst. "Vincent Keogh," said Furness. "My God," cried the President. "Another Irishman!" Furness made a final protest. "Maynard," he warned, "Domna and Mulcahy aren't on good terms at present." "What does it matter?" cried Maynard. "The girl's honest, isn't she?" Furness raised a nonchalant shoulder. "But north-northwest, like the rest of us. She can tell a hawk from a handsaw." He waved and hurried off to his car.

CHAPTER XIII

A Tygres Heart
Wrapt in a Player's Hyde

HENCE IT HAPPENED that the President, Furness, Domna Rejnev, and the two lady poets were among the few people connected with the poetry conference not to have a hangover on Saturday morning. Furness' house, according to the brigade of students who came to clean it up, must have been the scene of revels; he himself, coming downstairs in the morning, renamed it the Mermaid Tavern. The informal ten o'clock session, held in Barnes Social around a table, was sluggish; the psychology student with the tape-recorder, who was stationed under the table with the poets' permission, was able to pick up several new hangover recipes and to witness exchanges of No-Doz and benzedrine. By a forced agreement with the Psychology department, this recording was later destroyed, at the price of Dr. Grünthal's resignation and the loss of the Rockefeller grant.

Young Mrs. Giolini, a pretty heiress with a black spit-curl, thought to be very stupid, read a paper on the mock-epic, which, according to the tape-recording, everybody believed she had had help with. She was in the habit

of subsidizing upstart magazines of verse with typograph-
ical eccentricities, and already among the older poets the
word was passing that she ought not to have been invited.
One choleric little poet in middle life, with sideburns and
short jutting whiskers, considered that they had each, every
man-jack of them, been personally insulted by being asked
to sit down at the round table with her; at the same time,
he held that the college had showed a shocking discourtesy
in leaving the two women to pass the previous night un-
companioned. This ill-feeling grew during the morning,
as the inevitable publishers' representatives began to ar-
rive, in very hairy tweeds, and to drop onto the floor,
cross-legged; they too, in most cases, had hangovers and
had driven all the way over from Bucks County on the
remote chance that another *John Brown's Body* or a novel
might be picked up at this conference. It was felt by the
older poets, most of whom held academic jobs, that this
conference, like every other one, was going to be shot
through with commercialism; the younger poets were less
incorruptible, and Herbert Ellison's two friends immediately struck up an alliance, considered very questionable
by the majority, with the youngest of the New York publishers, whom they pronounced "very intelligent." And the
worst fears of the majority were realized almost at once.
Consy Van Tour, who was chairing the session, had the
idiocy to call on the publishers to say a few words on the
subject of modern poetry as it looked to *them*. They did
not need to be asked twice. They all, it turned out, had
strong identical opinions on the subject of modern verse,
which they did not read much, they conceded (Translator's
note—"Not at all"), but which nevertheless they felt

qualified to judge by virtue of their position: "This is the way it looks to the man behind the desk." And to the man behind the desk, *it did not communicate.* The poets around the table indicated by their tight lips and wearied eyebrows that communication with these persons and their salesmen was the last thing they desired; but they did not have the rudeness to say so. And their restraint had the result of making the publishers more confident. Emboldened by an intuition of their own solid mediocrity, they became convinced that each of them, individually, was the audience that every author aimed and yearned to reach, and that if he did not reach them, well, manifestly, he failed. Having pronounced this sentence, they would calmly get up, stretch, stroll over to the window, like expert consultants whose part is done when the fault is pointed out, the execution being left to others.

The poets then took the joint hazard of asserting that their verse, all modern verse, was intelligible to any person who would take the trouble to read it—a perilous contention which was easily put to rout by the devilish kind of senior male student who had spent four years in college drilling holes in his teachers' logic. Such a tall, large-eared Mephistopheles suavely rose from his place and read aloud a passage by one of the poets present and asked for a show of hands of those who understood it. A few hands hesitantly went up all around the room, but to everybody's surprise but the poets', who had been through this all before, there were several hands at the table itself that simply refused to go up. And one handsome young poet rose and gravely tried to explain that understanding of a given poem and respect for it were not necessarily identical, that he himself was not certain of the meaning of all the details in the disputed passage, but, even while the Literature faculty nodded in approval, he was interrupted by a fresh member of the Art department, who popped up like a jack-in-the-box to demand, "Why don't you ask the author?"

At this instant, Consy Van Tour received a sharp poke in the ribs and a whole collection of scribbled notes, ordering him to call for the next question, but the students now were echoing the popinjay art teacher's question, though more in a tone of entreaty. "That question is inevitably broached by an audience if the chairman doesn't know his business," observed the choleric poet to his neighbor, taking care that Consy heard him. *"No,"* they all semaphored sternly, as the wilting, plump Consy hesitated. "To ask a poet for an explanation of his poem is a violation of professional ethics, like asking a doctor to prescribe for you when you meet him at a friend's house at dinner," said the whiskered little poet, a formalist and neo-traditionalist, to Consy, when the meeting had been adjourned—he was a specialist in poetic etiquette, or rather in the correct forms to be observed with poets. He had already checked off several violations in the manners prevailing at Jocelyn, and his eye now followed with acerbity the student crawling out from under the table. "Where is Mr. Furness?" he sharply inquired, cocking an eyebrow at Consy. Consy did not know; he only knew, he protested, that Furness had telephoned him very early to ask him to take over this morning's session. In reply, the poet took out his pocket-watch.

Hovering on the edges of this group, Alma Fortune

was nearly beside herself. She was furious with Howard
for not being here and with Domna as well, who had
promised to take a carful of poets for a drive before
luncheon. All around her, she saw poets covertly unfolding
train-schedules and glancing at their watches; she heard
muttered talk of their decamping after the afternoon session, before the buffet supper that was being prepared for
them at Furness' house by the best cook in the region. She
was not familiar enough with the poetic temperament to
know that this migratory urge was merely a passing one
—after cocktails, most of the poets would be amenable
to staying on, and some might not leave for several days,
if they found a congenial bivouac. Ignorant of these con-
trarieties, she hurried about the room with a nervous smile,
pointing out that the train being spoken of was slow,
crowded, inconvenient, and invariably late into Harrisburg. She stopped to glare at a publisher who was offering
rides in his Buick back to Bucks County, and then, on
second thought, invited him to stay for supper. She spoke
to her tenants, the red-faced poet and his wife, and all
the while her eye was on the door, willing Furness to enter.
Even Mulcahy, who ought to have been here, had rushed
out toward the end of the session, without any explanation,
on a note's being passed to him by a student. There was
nobody but herself and Consy—she discounted Ellison as
useless—to round up the poets and see that they had their
lunch properly and got to the chapel on time for the afternoon session. One of them, the poet of the masses, had
already failed to appear for the session that had just
ended, and now, as she was trying to make plans, three
more slipped out the side door. " 'And now for God's

sake, hock and soda-water,' " laughed the very handsome curly-haired youth who had spoken at this morning's session. Alma knew her Byron and knew what this meant; it was the *locus classicus,* she said to herself bitterly, of the hair-of-the-dog in literature. At this moment, when despair seized her, Furness debonairly entered.

What Alma did not suspect was that early that morning, before the session had started, the poet of the masses had been shaken awake by Furness and asked if he would mind driving in to see the President in his office. Dazed, breakfastless, and bleeding from a quick shave, he had tiptoed down the stairs behind Furness and out into the lucent morning, while the other poets still slept. This embassy was the fruit of the previous night's interview, which had lasted until three in the morning, with Domna, himself, the President, and finally Bentkoop, who had been summoned out of bed, arguing what ought to be done. The result was that Furness had overslept and had nothing to eat either. And as he drove along in his Pontiac, alongside the poet, who had a terrible breath on, Furness wondered whether the counsels of night had been ill advised. He seriously doubted whether the poet would tell the President anything.

It had been Domna's whim that they should ask him, a real feminine caprice. For, first of all, she had refused to believe that all three men—Furness, the President, and Bentkoop—had taken no stock in the wild story Hen had told her and that she and Alma and Aristide and Consy had accepted without question. "How could you 'know,' Dr. Hoar, that he was not a Party member? How can anyone 'know' such a thing?" "By instinct, simply," said Fur-

ness. "We knew it in our bones," he added, with a sour
laugh of self-disparagement. "But weren't you interested
in pressing it further?" she persisted, with widened eyes,
ignoring him, and keeping after Maynard. "If you thought
Hen deliberately told such a lie, why didn't you say so?"
"My dear," said Maynard simply, "it was a very hot
potato. I am an administrator, Domna. You people were
backing him—some of my best teachers. I had no belief,
or wish to believe, that Hen was a Communist—I could
hardly reinstate him on that basis; that's not the kind of
argument you use on the bursar or the trustees. I chose
to ignore the question. What was relevant to my purpose
was your feeling, yours and John's and Kantorowitz's and
Aristide's and Alma Fortune's. If you backed him you left
me no choice. I respected your opinion, but not enough,
apparently." He gave a sorrowful laugh. Yet Domna remained incredulous. "You too, John?" she murmured
when John came in, as though accusing him of perfidy.
What struck Furness, straight off, was that this strange
tone of hers and soft, reproachful eyes seemed to betoken
an intimacy that he himself had never enjoyed with her.

And then, almost at once, she and John had dropped
into a low-voiced colloquy, from which Domna had
emerged with one of her sudden, startling *volte-faces*. All
at once, backed up by Bentkoop, she had taken the curious
position that there must be some misunderstanding: Mulcahy could never have been a Communist Party member.
She knew this, she declared—with her strange, positive
logic—by the fact that she had found herself skeptical
when the story of the recognition scene had been repeated
to her, just now, by the President—she had been too far

away to catch the exact words herself—which showed her, she said, that she had never really believed Mulcahy in the first place and had been merely overriding her doubts, in order, perhaps, to think ill of the President or perhaps for some more worthy motive. But she now was certain that she had been half-consciously gulling herself. Furthermore, and it was here that Bentkoop seconded her, there was something very implausible, she insisted, in their account of Vincent Keogh's behavior. No anarchist who was a decent fellow, as Keogh appeared to be, would denounce a former comrade to the authorities, still less expose him, for no reason, in a public room, in the presence of his employer and his colleagues. "Anarchists are not informers," she kept repeating, over Furness' objections. This stubborn repetition and Bentkoop's deep-voiced assents had the effect, not of convincing Furness and the President, who after all had heard the conversation with their own ears and were not simply reiterating a maddening abstraction, but of persuading them that further investigation would at any rate do no harm. It was agreed that Furness should bring Keogh to the President's office at nine-thirty. As to what they could do next, if Keogh were to substantiate what he had implied the previous evening, none of them dared think. It was the President's vague hope, apparently, that the truth could be somehow suppressed. Furness did not concur in this; he had no hope at all; but only a suicidal compulsion to *know* at all costs. As he drove along the black-top road, dipping and rising through the newly plowed farmland, he was a prey to the darkest jealousies, including a jealousy of political activism.

When Keogh, rumpled, badly shaven, his dark-blue eyes bloodshot, was ushered into the President's wainscoted sanctum and saw there, waiting for him, the pretty Russian girl, a strange dark bony young man, and the President himself, he perceived immediately that this was a judicial occasion. Up to this moment, he had supposed that the President was going to offer him a job, which he was strengthening himself to refuse. Thinking over the previous evening, in the student social room, he could not imagine now what offense he had given, and a truculent heat rose in him, which he damped by reminding himself that these people were human beings. He concentrated his thoughts on the girl, who was wearing a handsome white wool dress, with a dark purple stripe down the center of it, which he mentally tagged as very expensive. Having been poor all his life and intending to remain so, he had a funny itch to know how much things cost, things, that is, that he would never have—yachts, custom cars, jewels—but this feeling was without rancor on the whole. Furness, whose wrist-watch and tie-pin he had already appraised, pulled up a chair next to him and sat down. The dark young man was sitting in the window-embrasure. To Keogh, it was like a scene from a movie, in the District Attorney's office.

The President, whom Keogh cast as Robert Mitchum, came rapidly to the point. "Last night, Mr. Keogh, you spoke to one of our teachers, whom you remembered as a former comrade in the Party." Keogh sat upright with a jerk. "Whoa!" he protested, but the President went smoothly on. "Don't jump, please, to false conclusions, Mr. Keogh. We—all of us, my two young colleagues, Mr.

Furness and myself—are asking you to tell us in strict
confidence what you know about this. We have no idea
of using this information in any way, shape, or form.
We're all liberals, believe me"—Keogh sat absolutely still
—"and there's not one of us who isn't shocked and sick-
ened by the reign of terror in our colleges." He reached
out and selected a pamphlet from one of the bookcases; the
others appeared slightly embarrassed, and out of the corner
of his eye Keogh saw Furness wink at the Russian girl.
"You don't have to take me on faith," continued the President, extending the pamphlet to Keogh. "I refer you to
my article in the New York *Times* magazine, which brought
me"—he faintly smiled—"a good deal of obloquy from
our academic witch-hunters." Keogh obediently opened the
text. "I deal there with my own problems as an administrator in handling an academic freedom case, the case
of a man charged, unjustly, as I thought, with communistic tendencies by one of our over-zealous state legisla-
tures." He chose another pamphlet from the bookcase.
"Here," he said, proffering it, "I deal with the problem
in a more theoretical way. Examine it at your leisure; I'd
be glad of your opinion. Out where you come from, in
California, you know a good deal more, I dare say, than
we do about the loyalty issue." Keogh nodded, rather con-
fusedly, as the President went on to say, warmly. "You've
probably been in the thick of the fight for academic liberties." The President leaned dynamically across the desk.
"But the man I describe there, the man I welcomed to
Jocelyn over the dissent of all the nay-sayers among my
trustees and my faculty, is none other than the man you
recognized as a former comrade—Henry Mulcahy!" A

prankish smile briefly rested on the President's fine features. "You can see that your revelation has left me, as a liberal pundit, in a rather delicate, not to say embarrassing position. But that of course is not the point. The point is our colleague himself. It would seem now that he perjured himself in his testimony to the legislature—a very serious thing, as you know. I'm not sure myself, without taking legal advice, what the best course is for him now. But to help him—rest assured, we mean to help him, every one of us—we need to know the truth, for Mulcahy's own protection. Look upon us, if you want, as his lawyers." He gripped the edge of the desk and his dark eyes gazed warmly into Keogh's. "Naturally," he interpolated, "there's no question of dismissal." Furness made a wry face, but the President firmly continued. "I can assure you, Mr. Keogh, that your conscience will be absolutely clear on that score."

Keogh twisted the President's two pamphlets in his hands; after the first cursory glance, he made no attempt to examine them. "You don't have to worry about my conscience, friend," he said with an insouciant smile. "I don't know what I'd tell you otherwise, but under the circumstances, I'll sing, gladly." "*Sing?*" wondered the President. "I'll talk," said Keogh, laughing. "This bird Mulcahy was never in the Party or near it." The Russian girl made a joyful sound and clapped her hand to her lips. The men looked sharply at each other. "To me," remarked Keogh, "that means nothing either way today. I don't know how you feel. Some of you liberals look on an old Party card as a testimonial to the bearer's manliness, like a first dose of the clap." "No," murmured

Furness, smiling. "We are not so innocent. You bring us great relief, I must say. You come among us like a *deus ex machina.*" Keogh, who was perfectly literate, felt offended by something slurring in Furness' tone and in the veering stare of his blue eye. "I'm not a worker-robot," he retorted. "I look on myself as a free individual." "Please go on, Mr. Keogh," said the President. "Please," said the Russian girl, giving Furness an angry look. "I don't object," said Keogh. "In the fraction, I was given the assignment of recruiting Mulcahy to the Party. He seemed to be close to us on some things, but when it came to an organizational question, there was absolutely no dice. If I may say so without damage to his present standing in this liberal company"—he bowed— "Hen was very cautious, very much the home-body. Has he still got that wife?" The Russian girl laughingly nodded. "She was there last night; she writes poetry." "What about the John Reed Club?" said the dark young man. "He came to a meeting or two," said Keogh. "Under my steering. He stood in the back of the hall, with arms folded, so." Keogh folded his arms, high on his heavy chest, and looked around the room, sardonically, while the company chuckled. "He asked some satirical questions. Later, he informed me that these *lumpen*-intellectuals had nothing to say to him. He was one of those birds that are more Communist than the Communists in theory, but you'll never meet them on the picket-line. A weird, isolated figure, with a talent for self-dramatization." Everyone nodded, and he went on for some time, analyzing Mulcahy in terms of his class background, his two years at Oxford, his Jesuit schooling, when he recollected that he was talking to Mulcahy's employer and pulled himself up short, with the sense that already he had perhaps said too much.

The meeting broke up, with the President's cordial thanks, and Keogh, to his sorrow, was sent off to breakfast with Furness at a coffee-shop in the old red-brick town. The Russian girl, so she said, had an errand and went off with the dark young man, their heads bent in close conference as they crossed the campus. Furness looked at his wrist-watch with the woven gold strap and called after her, sharply, to be on hand at the close of the morning session. It was already eleven-thirty, and he seemed suddenly peevish and preoccupied. From the moment they sat down to breakfast and he called out, "Miss," awkwardly, to the waitress, he rubbed Keogh the wrong way. The self-made intellectual dandy was a type Keogh disliked intensely, and he quickly saw that Furness was unsure with him, in some peculiar way, placatory, and at the same time eager to be off. He unfolded the Mulcahy case and Keogh was repelled, both by the story itself, and by the veneer of amused sympathy with which Furness coated it and that seemed to overlay, as in fancy furniture, what Keogh took to be a raw spite and envy. So far as Keogh could see, only the Russian girl and the woman named Alma and the fellow they had just seen called Bentkoop had behaved with a modicum of humanity, and he felt suspicious even of them, as Furness smilingly elaborated the later events of the narrative, like a salesman in a plush store demonstrating the fittings of a suitcase or swiftly knotting a four-in-hand in supple, hairless fingers. The more he considered it, studying the dap-

per Furness, who patently believed in nothing, not even
in himself, nothing, that is, but the *amusing* warp-and-
woof of events and persons, the more he began to feel
that the meeting in the President's office had not been all
it seemed. In the light of what Furness was telling him,
of feuds and fissions and reversals, their concern for Mulcahy seemed acted. He had a sudden inkling that they
would have liked to get the goods on Mulcahy, that whatever he himself had told them they would have been
pleased, pleased if Mulcahy were a Communist and
pleased, even more, if he were not, since this made him
out a liar, which was probably even worse, from a liberal-
respectable point of view. "We had to *know*, don't you
see?" Furness kept drawling in his peculiar, half-cultivated
voice, as if he were trying anxiously to drag Keogh in to
some disagreeable dark corner of the soul. This insistence
on their psychology seemed to Keogh quite spurious and
unnecessary. Though the President had assured him that
there was no question of a discharge, he wondered now
that he had believed him so readily, or rather, not believed
him, but dismissed the problem as irrelevant. It was possible, he saw, that he had been very cleverly taken in.
The idea that he might have played just now the role of a
stool-pigeon or an informer was offensive to his whole
sense of himself. He stood up suddenly and asked to use the
telephone. Furness, fitting a cigarette into his holder, looked
up with a flitting uneasiness, as though he descried his
intention; he did not, naturally, have the courage to challenge him. Keogh stepped into the booth, found the Mulcahy number in the telephone book, and got Cathy Mulcahy
on the telephone. He asked her to tell her husband, if

she could locate him, that he would like to have a word with him whenever it was convenient. Cathy Mulcahy's voice showed prompt and business-like understanding. "Where are you?" she demanded, succinctly. When he told her, she was silent for a moment, and then her voice came rapidly over the wire. "Tell Furness you want to look up something in the Library. Hen will meet you there, in ten minutes if I can reach him. If not, wait there till somebody comes for you. I'll try to send a student." As he came out of the telephone booth, Furness was paying the check at the counter only a few feet off, just barely out of earshot.

Keogh's suspicions were fortified, both by Mrs. Mulcahy's response and by what he took to be an attempt at surveillance on Furness' part. He held no special brief for Mulcahy, less, if anything, when he saw him again in the Library, but it seemed to him, nevertheless, that he owed Mulcahy this much: to let him know that the President and certain staff-members had been asking questions about him, which he himself had answered, he now thought, too freely. Mulcahy thanked him, pressed his hand effusively, and sped off. He showed no interest in renewing the acquaintance, which relieved Keogh, who watched the tall, pot-bellied figure bolt out the swinging doors with a slight new feeling of dubiety. Should he have kept his mouth shut? He paced up and down, staring into the glass cases, where the books of the poets, including all of his own, were displayed. The middle-aged librarian respectfully bustled up and offered to help him, and this kindness softened him to the college, which looked to him once again like a pretty decent place. He left the librarian and strolled out onto the library steps; across the evergreen-shaded campus, where boys and girls were walking arm in arm, he saw the Russian girl hurrying toward one of the buildings. He had a sudden impulse to call out to her. Did he owe it to her to tell her what he had just told this shit, Mulcahy, etc., etc.? But as the ridiculous question, like a repeating decimal, propounded itself to him, he struck his open left hand a blow with his right fist. *No,* he inwardly shouted to himself; *Keogh, keep out of this, or they will get you.* The chapel clock struck one. Within twenty hours, he perceived, they had succeeded in leading him up the garden path into one of their academic mazes, where a man could wander for eternity, meeting himself in mirrors. *No,* he repeated. Possibly they were all very nice, high-minded, scrupulous people with only an occupational tendency toward backbiting and a nervous habit of self-correction, always emending, penciling, erasing; but he did not care to catch the bug, which seemed to be endemic in these ivied haunts. He drew a draught of spring air, flexed his chest muscles, and signaled to a tall blond girl in a tight turtle-neck sweater, who rode up to him, questioningly, on a bicycle. He knew that he was supposed to be somewhere at this hour; they had given him several purple schedules which he had promptly thrown away, on principle, just as he had tossed the President's two pamphlets into a large green can under an elm-tree.

Meanwhile, over fried sausages, red-apple rings, fried potatoes, fried chicken, fried onions, in the coffee-shop of the old hotel, the poets who were still on schedule were

relenting somewhat toward the conference. The old mountain town was very picturesque, with red-brick dwellings,
trimmed in white, with green shutters, fronting directly
on the single street, which, from its open end, looked
out onto rolling farm country, stone houses and great
barns, as onto the land of Canaan seen from Mount Nebo.
The young poets were insensible to scenery and to the
spirit of history, as well as to good farm-style cooking,
but the older poets' lyres were more attuned to the atmos-
pheric. The resemblance to the Promised Land, first
pointed out by Miss Mansell, tempted them into specula-
tions on the influence of the Old Testament on American
history. They wondered whether this likeness to the prophesied Canaan had not been seized upon by the early set-
tlers as a form of verification, which had led them into
the theological controversies so characteristic of this region,
and so much more prolonged and literal than the theocratic
rivalries of New England—"These people," proclaimed
the red-faced poet, with a billow of the arm that included the startled waitress and the cashier, "still imagine
that they are living in the Bible." "And up there on the
hill, we still imagine it, in our own fashion," edged in
Furness, with a plaintive smile, trying to draw the conversation back to Jocelyn itself. "Our progressive methodology," he announced, "with its emphasis on faith
and individual salvation, is a Protestant return to the
Old Testament." Miss Mansell turned to look at him
politely, but the others went on eating, as though he had
not spoken. "And our presidents, poor fellows," he continued, on a diminishing scale of assurance, "live the
dishonored life of prophets, a life of exposure and con-

tumely, for trying to put into practice literally the precepts
of a primitive liberalism." The poets still ignored him,
except for the whiskered poet, who threw him a glance of
fiery rebuke—this was the sort of observation that the
poets were supposed to frame, and it was unseemly to
have it supplied, ready made up, by jackanapes on the
faculty.

The poets had no interest in Jocelyn or its President,
whom they took for granted as the usual money-raiser,
not too successful, to judge by the size of the fee. The
President they knew generically, and this was sufficient.
At a given point in the afternoon's proceedings, he could
be counted on to rise from his seat and put a question
that had long been bothering him—why did not modern
poetry communicate to *him?* Somewhat more perplexed
than the publishers, but vigorous and manly, he would
call on modern poetry to step down from its pedestal
and meet with the ordinary man in the marketplace; he
would ask for a positive contribution to the vexed debates
of our times. This speech, which was not yet known to
the President or his faculty, was foreknown to the poets
down to the last metaphor, just as the red-faced poet's ex-
tempore speech attacking Eliot was as well known to his
confrères as it was to his own wife. And they could anticipate with equal lucidity the attack on themselves that
would be launched from some unexpected quarter in the
Literature department, an attack which would be backed
up, since this was a progressive college, by a sudden
foray of students from the audience who would hurl a
daring question or two and then fall into silence, nudging
each other vainly to start the assault again. The deadly

animosity between the professor and the poet was somewhat muted here by the fact that, strangely, there appeared to be only two literary careerists in the Literature
department, the young versifier, Ellison, and his ally,
Mulcahy, whose empty place still gaped at the long table
—both of whom, naturally, were supposedly managing the
conference, for ends of their own that had not yet become
manifest but which, predictably, had something to do with
a power-struggle within the department and a drive toward prestige in the literary world outside. Of the two,
the poets preferred Mulcahy, who was a man of some
acuity, but they did not indicate this, any more than they
gave way to the natural attraction they felt to the little
Rejnev girl and her friend, Mrs. Fortune—they had
learned not to take sides, even with the losers, which in
this case was their instinct. They came to Jocelyn in the
same spirit that dentists or doctors attend a professional
convention, knowing that the public speeches would be,
on the whole, very tiresome, but that, if they could keep
out of the way of the faculty, they could drink and visit
with their friends. The more experienced they were, the
more they considered the whole project to be an affair
of mutual exploitation—a contract, like any other, in
which they did not intend to be worsted. They gulped
their caffein tablets, therefore, and smiled encouragingly at
the little Rejnev girl, who looked very white at the prospect
of taking the chair. The red-haired man, Mulcahy, was
still absent, which they put down as a black mark in their
book.

An hour and a half before, the President had had a
shattering experience that altogether eclipsed the poetry

conference from his mind, so that he did not, as it happened, make the speech that he would certainly have made under normal circumstances. Without knocking, brushing by the secretary, as she explained later, Henry Mulcahy had burst into the President's private office, white-faced, malevolent, trembling, and demanded to know what the President had meant by interrogating a visiting poet about Mulcahy's political affiliations. A shocking scene followed. Mulcahy, as Maynard told Bentkoop, as soon as he could get him on the phone, literally shook his fist in Maynard's face, threatened to expose him to the A.A.U.P., and to every liberal magazine and newspaper in the country. He was going to write a sequel to the President's magazine article that would reveal to the whole world the true story of a professional liberal: a story of personal molestation, spying, surveillance, corruption of students by faculty stool-pigeons. A girl-student, he shouted, had already confessed to him in his office, when he faced her with it, a sordid tale of spying assignments given her by the White Russian, Miss Domna Rejnev.

"What could I do, John?" pleaded the President. "The man is quite mad. My first idea, naturally, was to throw him bodily out of my office. But then, God forgive me, I hesitated. I saw very clearly that he had me in a vise of blackmail. The campus was full of outsiders—these poets, other teachers, publishers, parents. What was I going to do? Fire him? I *can't* fire him. He has a contract. I would have to show cause and that would mean, in all probability, a lawsuit. The college can't afford it. The terrible thing, John, is that, on the surface, everything he says is true. We *did* interrogate the poet; the people in the Literature department *were* keeping tabs on him. It's all twisted, of course, by his warped imagination to give a sinister meaning, but still those things *were* done. I sat there looking at him and I lost all faith in the power of my denials to convince anybody, even myself. Maybe our behavior did have an ugly little kink in it: *I* don't know; I've lost the ability to say. Tell me, John—you believe in religion—what am I being punished for?" John made an indeterminate sound. "At that moment," continued the President, his voice desperately rising, as he tried to laugh, "I looked out the window and saw nuns, *nuns* on Jocelyn's driveway, going into the chapel. I thought I had gone mad." John laughed. "They came for the afternoon session. One of the poets is a convert." "I know, I know," said the President, impatiently. "But listen to me, John. Then I said to myself, 'I will bribe him.' I actually thought of offering him five years' salary to leave the campus today. But then of course I saw that that was what he wanted. He would have a club over me for life. He could always say, with truth, that I had tried to bribe him into silence."

"So what did you do?" said John, as the President's voice died away. "I didn't do anything," retorted Maynard. "I just sat there. Miss Crewes opened the door a crack to find out what was going on and she saw me sitting there, with my head in my hands, and Hen sitting opposite, cool as a cucumber. She thought I had had a nervous breakdown or a stroke, like the last president, till I looked up and told her to go away." John laughed. But the President was beyond resentment. "Finally, I raised my eyes and I said to him, 'What is it you want of me, man? Do you merely want to ruin me or have you an ulterior purpose? Tell me that, please,' I said, 'just as a

matter of interest, just between ourselves. Are you a conscious liar or a self-deluded hypocrite?' " Over the wire,
John whistled. "You know what he answered?" asked the
President. "He quoted the famous old paradox, the paradox of the liar. 'A Cretan says, all Cretans are liars.' That
was his answer. As for interpretation, he informed me
that the problem was subjective. 'We're none of us certain of our motives; we can only be certain of facts.' And
these facts, which he'd already enumerated, could not be
denied by me." John sighed. "Then," said the President,
"he quite changed his tune. 'I'm not concerned with
truth, Maynard,' he said to me, very straightforwardly.
'I'm concerned with justice. Justice for myself as a superior individual and for my family.' "

The President's voice sounded weary. "He claimed the
right to pursue his profession, the right to teach without
interference or meddling, the right to bring up his family in reasonable circumstances. What could I say? I
spoke of my own rights and duties, to the trustees, to the
student-body. And he snapped me up immediately. 'And
does that include the duty to interrogate visiting poets
on my political affiliations?' " Maynard laughed. "I admitted that that had been misguided, and he offered, very
sweetly, to accept my apology." There was a protracted
silence. "So?" said John, anxiously. "So," replied the
President firmly, "I concluded that it was best for me to
resign." He heard the young man gasp. "Yes," he assev-
erated, with something of his old buoyancy. "I saw that
I was too much incriminated. The college would never
get rid of him as long as I was at the tiller. With another
skipper, who can't be blackmailed, there's a fair chance

of getting him out. I confess I thought of Samson, bringing down the temple on the Philistines and himself."

"Maynard," cried the young man, protestingly. "You haven't told him?" "No," said Maynard. "But Miss Crewes knows and Esther. We've already sent off a letter to the head of the board of trustees." He sighed. "Are the poets gone, by the way?" "I don't think so," said John. "I think the party at Howard's is still going strong." The President chuckled. "That Miss Mansell, you know—I think she had something to do with giving me courage to do it." John made an inquiring sound. "I used to be quite a classicist," said the President, "when I was a kid in high school. I wanted to be a lawyer and Cicero was my hero. That talk on Virgil and that reading brought it all back to me. It was running through my head all the time I was talking to him and he was quoting paradoxes at me. 'You damnable demagogue,' I kept cursing him under my breath as I watched him. And then I felt guilty. A demagogue— what does it mean? A leader of the *demos* or the people. I suppose, in a certain sense, I must be saying farewell to progressivism. At any rate, John, at the very end of our talk, I just looked at him and declaimed the first line of the first Catiline oration." Taking a firm grip on the telephone, he threw his handsome head back and brave tears of oratory rose into his forensic eyes. " '*Quo usque tandem, Catilina, abutere patientia nostra?*' 'How far at length, O Catiline, will you abuse our patience?' " At the other end of the phone, the young man signaled to his wife, who crept up and put her ear to the receiver as the President's noble voice rolled on.

THE END